Rainbow Curve

At the manifest level this is a story about baseball. But it is much more than this. Baseball is a metaphor used with great virtuosity by the author Michael Boylan to explore at a deeper level larger universal themes of love, friendship, loyalty, betrayal, political intrigue, cultural conflict, and corruption. As the author intends, this is a novel of fictive philosophy that examines perennial philosophical issues concerning the human condition. Jean-Paul Sartre, the French existentialist philosopher of the 1950s, did it with his famous literary classic *Nausea*. Boylan does it with *Rainbow Curve*. The two main characters of the novel Rainbow Billy Beauchamp, a former pitcher in the Negro Baseball Leagues, and his young protégé Bo Mellan who ends up playing in the Big League for the Chicago Cubs, reminded me of Aristotle, the famous Greek philosopher, and his young gifted student Alexander who goes on to conquer Asia and become known as Alexander the Great. Just as Aristotle before him, Rainbow Billy Beauchamp tries but fails to instil in his headstrong baseball player Bo, the importance of a temperate and balanced virtuous character. And just as Alexander before him who succeeds to conquer the world but not his flawed character and well-intended but wayward ambition, so too young Bo succeeds to conquer the baseball world and become a legend but fails to master his own unruly passions. Ultimately, both young men are victims of political intrigue and corruption. Although set in America, this is a novel of universal dimensions. Boylan's novel reminds us that ethics and responsible refection on our actions as individuals and communities are just as important now as they were in Aristotle's time.

Edward H. Spence (PhD) is a Senior Research Fellow at the Centre for Applied and Public Ethics (CAPPE), Charles Sturt University, Australia.

Rainbow Curve

by Michael Boylan

PWI Books
Bethesda, Maryland

Cover Design by Greg Simanson
Edited by Joanna Jensen
Proofreading by Samantha March

ISBN 13: 978-069-2729090 (PWI)
ISBN 10: 069-2729097

Library of Congress Control Number: 2014921899

THE DE ANIMA NOVELS

Rainbow Curve

The Extinction of Desire

To the Promised Land

Maya

FORWARD
CHARLES JOHNSON

Baseball fans are going to love *Rainbow Curve*. And even readers not familiar with the intricacies of the game, like me, will find themselves drawn in by the drama Michael Boylan conjures from the lives of multi-racial players who make baseball America's national pastime and in Latin America a game "more serious than life itself." As Buddy Bael, field boss and general manager of the Chicago Cubs, says to a crowd of Rotarians, "Baseball is just like life...It ain't just no symbol of life; it *is* life. And you know it."

Boylan knows it, and you will know it, too, because on these pages there is life aplenty: a sports world filled to overflowing with corruption and political intrigue, loyalty and love, aging and coming of age, betrayals and human barracudas all vying to make a profit from the players. At the story's center is talented, blue-eyed, left-handed pitcher Bo Mellan, the quiet and good-natured protégé of Rainbow Billy Beauchamp, once a star pitcher in the Negro baseball leagues. Boylan describes those bygone days of glory with prose that makes palpable a very special era in sports history:

"It was in Chicago that the Negro Leagues held their All Star game. 'My, that was a special game,' Rainbow used to say. He had played in four All Star Games. The first in 1934 was when he threw for the Crawfords. Gus Greenlee had paid him a hundred fifty dollar bonus for being selected and for pitching several scoreless innings against some of the finest hitters in the country. They played to 30,000 paid customers. It was a fine day…Robert Cole, owner of the Chicago American Giants, had thrown a giant party for them the night before. It lasted till almost game time the next day. There was music, women, whiskey, and a big-time crapshoot bankrolled by some of the high rollers in the league. Thirty-four had brought in a lot of gate even though it was in the midst of the Depression. Perhaps people needed entertainment more than ever."

Beauchamp feels he has one "last chance to hit the road again" and relive a little of that glory. After raising money by selling his dry cleaning business, he puts together a team—the Pan-Am Elite Giants—to barnstorm its way across South America. Among the players are whites, Mexicans, a Venezuelan, and one player who, like Judas Iscariot, masks his real reason for traveling with the team.

We travel the small town circuit with the eleven players, watch Rainbow sharpen their skills as players and entertainers, and see the ball club at play both on the field and in nightclubs. We also witness the political graft, "La Mordida" and the mounting danger that the Giants must deal with, specifically from a corrupt and sleazy baseball entrepreneur named Juan Cortez. Rainbow knows Cortez is "out to ruin us because we're cutting into his territory." That effort at sabotage reaches its disastrous peak in a field near Zacoala when they play a team from a local stone quarry, not knowing how they've been set up for an ambush. Boylan masterfully handles the suspense of this deception and its consequences for young Bo Mellan and Rainbow Billy Beauchamp.

But if playing ball in South America is dangerous, how much more so must the risk, treachery and reality of corruption be in a city "run by influence and infiltrated by organized crime?" Entering the Major League and becoming a star player for the Cubs, Bo Mellan finds himself in a snake pit of politics, and a "people's war in Chicago." Ruppert Cakos, the puppet-master who pulls Buddy Bael's strings, is the Mogul who "owned a major Chicago newspaper (the Sun), TV and radio station (WDRT), Major League Baseball team (the Cubs), the largest construction firm in Illinois (Advanced Building Contractors) and extensive land holdings in Chicago." Predictably, the power structure in the Windy City is feudal. "Beneath Dailey were his four lieutenants: Adam Wojciuk, Tony Ballestrieri, Sean Patrick O'Neil, and Jesse Jefferson. They controlled the Polish, Italian, Irish, and black voting wards respectively. O'Neil was Council president and Ballestrieri headed Advanced Builders as well as being the mob liaison with the ruling Acardo family. Jesse Jefferson and Adam Wojciuk also had indirect ties to Advanced Builders." Bo learns from his childhood friend Angela that blacks in the city have pulled together what remains of the Black Power factions of the sixties into a new coalition, called Krakatowa, that aims to topple the existing power structure.

"You see," says Angela, "there's this big Federal contract called the Loop Redevelopment Project. It's really for the whole city and is it huge! Ten billion dollars according to the papers...It just seemed as if Advanced Builders was going to get all of it by default. That's why Krakatowa was started. They wanted minority businesses to get an even break on some of the money."

"But doesn't Advanced hire blacks?" asks Bo.

"Sure they do, but only if they work for the City Machine. It's all so cozy. The blacks who take that money are either crooks or Oreos—because no self-respecting Afro American would work for Dailey."

Bo hits upon an idea to help the city's poor, disadvantaged blacks. He starts the Chicago People's Project, a non-profit lending institution devoted to helping minority businesses, thus creating an alternative to Advanced Builders and the militant Krakatowa group. But Ruppert Cakos is Bo's boss, and Bael feels he owns the player, and insists that Bo use his celebrity to "tell everyone how Advanced Builders are good for the city."

The uncompromising ball player, now a "marked man," finds himself between a rock and a hard place. He's assaulted by two of Balestrieri's goons, and told by al Sulami, a founder of the Krakatowa group, that, "If you're not with me, you're against me."

With everyone bent on killing him, including a powerful figure from his days with the Elite Giants, Bo Mellan wonders, "How could he fight back? Could he get something on Cakos as Rainbow had with Juan Cortez? Coretz was a considerably less formidable opponent, but the same principle ought to hold."

Readers will keep turning pages eagerly for the answers to these questions, because the fate of Bo Mellan triggers surprising changes that sweep through Chicago and beyond. Like the special curve ball of Beauchamp, *Rainbow Curve* will keep catching you by surprise right to the very end.

From Behind the Caravan

Standing at the threshold without demanding the vainglory of Fame
    We have come.

Seeking a refuge from the cruel battering of Fortune
    We have come.

Traveling along love's journey,
From the borders of nothingness to states of being
    We have come

Seeing that vital cenacle from the Garden of Paradise
In search of Love's greenery
    We have come

Yearning for that most precious, guarded treasure
As humble supplicants to the door of the King
    We have come

Pride and Honor are at stake; clouds release your purifying showers
For to a Sovereign Judge whose black book lies open
    We have come

Hafez, throw off your overcoat!
It is with the breath of fire, behind the caravan,
    We have come.

By Hafez of Shiraz, rendered into English by Michael Boylan

Chapter One
1984

IT WAS HOT. Too hot to live. But then there was no other time to live. Spring training. The only time a man could make it.

Sun City, Arizona. Most of the geriatric population was still asleep, eating breakfast or taking their medication. No cars were moving on the street and the sidewalks were vacant. The air was still except for the grumbling and the blare of a small transistor radio that was almost pulling in its station of country-western music.

It was nine o'clock and even the eager rookies groaned as they began stretching out on the all-dirt infield. If it's eighty degrees at nine o'clock, what the hell is it going to be like this afternoon? Who the devil does Bael think he is putting them through all this as if they were high school legionnaires?

The bald headed, pot bellied manager, Buddy Bael, got up from the bench. He had been talking to the coaches. Before him spread artificial green: four practice fields built by the Chicago Cubs in the desert to prepare young athletes to fill the grandstands in the spring. Bael took off his hat and snagged an oversized handkerchief to wipe his forehead. It was time to clear his mind. It was also time to clear his face. The brown-spotted skin showed of the residues of mucous and tobacco juice that still lingered on his lips and mustache. It was oppressive and going to get worse.

These laggards had better clam up or he would give them something to cry about. They were worse than the Class A kids on the

Iowa farm team after a six-hour bus ride through the hot, dusty plains. What would these pampered, overpaid brats do if they had to wear the real wool uniforms that he had been forced to wear when he was a ball player? None of these air-conditioned clubhouses and fancy equipment-why, even the water these pansies drank was brought in specially prepared glass coolers! What was the matter with the local tap? In his day, you didn't take nothing 'cept another chaw.

"Get going you lazy bastards, or you'll be wearing those polyester jump suits in Iowa."

More grumbling. The calisthenics continued as the non-roster players began to get into the routine of stretching their sore muscles. Behind this menagerie of trainers, coaches, scouts and groaning athletes was a solitary figure who was sitting on the metal and wood bleachers. He sat hunched over so that he appeared shorter than his still youthful six-foot two-inch frame. The unnoticed spectator sat with both hands thrust deeply into the pockets of a faded blue chenille jacket that was zippered, despite the heat, almost to his semi-shaven chin. The man had a somewhat decadent air about him such that if Sun City's finest had not still been eating their eggs and bacon, this scruffy, sunburnt stranger might have been taken for a vagrant and been asked to move on.

Only the pale blue eyes of this indeterminately aged visitor could be witnessed to move as they darted back and forth, carefully taking in the proceedings. When the coaches broke the congregation into its specialized units, the onlooker deliberately and gracefully arose and carefully made his way off the aging gray structure, whose raised grain stood almost as if determined to yield part of itself into the body of the impetuous.

This mysterious figure stood in sharp contrast to the scattering ball players, who were jogging to their respective stations just ahead of cajoling coaches. He was out of place but not uncouth in this arena, carefully following the pitching coach, Sam Dowel, and his cache of young arms. Nobody paid any attention as the workout began. It wasn't until there was a break, forty-five minutes later, that Dowel noticed and approached his singular audience.

"This ain't no open practice or nothin'. You a scout or a reporter?"

Dowel was a thin man with premature gray hair on the sides. Before any answer could be given, the nervous, skinny forty-two year old answered his own question. "You ain't no reporter – no press boy done wear a thing like that." Then he motioned to the chenille jacket. "What do you want, anyway?"

"I'm a pitcher," replied the stranger firmly.

"A pitcher?" cried Dowel.

"That's right."

"You mean you *were* a pitcher. Hell, up here we don't look at nothing that ain't the near side of twenty."

"I can throw a baseball over ninety miles per hour."

Dowel pouted and scratched the back of his head. He screwed up his eyes as if he were trying to see something. "Nope. You're too old. By the time you gets seasoning..."

"I'm seasoned."

"Oh yeah? Where? They done got rid of the Texas League, you know." Dowel turned to go back to his resting crew.

"Wait a minute. Let me throw you a few pitches. You're on a break anyway. What have you got to lose? Take out your radar gun and time it for yourself." There was a slight edge to this stranger's voice, a plaintive note that was not discordant.

Dowel stopped and scratched his head again. "There's a catcher over there who you can throw to, but if you hurt your arm—understand me—you're just a guy who wanted to play catch with a big leaguer."

Without a reply, the curly haired pitcher showed the first signs of energy he'd displayed all morning. Not a minute had elapsed before the stranger was on one of the practice pitching rubbers and moving his arm about. A young, seventeen-year-old reluctantly put on a receiver's mitt and with a condescending smirk yelled, "Okay, old boy, send a few down." The other pitchers and rookie catchers smiled with amusement. The curly haired pitcher responded by tossing a half dozen easy pitches to the catcher. The gallery resumed their conversations and the catcher decided to get out of his crouch as he mockingly slipped down to a sitting position as if to let this neophyte hurler know that his break was being interrupted and the favor was not appreciated.

The pitcher reared back and smoked a pitch that bowled over the dumbfounded catcher. Suddenly there was no talking. Every eye was on the young man sprawled on his back and then the gaze shifted to this stranger with the redish brown, short curly hair that seemed to brighten in the midmorning sun.

The catcher righted himself and tossed the ball back. Again the pitcher brought the ball. Nobody needed a radar gun; the sound of the ball into the mitt told the tale. Then, a sinker that dropped so fast that it looked like a spitter. The break was so pronounced that the receiver couldn't manage it and the ball popped out of his glove and hit the brash young catcher in the throat.

Now the gallery was laughing again, but this time the object of their mirth had changed. Sam Dowel yelled for another fastball. He wanted to time it. Ninety-six.

"Where did you say you played ball?" asked the pitching coach in an all-together different voice.

"South."

"Class A?"

"Nope. Class A-merican. Latin American."

For most major leaguers, Latin America is a mysterious realm in which baseball is taken more seriously than life itself. Because of extreme poverty, this one sport is greedily embraced as an escape that makes living possible. Some great ball players had come from Latin America, yet no major scouts wanted to go there because the climate and politics made such expeditions seem dangerous. Besides, most of the towns were in obscure locales and the hotels weren't air-conditioned. Still, the words conveyed an exotic, powerful effect. Sam Dowel shook his head and rubbed the back of his neck. Then he screwed up his eyes and looked at the stranger. He peered straight into those pale blue eyes.

"What's your name, anyway? I think Buddy would like to meet you."

Chapter Two
1970

"MELLAN."

"Spell it." The tones were delivered without delay by the impassionate, uniformed man who started to fill out the government-sized monochromatic form beginning at its perforated top. The man bowed perceptibly before his task, his heavily-set squared jaw jutted forward from his face.

"Why it's just like it sounds. M-e-l-l-a-n."

"First name." The blunt words that should have formed a question instead became an obdurate command. The whole impersonal transaction was created for efficiency. Human interaction was superfluous. It did not promote the desired end.

"Phil. P-h-i—"

"Phillip. Fine. What is your middle initial?" The interrogator had to stay in command. It was his place. His superiors had told him so. Any interrogator worth his pay does just what his superiors say.

"No. Just Phil. I'm not Phillip. In fact, generally I'm just called Bo. That is what I like best."

"Your middle initial, Phillip." It came back even as Bo was finishing his reply. The words were heavy and threatening. His superiors allowed the interrogator to be that way. Any interrogator worth his pay will do whatever his superiors allow.

"I don't know what your problem is, mister, but I just told you my name is Phil. My birth certificate here says—"

The interrogator snatched the black and white certified copy brusquely so that Bo was left holding a jagged corner of it. The bureaucrat began making his own notations. However, the applicant was not satisfied with this behavior. He looked down at the corner of the birth certificate for which he had paid four dollars to the clerk of Milwaukee County to obtain.

"Listen mister, that was not very polite."

The man continued to write. Any good uniformed clerk knows that he is to give the applicant a certain leeway. His superiors had always said to be tolerant of customers' complaints. He made no exterior sign of disapproval, save a rhythmic thrusting of his threatening jaw forward and back.

Bo looked again at the jagged scrap of paper in his hand. "Mister." No response. "Mister!" Again nothing. Finally, Bo grabbed the clerk's arm to stop him from writing.

"Let go of my arm, son." The words were measured.

"But you tore my birth certificate. See, here's the corner of it in my hand."

"You're going to have to go to the end of the line, son." The clerk was now an officer of the immigration service. Any customs/immigration officer worth his pay knows that his superiors won't care what he does to some young kid without money or position.

"But my birth certificate," began Bo, still holding the arm of the bureaucrat in exasperation.

The man behind the counter pressed a button with his foot and before Bo could stammer anything further, a uniformed guard came over and twisted Bo's free arm back violently and forced him to the floor. The long line of petitioners for passports silently parted as the young troublemaker was escorted outside.

The guard threatened to break various bones if Bo tried anything else.

His words were unnecessary. Bo moved passively, fully expecting to be taken to jail. But, of course, there would be no charge. The guard outside led Bo to the steps of the Dailey Center. The guard knew his charge was scared and that any rough stuff would go unreported. He smiled. His superiors were out to lunch. Besides, they wouldn't mind a kidney punch or two. Any guard worth his pay knows what the perks are in his line of work.

After Bo was led out, the mechanical process did not immediately begin again. It took the heavy voice of the man behind the counter and the threatening movements of his massive jaw to resume normal operations as meek petitioners filed forward.

In the back corner of the room were two eyes that observed the movements of the officious civil servant as he crumpled up Bo's birth certificate and tossed it into his wastebasket. Those two eyes, marked by the softness of chocolate brown irises, did not miss the actions of the black janitor as he dumped box-jaw's wastebasket into a large plastic garbage sack while he shuffled about his humble task. The sack was thrown into a large metal pushcart waiting in the hall. Along the sides of this functional receptacle were catches and metal brackets that held the tools needed for sanitary engineering. The thin, aging spectator waited and watched with care until another plastic bag disappeared into the next office before he made for the cart.

In another part of the city, south of the Loop, the thin black man made his way carefully into an unpretending brownstone hotel. The aging figure moved with an athletic grace that seemed to flow and could not be hidden even by his baggy, blue, brushed cotton trousers.

This man strode up to the front desk, asked a question and then proceeded over the thick, worn and musty carpet that seemed to stick to the very soles of his shoes as he ascended the stairs. After jiggling the lock, he opened the door with his key and beheld the figure of Bo supine on a sagging mattress.

Bo turned at the noise. His curly hair was long and somewhat unkempt from lying on the threadbare, gray coverlet which once was white with puffy threaded loops that at one time formed an intricate design. A breeze blew the gray window sheers that stood in front of greasy brown shades that were wound loosely atop crooked, double sashed windows.

The figure in the doorway stood staring at Bo. Then he closed the door with a sharp push, walked over to the window and opened it with a determination that overcame its natural stubborn reluctance to budge. In one motion he pivoted toward the horizontal figure and menaced above, hands at his side, elbows out, and chest expanded. It all happened in an instant even as a dried piece of aged caulking fell noiselessly from the window behind.

"That was some trick you pulled back there, boy."

Bo rolled over in the bed.

"We've got two train tickets for New Orleans tomorrow at noon." The older man pushed his lips together tightly. "I'm not going to miss it. I've got business waiting for me." Then the tall, lanky man took out a crumpled piece of paper from his pocket and tossed it underhand toward the reclining figure. The light paper bounced on Bo's hips and then rolled back onto the gray bedspread.

Then Bo was alone. All the while, Bo had not looked at Billy Beauchamp whom he affectionately called by his nickname "Rainbow." His eyes instead had been focused upon an irregular crack in the plaster ceiling. Scaling the fissure was a light brown roach, trying to get inside. While Rainbow talked to him, Bo watched carefully as the insect searched for some angle that would allow him entrance into that land of prosperity that undoubtedly awaited him within the interior domain. Bo watched skeptically as the tenacious creature first tried one leg and withdrew it and then walked farther to test the opportunity from another angle. This seemingly futile struggle fascinated the aspiring pitcher. His eyes only left the creature's ambitious project for an instant as he picked up the crumpled piece of paper that Rainbow had left behind. It was his birth certificate. Bo was taken aback. He had forgotten that he'd been without it.

Bo bit his lower lip hard so it almost bled. Then he looked up again. But the cockroach had vanished.

Chapter Three

"WHAT CRACK DID HE FALL OUT OF?" asked the bald headed, pot bellied Buddy Bael. The manager and the pitching coach stood together facing east. The early morning sun slanted down in a powerful stream so that it seemed to illumine the short ends of the pitcher's curly hair.

"Said he played in South America," said Dowel as he moved to his left so that the sun would not shine in his eyes. But no matter how he moved, the pitcher's hair seemed to reflect the potent rays of brilliant Hyperion.

"South America's a big place," replied Bael. The large man perspired freely in the heat. This gave him a unique air which, when mixed with the tobacco juice residue, presented a singular aura indeed. The manager's uniform shirt below the breast was black with his perspiration. This triangular area seemed to rest on an angle just above his stomach, almost as if the stain were reclining for a snooze.

The pitcher's blue eyes glanced at the chest of Bael and then to the wide set, green eyes of Dowel, which always wore a look of surprise except when he squinted.

"He can really bring it, Buddy," offered Sam as he caught the gaze of those faded blues.

The manager tried to get a look at this prospect before him. But his beady, hazel eyes could not rest on this figure for more than an instant. With his left hand he reached for his bandana, but this time the nimble fingers fumbled it. In an angry voice Bael exclaimed,

"I've seen a lot of guys who could throw a pea and most of them are selling insurance!"

It was not easy for Bael to bend down and retrieve his lost handkerchief. Dowel moved back a step and slapped his fist anxiously into the palm of his open hand. The faded blue eyes noted this and did not offer to aid the aging, overweight captain.

Bael got to the ground by bending his legs and then groping blindly for his property. His first attempts were not rewarded. He reacted through intermittent expressions of tobacco that described a trajectory that terminated two inches from his pitching coach's feet. The perspiration seemed to flow more freely until he had it. Then Bael rose hurriedly and unsteadily—almost falling. Dowel offered a hand that was disdainfully rejected. The manager turned and began to walk away. He stopped and motioned for Dowel to come over with him.

"Hey Sam, what is this? A joke? Are you getting even for my trading Ramos away from your crew? I admit we didn't get a hell of a lot for him, but shit, Sam, that greaser was a trouble maker."

The pitching coach stood imbalanced: his weight shifted from one leg to the other. He swung his arms loosely as his cupped left hand slapped against his right fist. "Hey, Buddy, what's past is past. I'm just trying to put together a pitching staff here."

"And you think you can do it with the likes of him? C'mon, Sam."

The manager's right index finger was pointed at the pitching coach's sternum. As he talked, Buddy Bael jabbed that digit as if he were going to implant it into the other (though he never so much as touched Sam's uniform). "I mean look at him, Sam—standing there like a bum." Buddy spat tobacco juice for emphasis. He adjusted his chaw and started to put away his handkerchief as he cocked his head and smiled. "Tell the truth. Is he just some wino you rousted out of the bleachers this morning?" Buddy laughed.

Sam stopped swinging his arms. He backed a step away from Buddy's jabbing finger and then widened his stance, evenly distributing his weight. As he was adjusting his posture, Sam also folded his arms. When the manager laughed, Sam frowned and screwed up his eyes.

"You can't be serious, Sam." The manager was no longer laughing."Look at him. That don't look like no ball player. How old is he?

And that jacket. I mean, holy mother, them's the things coons used to pick up in Cuba. Strictly bush, Sam."

Bael took a step towards his pitching coach as he delivered these words. It was very hot but suddenly Sam was no longer sweating. He didn't back away this time.

"I want to give him a shot. I think he's got something."

"What he's got is *you* bamboozled."

Bael moved closer and Dowel wiped his nose. For a moment the two stood there, motionless. Then the manager spat to the side and pivoted away. "Go ahead if you're really serious. But if this is a joke, it's the damndest I've ever seen."

Dowel walked back to his pitcher who had been standing only five yards away. "Well, Bo, that rotten son-of-a-bitch thinks you're too old and that you're some kind of a wino." Sam stopped and stared again into the fathoms of those pale blues. Then he stepped forward, drew his lips into a wide smile and put his hand on Bo's shoulder. "You save my ass, will you? And show him he don't know *shit* about pitchers." The two men were still. They stood in the middle of the field together. Bo raised the right side of his mouth hesitantly and tentatively into a smile. The pitching coach took Bo back to the practice area. He strode close to the unknown prospect, muttering just under his breath so that his words did not even reach the ears of the man in the chenille jacket.

"Don't know shit."

* * *

After a week of calisthenics and running—pitching and running—and more running, Bo was taken out to eat by Sam Dowel.

They seated themselves at the back left corner of the restaurant's main room near the 'Superstars Video Carnival' game. "Right here's the quietest spot in the whole joint. This game here's silent as you please," said Sam as he slid into his chair. The forty-two-year-old former pitcher for the Giants still moved like an athlete. "The only time it's loud is when you win and become a superstar. Then it goes haywire. It's the darndest thing."

Bo Mellan sat down and looked about him. It was unlike anything he'd ever seen before. The restaurant consisted of one large main room and a smaller room off to the right just as you came in. In the large room there were video games along opposite walls, left and right. On the back wall were boxes of hats and balloons that could be used to adorn the younger patrons, and the windows at which one placed his order. There was also a player piano that was continuously rolling out old-time melodies. In the center was a four-sided screen with an interior projection unit that displayed the old silent comedies of Harold Lloyd, Buster Keaton, et. al.

It was the only thing silent in the place.

In the side room were centered pieces of playground equipment with tables fashioned around in a horseshoe. The background music for this section of the restaurant was sixties rock and roll.

The combination of noise from the video games, player piano, sixties music and the constant modulation of children's voices was at first confusing to the rookie prospect. Where did one place his attention? The sights were no less incoherent. Little bodies and teenaged ones hopped energetically about. Lights from the games splashed vibrant color while the movie screen flickered black and white in the semi-darkened room.

"What would you like, Bo?" asked Sam after they had seated themselves and the pitching coach had reviewed the familiar menu imbedded in its clear plastic home within the table top.

Bo did not hear the question. He was still looking about. Sam noticed his guest's wonder and took out a cigarette. "Quite an idea, isn't it? Recreation hall and pizza joint all rolled into one. You can take the kids and keep them out of your hair at the same time. Wish they'd had one of these when Linda and me was bringing up Bobbi. You bet. Quite a place." Sam smoked in quick puffs that never interrupted his conversation. He just took it in with one breath and let it emerge with his voice. "See anything you like?"

Bo listened to Sam, but was astonished by the thundering machines that he'd never seen before. In this way he did not completely register what was being said. The scene was extraordinary but Bo was not certain whether the 'extra' was positive or negative. "What are these games, Sam?"

The pitching coach cocked his head and blew out a long, easy column of smoke. "You have been away a long time, haven't you?

Say, I'll tell you what. I'll show you on this game Superstar, here."
Sam put out his cigarette and took Bo over to the game.

Bo tried playing and was thoroughly unsuccessful. Then Sam
showed him how. The former Giants pitcher skillfully passed the
magic number of points.

Suddenly a siren went off and an electronic synthesizer played
the "Washington Post March" while lights all over the game flashed,
"You're a Superstar!" "You're Number One!" "You're a Superstar!"

Bo returned directly to their table. Sam laughed softly at his skit-
tish companion and lit up another smoke.

"It's not so bad, you know. It's just like pinball. You remember
that, don't you?"

"They make so much noise when you win."

"Naturally, I was a superstar."

"I still don't know why they have to be so loud about it."

Sam laughed again. He liked this fellow who Bael wanted to
cut from the club. He liked him though he knew it would take a
surprising event to force the manager's hand. In three days the
non-rostered players would be divided and Sam wanted Bo to stay.
He had to create a situation that would make it impossible for the
manager to cut this prospect.

"So, what'll it be, Bo?" put in the pitching coach again.

Bo could see the menu imbedded in the table, but something
pulled him away from examining it closely. Instead, he folded his
hands atop the table where the menu should be placed and replied,
"I'll have what you're having."

"How do you know you'll like what I'm having?"

"I like most things. I'm not very particular that way." Bo looked
down at the knuckles of his folded hands.

Sam laughed. "Well, I'm having a large pepperoni pizza and a
schooner of beer."

"That sounds good to me except I'll have a coffee to drink." Bo
watched his knuckles grow white, though his hands and arms did
not appear to move.

"Coffee?" exclaimed Sam, putting out his cigarette before it was
finished. "Pretty warm day for coffee."

"A hot drink on a hot day makes for a sizzling fastball," responded
Bo, looking up with a grin.

"Well if that's your secret, stick to it. You've got a sizzler, all right," replied Sam with equal levity as he left his guest to place their order.

Sam was into his third schooner when the pizza arrived. He had been telling Bo stories concerning his late hurling days. "You know, I always say there are two kinds of pitchers: those that throw and those that pitch. Eighty percent of the guys they stick on the mound can only throw. That's why they have a couple of good years and fade away.

"Not me. I'll tell you. I was a pitcher. I could find the spots to put the ball at different speeds so they was always off balance. A guy like that can go on forever. I'll tell you." Sam put down his beer as he reached for another cigarette. Sam liked to hold the glass and cigarette in the same hand.

"What made *you* stop, Sam?" asked Bo, who was still on his first cup of coffee.

Sam's lighter missed twice. Then he got it and took in a deep draw. "Bael."

"Bael? Buddy?"

"Yeah. I was pitching for the Giants and he was manager. Just hired, you understand. He was the man to turn around a losing team at the All-Star Break. Buddy Bael: the baseball genius who never won a pennant." Sam signaled the girl who poured coffee and brought the pizzas to get him another beer. "Buddy decided I was through. I was six and four with a solid earned run average. Washed up, shit. I was third best on the staff at the time. He told me that the general manager had asked around the league to try to trade me. 'Nothing doing,' he said. Claimed they wouldn't even part with a B-level minor leaguer for me. Said that if I wanted a job he'd make me pitching coach. We didn't have a separate pitching coach then—old Ruddles, the manager before had always done it himself. Well they said that they'd give me a job because I had a little following there in town, you know. They'd get mad at the club for just dropping me after all the years I'd put in for them. So they said they'd give me a job or my release—either one. But if I took my release and tried to hook onto another team and couldn't, why there wouldn't be that pitching coach job either. If I took the release, the fans would yell at the front office and they'd get no positive PR. You see, they wanted me to announce my 'retirement' and then people would think I'd left on my own. They'd look really rosy in offering me a coaching position and everybody would be happy."

Sam's beer came. He took out his last cigarette and dropped the crumpled pack on the far side of the table. Bo signaled for another coffee.

"So there I was. If I split, I could be out of baseball. And I wasn't getting any younger at thirty-seven. I was no all star, you understand, but I could get them out as well as the next guy. The trouble was that the next guy was twenty-one. If I didn't latch on... . They said they'd asked around, but fuck, that was when they still had the reserve clause and them owners was tight-lipped. You couldn't 'test the waters' like the agents do now.

"I was in a bad position." Sam took a drag, a sip and a slice of pizza. He chewed it over thoughtfully. His eyes were fixed on the partially eaten dinner in front of him. Bo's lonely blues set softly on his companion.

"Well, you can tell what I chose."

"They just forced you out?"

"I've often thought about whether they were feeding me a line or what. I know they were. I've seen how Buddy operates. He likes to get his way. But what can you do? He's the boss." Sam took another slice.

"So when he went over to the Cubs he took you with him?"

"Sanchez, the third base coach, and me. I don't know why. I think he likes to let me know that he can pull the strings." Sam put his drink and smoke down. "I was still married then and not getting any younger. What did I know except baseball?"

"I think I would have done the same thing in your position."

The two men sat on opposite sides of the table. Sam was staring at the smoke from his dying cigarette, the last from the pack. Bo watched in silence. Then Sam looked up suddenly. He smiled at Bo. He picked up his cigarette again. "You know, I'm going to put you into that big inter-squad game tomorrow. We're playing the Brewers and there'll be a lot of press people there." The smoke was finished. Sam was all business again. "Now you have to understand this. See, I'm going to put you into the game—that's why I'm telling you this—but I'm not going to pre-schedule it. Buddy'll be with our "'A' team and I'll coach the 'B's with Solly. I'm going to put you in there in front of all them reporters and see what they'll say when they see you pitch."

Bo set down a piece of pizza he was eating. He didn't quite know yet whether he liked the seasoning.

"I don't have to tell you how important it is for you to wow them. You know those reporters come down here partially for a vacation. Who wouldn't trade eight degrees for eighty-eight? The club PR man gives them some stuff about this guy or that who might make the big team—you know, fuel for the old hot stove. So then reporters get their copy and just have to retype it with a story lead and presto: one day's column!"

Sam laughed and took some more pizza. His appetite seemed enormous as he bolted down the cheese and tomato mixture. He had finished his beer and had switched to water. His conversation now was squeezed between bites.

"Sometimes they write something which really catches on back home. You remember Joe Hall?" Without waiting for an answer Sam said, "Well, they sent him down a few years ago, but he had made such a splash in the local press that they had to bring him up right away. A winning club can keep somebody down for as long as they like. But a loser has to show the hometown fans that they are trying. And nothing fills up the seats faster than new faces and new promise."

Sam stopped. His pizza was finished. The thin man could really go through the food. Bo nodded his comprehension and offered Sam some of his pizza that was still whole save a few pieces.

"I'll just take a couple," replied the pitching coach, taking one in each hand. "You know, I like you, Bo. You don't knuckle under to 'em and I like that. You're also kinda quiet, but not timid. And you've got a great arm. A great arm. But the only way you're going to make the big club is by forcing Buddy's hand."

"I'm not sure I follow you," said Bo. "I don't think I'm very good at forcing people's hands."

"Don't worry about that. I've learned a lot in five years from that son-of-a-bitch. He doesn't know it, but I've been watching him careful. Leave it to me, Bo, and I'll make him put you on the Cubs." There was fire in his wide set, green eyes. Their natural look of surprise had sharpened to an intensity that was frightening. As he continued to go through the remainder of Bo's meal, the Italian spices seemed to fuel his spirit. "Just leave it all to me," repeated Sam, "all you've got to do is pitch like hell when I put you out there." Sam laughed to himself. He was now leaning over the table as he animatedly made his points. It almost seemed to Bo that Sam was talking to someone else at the table. But he could not be sure. "Just leave it all to me."

Bo nodded. Sam had just taken his last slice of pizza.

CHAPTER FOUR

THERE'S A LITTLE HOTEL in New Orleans called Le Bout that is just outside of the Vieux Carré towards the Elysian Fields near St. Claude Avenue. It is just a stone's throw from the river and is run by an old Haitian named Duvaier. The hotel has only seven rooms to let: three on each story plus one on the main floor. There is not much to distinguish this dwelling from scores of others whose balconies and intricate ironwork decorate their facades. It is an old establishment with a regular clientele that take up four of the seven rooms and enable Duvaier to pay his bills and not worry much about his three vacancies. The clientele are mostly old and dark skinned. Also, each had formerly been connected, in some way, with the entertainment circuit. Duvaier, himself, once owned part of a local club where several of his current tenants used to stop for an engagement.

There is a different pace of life at Le Bout that most visitors cannot understand. Breakfast is served at noon and Duvaier informally provides drinks at midnight in a small room just off the front desk. Between these exist rituals of living that cannot be hurried. Life proceeds at a low frequency, and each resident transmits his life pattern with a resolute determination.

One evening just before drinks, a tall, aging black man and a young, curly haired white boy walked into Le Bout. Though it had been many years between engagements, it did not take the manager long to recognize his visitor.

"Well, mon dieu, if it isn't Rainbow Billy Beauchamp hisself," roared the seventy-five year old hotelier and former entertainment entrepreneur as he slapped his hands on the high-gloss, dark mahogany reception desk (which also doubled as the bar at midnight). "Step right up, my man, I haven't seen that magic arm of yours in très longtemps."

Rainbow rocked back on his heels and smiled. The tall, aging man in the brushed cotton pants stood erect and surveyed the lobby of the Hôtel Le Bout. A cigarette stuck straight out from his lips.

"What you been up to, Rainbow? And who's your friend here?" asked Duvaier motioning at Bo.

"This here's my pro-ta-gee, Bo Mellan. He's an as-p-i-r-ing pitcher." The words were burlesqued by Rainbow's dramatic delivery. Bo shied his bright blue eyes down and away, though there was no one else about.

"Bo? Like a little Rainbow, eh, mon ami? He must be a pitcher, aussi, yes? I always remember you tell us très fort, 'I shall return with a pitcher,' and he is it?"

Bo kept his eyes on the bare stone floor and the old embroidered rugs atop. Then he looked at the anteroom that hosted afternoon breakfast and midnight cocktails each day. Rainbow turned to his young companion and nodded. "A regular Douglas MacArthur I am; 'cept I always planned it to be my kin, but Bo here is all I was able to drug up."

Duvaier's grin exploded into an enthusiastic laugh, a vestige of his early Haitian life. It was the laugh of a man far younger than his actual years. "Yes, he's a little light for a son. But for you, peut-être, he's the light at the end of the rainbow?" Duvaier's mirth redoubled at his verbal cleverness for which Haitians are famous.

"Well, maybe you right about that. But you know a rainbow's light means the storm's a windin' up."

Duvaier slapped the desktop again over the continuation of the metaphor. Bo turned away and wandered to the anteroom to look inside. It was a respectable room with ceiling-high windows and a few pieces of sleek, dark furniture. Nothing was crowded. This left much of the room quite open. There was a blonde wood floor and an intricate Persian octagonal rug in the center that stood under a beautiful, though simple, cut-glass light fixture.

Bo put his fingers gently upon the strips of lead that connected the panes of glass that made up the entry door. The room was dim despite the long windows. A reflected flickering came from the sparkling light of the square, black iron coach lights outside.

"Is it true, then, you are going back to base-se-ball?" asked Duvaier.

"That's it," said Beauchamp, now leaning on the opposite end of the front desk.

"On the old circuit? You are planning to—"

"Got to put together a team, of course. Get me some kids with talent and some showmanship. We'll put it on the road for a couple of years to get seasoning and then, maybe, I'll enter it in the Mexican League in the spring and in the Caribbean League in the winter. Be a real push, I think."

"Magnifique, Monsieur Rainbow. I applaud you." Duvaier clapped his hands together in slow motion rhythm. "It is not easy to start up a team." The Haitian drummed his fingers on the wood. "Today, not so easy, but—ah—in the old days one could... . But there was a different climate then." The hotelier looked toward the ceiling and shook his head.

Then he took out his register and pretended to search for an empty room. He started to say, "Where will we put you?" when the door opened and in stepped three of the hotel's four residents: Johnny Rae, Cadillac Joe Gentry and Dixie Lee Rose. The three men made a casual entrance when they stopped suddenly. Johnny Rae, the former booking agent and sax player, stepped in front of his two comrades and straightened his arms out from his five foot three inch frame to form a barrier.

"I say, what do we have here?" mugged Johnny.

Rainbow laughed at the sight of little Johnny Rae restraining his two taller companions (especially Cadillac Joe, the former singer and comic who weighed at least two hundred and seventy pounds).

"This like old times at the R & B," said Duvaier with a grin. Then the five of them converged in an instant and began getting the details of what life had brought to them since they had palled around in the forties.

As they talked, Bo opened the door to the anteroom and walked about by himself into the semi-darkened atmosphere. The reflected light lent an ethereal quality to the room. It was as if he were shut off from the world's noises and troubles. It was his haven: a hidden refuge from impinging sights and sounds.

How quickly he had been whisked away from Milwaukee and Marshall High School where tomorrow, if he had been allowed to stay, he would have been marching in the school's graduation ceremony. But then there had been the upset: Rainbow and Willie. They had always been at each other's throats as long as he had lived there—even before his mother had died and left him alone.

There was never any question that he would go with Rainbow. It was just a little sooner than he had planned.

Then there were the passport problems in Chicago, and more and more Bo wondered who he was apart from those curving streets, high arching elm trees and sturdy red brick homes on Milwaukee's northwest side. Now he stood in darkness. The closed door muffled the raucous voices in the other room. The low illumination within was just enough to see the dark outlines of everything about him, but not enough to make out any detail. Bo made his way to one of the large windows and looked at the quiet narrow street outside.

Then there was light. In stepped a smartly dressed, elderly black male who carried an ebony cane with silver ferrule. In the center of his tie shown a diamond stickpin, and on his French cuffs, which slid out one and a half inches from his coat, were pearled cufflinks. Bo's jaw dropped as he gazed at the total effect of this stunning man in his shining silk evening attire.

"Hello there," began the elderly man, who moved gracefully despite some obvious stiffness in his joints. "You must be Bo. My name's Louis Reed." Louis Reed spoke with precision (though he elongated his Christian name to Lou-ee). His dress and grooming were acute. As he strode forward to shake Bo's hand, the young hurler from Milwaukee noticed the results of a professional manicure that Mr. Reed required twice a week. His cuticles were angled so that they formed a precise border between the pink skin under his nails and the darker skin around.

Bo shook Mr. Reed's hand and stood perfectly still with his mouth slightly open.

"Come over to the table and sit down. Would you like a drink? I generally have a gin and tonic this time of night, but perhaps you have a particular favorite?"

Bo moved clumsily over to the round table and sat down. He could not take his eyes off his new acquaintance. Mr. Reed took out a deck of cards from his coat and began to shuffle. "Would you like to play cards? I think we can get a five-some going while Johnny Rae and Rainbow have their tête-à-tête in the lobby."

Bo nodded. He liked playing cards even though he wasn't very good at it. Some of the baseball players at Marshall High used to play for nickels and dimes and Bo had, more often than not, gone home without his next day's lunch money. Despite his lack of acumen, Bo liked placing bets and the feel of the cards. The end product was not as important to him as participating in the game and the comradeship with others. Bo always played for the big hands against the odds. And strangely enough he generally pulled pretty good cards. However, this advantage was negated by the fact that Bo's face reflected his hand. Everyone at the table knew when Bo had a full house or a bust hand. He couldn't hide his elation over a good hand or his disappointment over a bad one.

Soon the others filed in except Rainbow and Johnny Rae, who were alone talking over the prospects of the new team. Cadillac Joe and Dixie Lee came in with drinks. It was decided that Bo should have beer. Five cans were set in front of him like a hand of draw. Everyone laughed and the group proceeded to play cards.

Out at the desk, Johnny Rae had lit up an enormous cigar and poured himself a glass of Jack Daniels, neat. The former entertainment-booking agent had much experience in arranging dates for entertainers, circuses, auto races, carnivals and barnstorming baseball teams throughout the South and northern Mexico.

"It ain't like the old days, Rainbow. People don't turn out for road shows much anymore. You've got to either be a real big outfit or else hit the sticks. Ain't much money in the sticks. You work your ass off for a buck, I'll tell you." As Johnny talked he licked his thick lips together. Johnny was a small man. His lips were the only things big about him. "Don't know if it's TV or what, but folks don't turn out as well as they used to."

"Times have been tough," said Rainbow as he sipped a glass of steady claret that Duvaier had opened for the occasion.

"I don't know if they don't comes out better when times is tough. Needs to forget the hand life's dealt 'em."

"Dunno, Johnny. Back in '32 I was with the ABC's and we rarely drew our full pay." Rainbow drained his glass. He had strong feelings about his years as a star pitcher in the Negro base-ball leagues.

"Thems was bad years for the ABC's even with that singing act you used to have. Not bad neither. But that ball club lost a lot of games, I remember."

"That ball club," rejoined Rainbow as he poured another glass, "was just too tired: fifteen, seventeen games a week—and that don't count the traveling."

"But that was the beauty of barnstorming back then. A ballplayer kept going so hard that he didn't have no time to fuck around much. Too damn tired. Shit, you could put jist about anyone on a team like that and t'wouldn't be no messin' neither. Nuttin to do 'cept sleep 'n travel 'n play ball." Johnny laughed high. All of it came from his throat on up. The rest of his body hardly moved. The laughs would emmanate all at once and then die suddenly as the small, delicate man would re-insert his long cigar between his large lips.

"You got that right."

"Nope. Nothin' wrong with a travelin' team. Booked plenty of them, I did. Nothin' to it. I could do it again, 'cept there ain't much margin in it for a man who wants ta make the big payday."

"Not fixin' ta break the bank, Johnny Rae. Just felt it was my last chance to hit the road again."

"Hells bells, why you want to hit the road again at you age?"

"What do you mean at my age? I'm only sixty."

"You and Satchel Paige. That man was ten 'fore he was born."

Rainbow laughed at the light jibe against his ageless mound companion of the Pittsburgh Crawfords and Homestead Grays, two premier clubs for which Billy Beauchamp once pitched. Rainbow took another long drink and let a few images bounce about his head. It was only a moment, but Rainbow felt the reverberations of decades. "Once you got travelin' en you blood, ain't no way you ever get it out," replied the former legendary pitcher of the Negro Leagues. "'Cides, there's that boy in there. I think he could be a good 'un. Needs seasoning, though. The right kind."

"What you going to call your team? Where do you aim ta play?"

"Well, thought we'd play Mexico, mainly. Maybe some Panama, Venezuela, Dominican Republic and Puerto Rico. Travel around and play the local team or a league team on an off day." Rainbow held up his glass and studied the red color as the incandescent light of the evening showed through. "Don't know yet what I'd name 'em."

"Put 'Pan-American All Stars' in there somewhere. They like the name 'Pan-American' down there. And get a mix of players from all over if you can. Be like the 'All Nations' team. Remember them?"

"That was 'fore the First World War, Johnny Rae. Can't remember that far. But I think I'll stack it with U.S. boys 'cause there's less passport problems." Rainbow lit his cigarette with a match he'd ignited by snapping it off his fingernail. "Maybe I'll call us the 'Elite Giants.' The 'Pan-Am Elite Giants.' How'd that sound?"

"I think we gotta get down to business," replied Johnny Rae. He re-filled his glass and got out a book from his breast pocket as the two of them talked for several hours on the practical details necessary for putting together a first-rate outfit. There were going to be some capital expenses, like uniforms and equipment and an RV to carry the eleven men who would comprise his outfit. But Rainbow had a stake from the proceeds of his dry-cleaning business that he had sold a month before. What he wanted from his old friend were connections to people who could get him engagements and provide publicity.

Rainbow had gone in hoping for a contact from his friend. What he got was a promise that Johnny Rae, himself, would start them off by fixing up a tour. After that, arrangements would be provided by the key contact, Hector Ramirez, a successful promoter of traveling carnivals and circuses through Mexico and southern Texas.

In the other room things were breaking up. It was three o'clock, and in only three hours Bo had dropped fifty dollars (half of all the money he had in the world). He had gotten through the drinks and camaraderie in high spirits. It was time to retire. The young man could not wait to describe to Rainbow everything that had happened.

"Did you know that Lou-ee Reed has a pair of cufflinks with pearls in them that come all the way from Borneo? He told me they were rare black pearls worth over a thousand dollars each!"

Rainbow smiled and nodded his head. He had, of course, known all of this before. But his mind was now on other matters. Johnny Rae had painted a picture full of potential gloom. It was so expensive to start a team and even more so to keep one going. Most of the figures he had been using were on the conservative side, according to his friend. Almost all of his savings would be invested in setting out the team and seeing it into its first month of operations. It was a frightening proposition to gamble such a large stake. It was one thing for a boy like Bo to shoot for the stars – quite another for Rainbow to do so. A mature man should know better.

And what if they failed?

Everything would be gone. His fight with his son-in-law made returning to Milwaukee impossible. There was no one else. Why was he doing it? The old pitcher looked over at Bo. His young friend was already stretched out asleep. A moment ago there was so much energy and talk—then in an instant it had transformed into the balm of slumber.

Rainbow sat on his own bed fully clothed. He kicked off his shoes and propped himself up with some pillows. He was far from sleep. A light breeze blew in through the window. Rainbow Billy Beauchamp lit a cigarette and for hours watched the smoke curl and twist as it rose and dissipated into nothingness.

Chapter Five

The latest story from Sun City and the Chicago Cubs is that the perennial deficit in left-handed pitching may finally be filled by a young prospect named Phil "Bo" Mellan. The Milwaukee native is a veteran player from the Latin American Leagues. Yesterday he pitched sparkling baseball for three innings as the Cubbies' "B's" edged the Brewers' "B's" 3-1.

Catcher Jody Hill scored the Cubs' runs on a first inning three run blast. The Brewers scored on a one out squeeze bunt in the fourth.

The real excitement came when Mellan was brought on into the game in the seventh inning with runners on first and second and nobody out. The thin left-hander threw so much heat that he only needed eleven pitches to strike out the side. It was an "opening day performance" by a complete unknown who will be an unexpected surprise to Cub's field boss and general manager Buddy Bael...

IN THE MIDST OF ONE OF THE UBIQUITOUS, quiet residential sections of Sun City, near the end of a dead-end street, was an unassuming two-story house with white vinyl siding. Electric lights from upstairs and down sent their bright luminescence into the dry, cooling night air. Seated in the living room were Mr. and Mrs. Michael Rossi with drinks in their hands, waiting for their guest to return from making his "short" phone call. The hot hors d'oeuvres were cold. The ice was melted in the freshly made pitcher of margaritas and specially prepared rock salt tumbled from glass rims once chilled and painstakingly ornamented.

"Do you think we should put the dinner on?" asked Michael to his wife, Joan.

"It is nine-thirty. Perhaps it's too late for dinner," replied Joan as she fussed with her freshly prepared hairdo that seemed to be wilting despite the fact that the coolness of the evening was now descending upon the desert and its artificial oasis.

"Do you think it will save?" Michael's voice was thin as he put the inquiry to his spouse of forty-seven years. He wore a white evening coat and a red and white polka-dotted butterfly tie that he had arranged slightly off center. His wife wore a chiffon, pajama-like hostess combination that sported large scarlet and violet daffodils against a background of light brown, loosely fitting material.

Their party area was simply, yet expensively, decorated in a mixture of Swedish and Navaho decor. Though the cool night air began to blow through the large, open windows, both Mr. and Mrs. Rossi continued to perspire even as they raised and lowered their semi-consumed potations.

"Oh no. It will never save once it's been dethawed. But that's not important. After all, an eminent man like Buddy Bael—"

"Screw Buddy Bael: he's just a bloody *baseball* manager. When I worked for General Electric I had forty people under me. I don't know who he thinks he is to come here on our invitation, and then without so much as a 'howdy-do' use our phone for some long distance conference call."

"We should be gracious, I suppose," interrupted Joan as she tried unsuccessfully to fix one side of her hair.

"Gracious, shit," began Michael in a thin wavering voice. "Why, if someone had tried something like that with me when I was at GE, I'd have given him a tongue lashing he'd remember. You can be sure of that."

As Michael was finishing his speech, he gestured vigorously with his glass, splashing tequila over an authentic Navaho blanket which had cost him three thousand dollars. Joan cried out, and half of her hairdo fell completely apart. Just then, the general manager and field commander of the Chicago Cubs made his way down the stairs.

"I'm sorry to be so late, everybody," began the bald-headed baseball man.

The sides of his hair were slicked and combed upward on a slant so as to cover much of the back of his head as possible. His large stomach was somewhat masked by his steel gray sport coat which he wore over royal blue pants. Around his neck he wore a string tie that ran through a hand-fashioned silver and emerald clip that was pulled only to the top of his sternum.

"I got time and charges for the call—really urgent, you understand. It was around forty dollars or so. I left a check for an even fifty by the phone."

Buddy descended the stairs easily and went over to the now cold appetizers. He tossed a few in his mouth and filled his hand with several more. "I'll tell you, that baseball wheeling and dealing can really take it out of you."

As Buddy had made his entrance, Mr. and Mrs. Rossi were dumb as their tilted heads and frozen expressions revealed their total stupefaction. When Buddy had seated himself and taken his drink, Joan Rossi instantly got up to put dinner in the oven.

"Let me tell you, Michael, you are smart to stay out of the day to day operations of a modern Major League baseball team." Bael poured himself a drink and motioned to the kitchen for some ice. Michael, whose connection to baseball amounted to a part ownership in the concessions sold at exhibition games, began to react physically to his guest's comments. He stiffly made the trip to the refrigerator and back.

"We have one problem after another. It's a miracle that we can hold it all together," continued Buddy as he filled his glass with an inordinate amount of ice.

Michael set his drink down and placed both hands on his knees. "Well, what's this about the new kid, 'Mellan'? Caused quite a stir, you know. He really has a hummer."

Buddy laughed. "You know how it is, Michael. In spring training lots of guys seem to have the stuff to make the majors. Believe me.

This kid's a flash in the pan. If I put him into a full fledged 'A' team exhibition game, he'd fold soon enough. You can be sure of that." Bael took a long drink and refilled his glass. "If you want to know the truth, I was on the phone just now with Mr. Cakos in Chicago. He wanted the low down on this Mellan—who, by the way, is no kid. Looks over thirty to me. Not much margin in bringing along an arm that old. You'll see: one big performance and that amateur will be hit so hard that they'll have to bring him out on a stretcher."

Buddy laughed hard at his own joke as he took out his hand-kerchief and polished the back of his baldhead with a few quick circular motions. Michael didn't laugh but started to reach for an appetizer. He stopped and sat down again without retrieving any of the now cold, semi-edible fare.

"Seems the papers think you need another pitcher," put in Michael as he tried to resume the conversation in thin, confident tones.

"I'll agree," replied Buddy amiably enough. "And when I find one, I'll be the first to celebrate." These words were delivered forcefully.

At their conclusion, the general manager and field boss of the Chicago Cubs thrust two miniature wieners, which he held in the stubby fingers of his left hand, into his open mouth and, after vig-orous masticating movements, swallowed hard – even as he wiped the thick, cold lard off his fingers onto a rare Hopi table cloth. The congealed grease clung to the rare material and began to penetrate into the finely woven design.

Then Bael announced that he had to leave, mumbling something about a coaches' meeting at ten-thirty. And in a moment the field manager was gone, just as Joan came in to announce dinner. All that she saw was her husband staring blankly at their prize Hopi cloth lying stained and crumpled next to a small stack of brightly colored, Navaho-designed paper napkins.

*   *   *

The spring training office of general manager and field commander Buddy Bael was not an executive suite. It consisted of a single ten-by-fourteen-foot room with peeling, off-white walls that sported a number of travel posters interspersed with Cubs banners and advertising sheets. In the back half of this room was a large, gray metal desk with black rubber edges. The top of the desk was cluttered with all varieties of red and blue colored plastic shelving. Each was crammed with papers. On the right side of the desk was a peach-colored dial phone with an answering jack inserted into an expensive machine designed to catch calls which might not coincide with the ninety minutes or so he spent inside his cubicle each day. In the bottom left drawer was a bottle of English Gin and several partially-used pouches of chewing tobacco.

On this particular day, Buddy was leaning back in his chair trying to decide his final roster selections for the new season. The team had been on the skids for the three years he had been GM and field manager. This would be his last year if things did not work out. He knew that, but it didn't bother him. Buddy had invested his money wisely and had a number of friends in high places. He didn't need a job—this or any other. Sometimes he wondered why he put up with all the aggravation. Wouldn't he rather be spending this March in his Palm Springs home and enjoying golf at the expensive club he belonged to? After all, membership had cost him fifteen grand. It seemed that he could only squeeze in games for about three months a year. Still, he had two years left on his contract. And there were other reasons Buddy remained in Chicago. Besides, he had to admit that he enjoyed managing a ball team. It was hell, and he liked the heat.

Buddy had one more appointment left for the day. He had just disposed of Freddy Feinstein who had tried to sell him on installing a new computer system. "Computers, shit," Bael had said contemptuously at young Freddy. "We pay good money for scouting reports and we have a stats man who can do what needs to be done. Computers eat numbers. And you're going to eat shit if you ever come here with a half-assed idea like that again."

Freddy was really scared when Bael threatened to can him. The young man left shaking with fear about where he'd get another job now that spring training was over. Buddy got out a glass and poured himself a short one. It was only two o'clock, but sometimes a man has a right to reward himself.

Bo Mellan was only a couple minutes late when he knocked on Buddy's wood door. The left-handed hurler stepped in. There was nowhere to sit. Buddy liked to have everyone standing.

"Mellan. You're going north with the team," began Bael in a matter-of-fact tone. He didn't seem to look at Bo's face, but rather stared a hole through his gut. Bo was therefore surprised when the manager quickly added, "Don't get overly excited about this, boy. I'm going with ten pitchers for a couple weeks, but that's going to be cut by mid-April. You might be down faster than you got up."

The smile that had broken out immediately on Bo's face froze. The first words may have declared a sentiment, but the real passion was in the manager's retort. Bo thought about Juan Cortez. It could get up to eighty degrees when Buddy kept his door closed. There were no air vents inside. The ventilation was supposed to come in and circulate from the hallway, but Bael preferred it this way. He wanted people to sweat when they came to see him.

Bo felt a chill, however. It was a thick fog, and the chill of dampness made it difficult to see the rocks ambuscading ahead. The boat was not out of control, but it seemed as if disaster was in store for it.

Bael's jagged teeth shown as he bit off a chaw of tobacco. His private phone had been ringing all morning, but only one call had been returned. When the power beckoned, he had to reply. An erratic element on the club might be a good thing, particularly if, as Buddy had assured them, Bo was going to fold. Mellan had done well in spring training. He was a strikeout pitcher. But there had been a few lapses when lesser hitters had gotten to this unknown hurler. This only confirmed to the field commander that Bo was playing over his head.

This was not totally unheard of in the pre-season tune-up. Regulars often did not perform as well as they could because they knew their jobs were secure. It was the flyer, who seemed to peak his performance so that he appeared to be of comparatively higher caliber than he really was.

Buddy had taken kids north before who he knew he would send down in a fortnight. This case was different. A manager has to establish a certain control of his team. Every leader has a different method for dealing with his subjects. Bael knew how to control people.

There was something, however, about this Bo Mellan that made him uneasy.

When Buddy had been told that this unknown had sparked a lot of interest and that certain wise guys connected to the team, via the first aldermanic ward, believed a large amount of cash could be made off this prospect, then he knew his hands were not free. Ruppert Cakos could promote Bo and then cash in on the pitcher's demise. It was a perfect set-up. A sure way to make money – provided Bael was certain the newcomer would fail.

Even as he had talked to Chicago, Bael had fumbled for a chaw and a drink. But the normally sure-handed general manager dropped his tobacco into his drink and then knocked over his glass trying to get it out.

Buddy had to stay in control. He waited in ambush, always with the wherewithal to sink anyone who tried to make it past him. But the same fog that hides the shoals can also obscure the quarry. And it was a consummate fear that, despite everything he knew, some beacon might guide this wandering vessel into a safely protected port.

"Yes, sir," replied Bo, judging by the general manager's silence that the potbellied man had no more to say. Bo started to turn away when a grunt from behind the desk stayed his progress.

Bael was shifting around for the contract he had prepared for his new left-handed pitcher. It was a standard contract. Most of it was boilerplate hammered together by the player's union and the owners. In a new contract offered to a prospect there are virtually no deal points that can be negotiated. All the power rests with the owner. The player is his property for six years. All a player can do is take it or sit out. Careers are too short to truncate that quickly. Besides, only an established player has the leverage to get anywhere in a one-way negotiation. Prospects see a major league contract as a way to move up from the eight to ten thousand maximum of the minor leagues to the twenty-five thousand minimum of the majors (provided they aren't cut or sent down). Who wouldn't be thrilled at the prospect of playing in the big time? If only there weren't veteran players, the owners would roll over and over in their profits.

Bael grabbed the densely worded, thin-skinned declaration of future services and thrust it in the direction of Bo Mellan. "We're offering you a contract. I've got a pen. Sign it."

Bo took the paper and the pen. His eyes danced over the pre-printed sections. These were the same on everyone's contract – well, almost everyone's.

"What are you doing?" snapped Bael as Bo stood there with pen in hand but without the design to immediately sign as commanded.

"I'm looking over the contract," put Bo immediately in unhurried, measured tones. He flipped a couple pages to the part that discussed salary and conditions of employment. "You wouldn't want me to sign without looking at it, would you?"

"It would take a goddamn month to go through that thing, boy. You ain't no lawyer." The general manager of the Chicago Cubs began compulsively rubbing the spot where his drink had spilled. His thick fingers moved his handkerchief vigorously with short violent strokes in an attempt to rid the table of the liquid residue.

"It's a generous offer," began Bo looking up. "But I'd prefer an alteration."

"Alter—a—tion?" Buddy could barely get the words out. He had never had a prospect question his first big league contract. It was unheard of.

"Instead of thirty-six thousand you've offered me, I'd like to take the twenty-five minimum with the addition of certain performance bonuses." Bo spoke with the same even-measured tones.

"What?"

"Performance bonuses. If I strike out more than 100 batters, for example, I would get a thousand more per batter."

"I know what a performance clause is, son. What makes you think you're worth all that? You've never thrown a fuckin' big league pitch!" Buddy's voice quivered. Deep inside it was strong; the ambuscading rocks were ready to smash through the delicate wooden hull of the returning vessel. Buddy squeezed his bandana so tightly that the fluid he had just absorbed with it was returning to the tabletop between his prominent whitened knuckles.

"It doesn't cost you a cent if I don't perform. And you pay me less right off the top."

Buddy had told Mr. Cakos that thirty-six was too much. But the owner hadn't wanted to pay the minimum because it might make the club look bad – especially if Bo got any sympathy when they sent him down again. They intended to make money on this admittedly talented, green prospect. The public has feeling for anyone paid the lowest salary. But jack that up a bit – even a small amount – and the average fan's reaction immediately becomes, "Those bums are making too much already."

On the other hand, he thought, as a light coolness seemed to sweep over the general manager, a contract with incentive clauses (especially ones which never would be paid) could be used to make Bo appear to be an even higher paid player. If one assumed that Bo would amass statistics– as good as, say, the tenth best pitcher in the league – why that would probably put his pay at a hundred fifty grand. This is the figure that could be leaked to the press as Bo's salary. Then sympathy would go away from Mellan and onto the club that the public would perceive as being willing to take big risks for the sake of its fans.

They would get something for nothing.

There was no chance that this young upstart would even finish the season with the club, much less amass those stats. Mellan would get less money while everyone thought he was very highly paid. Mr. Cakos would love it. Interest and betting money would run even higher with such a compact. Bael would be a genius! He could make a tidy bundle himself from the owner's gambling connections.

Gradually the tight fist eased its hold of the wadded red and white checked cloth. The little ball fell on the gray steel desk and opened up its sides into an irregular-shaped mass, limp from dehydration. The water now flowed again over the menacing, jagged shoals. The time would come. Buddy smiled and reached out his hand to Bo Mellan.

"Incentives are fine with us. Work out a proposal and we'll go over it tomorrow morning at nine."

The field commander and general manager of the Chicago Cubs watched Bo leave. Buddy Bael got himself another drink and leaned back in his pivoting office chair. The time would come. There was no doubt in his mind. The time would come.

Chapter Six

"WELL, IT'S ABOUT TIME!" exclaimed Rainbow when the big, yellow school bus was rolled out of the truck barn. Johnny Rae had known a friend of a friend. They purchased and remodeled the used vehicle for a price normally paid for the bus alone. Rainbow had installed recovered reclining parlor railroad seats that swiveled with the pull of a lever. He also installed a sink-refrigerator-stove unit commonly used in RVs. The bus was completely outfitted including luggage racks, a lavatory—even a small shower!

Outside, the storage compartments were filled with bats, balls, bases etc. as well as three telescoping poles with lights, a generator, a collection of scythes, rakes and a lawnmower. They also acquired some assorted used mechanics tools, though neither Rainbow nor Bo knew anything about auto repair. Under the driver's seat, Rainbow installed a secret safe.

When it was finished they had a hotel and restaurant on wheels. Putting a team together was a more difficult proposition. It was important to find the proper mix of personalities and talents. They still had a couple more weeks for their visa and entertainment permits to be processed. Rainbow went around to all the leagues in the area to scout talent. He almost gave up.

Then, on the penultimate day, he found and signed Harold Law, a medium range short stop who could really give the ball a long ride.

It was time to leave. Every stop on their way to Galveston, Texas had the aging manager/owner of the Elite Giants eying talent as he scoured small towns and large along the way. A few people turned him down, but most liked the idea of a five hundred dollar signing bonus and the prospect of earning up to a thousand a month to play baseball. When they reached Galveston they had added four players to their roster—including one Hector Ramirez. They were only five short of their projected goal.

* * *

Hector Ramirez was a quiet man. He was the type of individual who preferred to react to what you were saying rather than to offer suggestions of his own. He wore glasses with thick, blue-colored lenses that tended to hide his eyes. While he sat and considered various proposals, the entertainment and carnival agent would smoke a short, thin cigar that resembled a cigarette.

"What I can do for you is to put you into some of the larger cities. They're the ones with regular stadiums. Most of my business is on the West Coast so I think you'd be better off there."

"How about the small towns?" asked Rainbow, who felt a little out of place in the tenth-floor plush office that had a spectacular view of the ocean.

"No margin for me. Too unstable. You can pick that up a few days at a time if you want. I suggest starting your own list of places and people willing to accommodate you. But the real money is in the larger towns. I can get you three to five thousand dollar guarantees for a series in the bigger towns—but some of those little places will only pull in few hundred, tops. It's not worth my time, you understand..."

Ramirez was somewhat pessimistic but agreed to fix things up. Johnny Rae had taken care of ten dates around the Mexico City area. With a little luck, the receipts from Mexico City should pay their bills for a while. The Texan booking agent also gave Rainbow some tips on where to find more talent. The advice turned up two more ball players, one of which – Roy Carnes – happened also to be an auto mechanic by profession.

The last word of Hector Ramirez was that they should watch out for local political graft "La Mordida" and small time hustlers or "paracaidistas." Rainbow nodded his head.

Rainbow took his elite eight through Houston and west to San Antonio where he found a Venezuelan center fielder who seemed to be able to catch everything hit into the outfield. His only drawback appeared to be a rather short temper. But he was likeable enough, and had such baseball potential, that they could not afford to let him get away. They now could field a team and headed south to Laredo to play a few easy games and to become a barnstorming club.

It was in Laredo that they played their first series of games as a unit. They mostly squared off against Mexican teams and came through it splitting the eight games they managed to fit in between Friday and Monday. The Elite Giants were getting experience. They also signed their final two players, both Mexican, who had been standouts on the teams they played against.

The group was now complete, but it was making too many mistakes on the field. Rainbow decided to arrange four games in Monterrey for the next weekend. These would be for money. They were getting short on cash very quickly. For the first part of the week Rainbow worked the team to its limit and got the players performing, more or less, at an acceptable level.

When they got to Monterrey, they immediately were impressed by the city. The team arrived Thursday afternoon and made a trek to the town square, Zaragoza Plaza, in order to promote their weekend games. They had printed up handbills that they handed out describing their team. The ball players, dressed in their new uniforms, moved in groups in front of the old cathedral and around the Palaclo Municipal, smiling and exhorting the locals to come and see them.

The people were friendly and seemed quite interested in baseball. It was a town that took recreation seriously. This was a festive city that sported bullfights and fiestas. Their people knew how to work and play—each with vigor.

Rainbow was surprised to see how many people were congregated in the town square until he realized that an event was going on that very evening. It was a band concert that was to occur right in the Zaragoza. Rainbow watched with anticipation as the musicians tuned and prepared. Most of the older people sat down in various shady spots even though it was early evening. The young people milled about.

Rainbow sat down at a cafe with Pedro Gonzales, his Mexican-American third baseman, to watch the festivities. The aging manager had sent the rest of his team to the smelting factories to spread the word and to hand out their leaflets.

As Billy Beauchamp sat back in his wrought iron chair with a local beer in hand, he realized that he had made his move. The team was a reality. Whether it would be a success was still to be seen, but he had his eleven players. All that was left was to see whether they would work well as a unit and put on a pleasing show for the people.

Rainbow took a short sip of beer and let the world come to him. The former legendary pitcher in the Negro Leagues thought back to earlier times when he barnstormed south of the border. Generally, he had hooked up with an 'All Star' team that went to Cuba, where baseball is more important than life itself. There they would play Cuban teams and white teams formed by Major Leaguers who wanted to pick up extra cash. Sometimes they would go to Mexico, but they never hit a full itinerary. Usually they would just play a couple of cities and head south to Panama and Venezuela.

Rainbow had never played in the Mexican League.

Jorge Pasquel dangled big money in front of blacks as well as whites in the early forties. Josh Gibson had gone to Vera Cruz for the '40-41' season, and many others made the jump for a longer stint. But Rainbow had gotten into a groove with the Grays. In 1940 he played in his third All Star Game. They drew fifty thousand into Comiskey Park. The Grays were first that year, as they had been in '38 and '39. It was the middle of an eight-season dynasty that dominated Negro Baseball. Rainbow had been a part of that dynasty.

But where were all the Negro League stars now? Cool Papa was a humble municipal worker. Others were employed as janitors or in similarly low status, low income positions. These men who had been the best there was! Had been. Had been.

Ahead stretched the Sierra Madres and beautiful rolling hills. Behind were the arid plains of Nuevo Leon. Rainbow felt he had been fortunate to have had his opportunity in dry cleaning. It was work. He transferred a stake he had saved and turned it into a profitable enterprise. How many others had ended with nothing? Had been. Had been.

And now he was beginning again. Another team. Traveling. Better than before. Modern luxury. His link with the old life.

His life in Milwaukee. Gone. Around him in the Zaragoza was the beautiful, traditional Spanish architecture of the old city. Monterrey was a town of many contrasts. The new city spread away from the old. The same time-honored streets connected the two worlds.

In the square before him, young teenage boys and girls were walking in concentric circles traveling in opposite directions. The ancient ritual began just as the band began its melody. The old interspersed among the young—connected by a fragile melody that drew everyone together. Old and new. An ancient cathedral and modern foundry—connected in such a way that the town was kept fresh and alive.

Old and new. Such an odd collection of ball players. His money was exhausted. There was no stopping. He had to pursue his direction or become nothing. Had been. Has been. Crumbling architecture ignored by modern technocrats. Alone: left to decay and rot.

* * *

The next day they had a double header scheduled against two teams from the local semi-pro league. They played in the city stadium and got a crowd of 8,000 loyal team supporters and boosters. Pre-game publicity had been good. Nothing sells the product better than word of mouth—and at the ten pesos, "one price admission," they were 60% cheaper than the town's Mexican League entry. After paying their quarter draw to the stadium promoter, they still netted $2,400 for their night's work (almost five days expenses).

In the first game they pitched Gypsy Joe Grandy, a short, hefty Texan right-hander. His specialty pitch was officially the forkball, but he really was a master of the spitter and the cut ball (two illegal pitches, which he carefully masked). His spitball began at the knees and dropped into the dirt. His cut ball sailed a bit, prompting the batters to go after it. But the ball wouldn't travel far because of the cuts. These cuts in the ball, applied by Gypsy Joe's belt buckle, interfered with the projectile's aerodynamics that usually resulted in medium fly balls that stayed inside the ballpark for easy outs.

The Elite Giants won the first game as big, muscular Roy Carnes, the first baseman, hit an eighth inning home run with Jimmy "Juice" Johnson and José Morales aboard. The final score was 4-2. But the hometown team in the second game was the better opposition. Bo started the second game. The thin left-hander had a two-hit shutout going into the seventh when he was greeted with a line shot to 'Mellow' Carmello in left field. It was a chance that Carmello should have fielded. Instead, the young left fielder broke back instead of forward. He tried to recover by rapidly reversing his direction and lunging for the ball, but it was too late. The ball bounced just ahead of the diving Carmello, and rolled to the wall where the vigilant José Morales prevented the mistake from costing the team an inside-the-park home run. It ended up as a triple.

Then there was a scratch hit off the glove of the charging Pedro Gonzales. Suddenly, the opposition had a run. Bo kicked the mound with his spikes and proceeded to yield in consecutive pitches: a double and a home run. The home team spurted out to a 4-2 lead. Rainbow replaced Bo with the right fielder, Sam Nuxall. The Elite Giants went on to lose 5-3.

* * *

"Why'd you take me out?" asked Bo when the game was over, the players dressed, the money counted and everyone was heading back to the bus.

Rainbow didn't answer. The team had split its first two games. But they weren't working together the way he wanted them to. It was also bad for the gate to lose so early in a series against the town's team. One of the reasons people come out to see an exhibition game is to be amazed. If the visiting team steadily defeats the homegrown talent, people tend to come out game after game in order to see if the visitors can lose.

Another thing they needed to work on was showmanship. A few stunts and lighthearted fun entertained a local crowd and made it an experience that the whole family could enjoy. Overly intense and completely 'straight' baseball tended to attract only the baseball fanatics. They needed a broader base, especially in the small towns where this added edge might make the difference between a crowd of two hundred and one of four to five hundred.

"I was going good. If Carmello hadn't—"

Rainbow spun around. "It's in the can, boy. You lost it out there. A pitcher's gotta bounce back. He can't cry over a few errors. Until you learn that you ain't going to be nothin'."

Bo stopped where he was. His long, unkempt curly hair was blowing in the chilly Monterrey night air. Bo felt isolated. He had been pitching so well. If only Carmello had been able to handle that easy chance. If only—

Bo couldn't let himself think about it anymore. Such an easy fly ball. A pitcher has the right to expect that the players around him will play competent baseball. He couldn't let himself think of it anymore. Still, he had had a two hitter going....

Rainbow and the others left Bo behind. It was ten thirty and Bo still had two and a half hours until curfew. He decided to go someplace for a couple of beers.

* * *

It was one forty-five when Bo stumbled up to the team bus. The young left-hander was walking with some effort. His body was bent and he held his gut tight with his right forearm. The curly haired pitcher panted with labored irregularity. His lower lip was puffy. Some coagulated blood clung to his chin.

When he got to the bus, Bo tried the door but found it locked. Without any further action he shuffled over to the side of the vehicle. All that Bo needed was a smooth, quiet place to set himself down.

Then a hand touched Bo's shoulder. The young hurler pugnaciously tried to react, but the pain in his gut slowed him down. The curly haired man staggered. He could not coordinate this maneuver. He would have fallen on his back except for the firm hand of Billy Beauchamp. Without a word, the team owner and manager took his young charge and led him docilely into the team bus.

The next morning the ball players were up by eight. They had practice at ten. Bo's condition and physical injuries were apparent to everyone. Rainbow ate before the rest and waited outside with a couple of smokes while his team went through their morning rituals.

It was nearly nine when Bo Mellan came out to Rainbow Billy Beauchamp. The manager was sitting on a bench staring at the mountains and hills stretching out before them. The early morning haze painted a translucent glaze of white over the deep natural hues of the imposing scenery.

"I guess I owe you an explanation," began Bo. His head was generally clear except for some localized pain where he had suffered bruises.

Rainbow took a long drag and continued his steady gaze at the almost ethereal, rugged panorama that would be his future.

"I went to a bar and had a few drinks. Honestly, that's all I intended to do was simply to have a beer or two. I needed to relax. Anyway, I'd forgot that I didn't have no Mexican money so I gave them a couple U.S. bucks and they give me a bunch of drinks I never tasted before." Bo took a deep breath of the fresh morning air. The rarefied mixture did not sit well with his body and he coughed. Suddenly, Bo did not feel as well as he had when he first awoke. The lanky left-hander tried to straighten his snarled, curly hair, but the light brown tangle would not respond. This morning the reddish highlights were subdued.

"Then there was this girl," began Bo as he shifted his hands to his pockets.

Rainbow leaned back and tossed away his cigarette.

"Nothing happened or anything. I mean between me and the girl. She just sat there smiling at me and so I smiled at her. You know. We seemed to have a—I don't know—a kind of attraction."

"Shit boy. You a fool." The words shot out of Beauchamp's lips. He turned and looked directly at his charge.

"Well, I moved a little closer. I thought I'd buy her a drink or something. Maybe we'd talk."

"You know Spanish, boy?"

"I don't understand it. She seemed so friendly across the bar there. She was smiling at me. Inviting me over with her eyes. Damned if she didn't."

"And when you got over to her some gaucho told you to hold back, right?"

Bo looked amazed. "How'd you know?"

"And you said you just wanted to talk with miss little lady and then there was pushing and shoving and somebody threw a punch."

"The next thing I knew I was laying on the street; my head aches and I don't know where I am."

"Did they roll you?"

"Yep. Took twenty dollars."

Rainbow got up and gazed at Bo. The boy did not look too bad considering what he had gone through the night before.

"Well, you're lucky you're not in the hospital. You'll be no good to the team, though, for this weekend series. I'm going to fine you $100 and post a fine notice on our bulletin board inside the bus."

Bo hung his head and shuffled away. He didn't have any money and now his next pay envelope was going to be $100 light. The coach was going to make an example of him. But Bo could not blame Rainbow.

The team's bonsai box, into which all fines arrive, would be 100 dollars richer come payday.

* * *

The other two games in Monterrey went well, though the attendance was not what it was for the first night in town. Still, the team had earned a comfortable sum that would see them through several weeks of playing the small town circuit.

Next stop was Mexico City, in which they had ten games in twelve days. This was a leisurely pace, but you had to bring around a team slowly. Mexico City has several professional clubs and scores of semi-pro outfits. The city itself sprawls high on the plateau between its large mountain protectors. Lake Texaco was dry and edged with miles of slum hovels. Around the city, which stands a mile and a half above sea level, was a blanket of smog that stretched almost to the dormant volcanoes Popocatepetl and Iztaccihuatl.

Among their ten games, six were scheduled for large stadia. Rainbow took his team into Mexico City a couple days before their first game. The old pitcher had to finalize some details, arrange some small town exhibitions and work out his team at altitude.

The first night in town, curfew was extended to 3 a.m. It was impossible to visit a metropolis like Mexico City without hitting some of the nightspots. Most of the players had barely touched their $500 signing bonus and a few others had bettered their stake by playing cards with Bo, who was always eager to play but rarely came away from the table with more than he started with. Despite his bad card playing, Bo talked with enthusiasm about his sharpening prowess. "You fellas better watch out. My hands are so fast that I can deal from the top, middle and bottom of the deck at the same time!" His teammates would smile, sit down and take his money. But though he was a habitual loser, no one had a better time at cards than Bo. And his easy attitude made the young left-hander a favorite among his teammates.

*   *   *

That evening around six o'clock, eight of the ball players headed out as a group to see what excitement they could find. Ramon Jimmerez, the stocky catcher, and Pedro Gonzales, the wiry third baseman, stayed behind with Rainbow Billy Beauchamp. José Morales, the Venezuelan, went off by himself while the rest of the team headed out for good food, good music and good times.

After several abortive efforts, the group finally found a little nightclub where they could get food and drink while being entertained by a Mexican instrumental group and exotic dancers.

Bo sat with Gypsy Joe, Harold Law and Juice Johnson, the big mouth second baseman who liked to jive with Harold. The two of them were almost a comedy act with Juice being the comic and Harold the straight man. They were both very skinny, but Harold's extra height made him seem like a pole. His almost natural expression of perpetual surprise created a visually entertaining effect that was heightened when Juice delivered his rapid-fire lines.

The two black men seemed to develop in friendship even as their lighthearted banter went past casual wit and ascended to a more developed form of comedy. Juice spoke pretty good Spanish and so addressed the waitress when she came over to refill their glasses.

"You've got some good looking women in here," said Juice to the scantily clad waitress.

"I've been noticing your roving eyes," the waitress smiled. "Thou must be married. It's married men who do most of the looking." Juice laughed and winked at the waitress. Bo and Harold, seeing Juice smile, put on smiles of their own. But the effect was forced. Juice laughed. His sparkling white teeth seemed almost to shine in the dimly lit room. His mouth was large and when he smiled the happiness spread over his entire face. The waitress thought that her customers did not understand her joke. "Do you understand what I'm saying?" she returned in very slow, drawn out Spanish that was exaggerated so that foreigners might understand. Juice pretended to a level of Spanish competence far below his actual fluency.

"Art—thou—m-a-r-r-i-e-d?" she asked deliberately, as she was intent on having her customers appreciate her humor.

"Us?" responded Juice, raising the pitch of his voice to emphasize his incredulity. "Married?" Then he looked over at Bo and put his arm over the other's shoulder, and in perfect Spanish he fluently replied, "No, signorina. We're not married, just good friends."

The waitress broke into a large smile and laughed from deep within her breast so that the reverberations shook her ample bosom. She enjoyed a good joke and rewarded the table with a round of drinks.

There were two groups of dancers who entertained the predominantly male crowd inside the little cantina. The first group seemed to dance to the music with some skill while the second group required the musicians to follow them. This latter group was more interested in arousing lascivious interests. Both groups of female entertainers appealed to the young ball players. The audience, in general, sang along with the music while the first group of dancers performed and clapped and stamped their feet while the second revealed their talents.

After a couple of sets and dinner and more drinks, the waitress came over and asked Juice if he and his friends would like to come to a small private party with her when she got off at midnight (only fifteen minutes away). A couple dancers from the first group of hoofers would be there along with the waitress' sister—a perfect match: four for four.

Juice agreed for his compatriots, who showed no reservations themselves. The four of them heightened their interest at the delightful possibilities awaiting them. At midnight their waitress, Maria, came over and asked Juice for some money for booze and something to keep their concierge content.

"How much?" inquired the nineteen-year-old second baseman.

"About fourteen hundred pesos should do it," replied Maria. Juice was not too good at math, but his rudimentary knowledge knew that at twenty pesos to the dollar, she was talking big bucks. But Juice was not the kind of individual to let money get in the way of his having a good time. He pulled out a roll of bills and paid Maria the money. At the same time he kept a close eye on her in case she should decide to split, all at once.

Juice came back to his friends and told them that they each owed him four hundred Pesos for their nocturnal adventures. No one seemed to mind much except Harold, who kept mumbling that he wasn't interested in professionals.

Finally Gypsy Joe replied that four hundred pesos was only twenty dollars and that you couldn't get a professional for that kind of money. Harold replied that twenty dollars went a long way in Mexico. Bo had to borrow from Juice, who was down to two hundred himself. After a wait of ten minutes or so, Maria came out dressed more plainly and completely than she had been in her waitress outfit. The two dancers accompanying her were more smartly attired. Juice took Maria's arm while Bo and Gypsy Joe each escorted one of the dancers out of the establishment. Harold walked behind with his hands in his pockets. He would get Maria's sister, though he was still a little unsure whether he liked the idea of this rendezvous. Though he was only twenty-two, hardscrabble experience had made this black shortstop a cautious man. As they walked, his eyes searched about the shadows waiting for something to happen.

It was only a four-block walk to Maria's apartment. They had to press an outdoor button before opening a large wooden door that led to a small packed dirt courtyard. On each of the four sides of the courtyard were apartments that could be reached by one of two entrances. The group cut across and up a square staircase to Maria's two-bedroom lodgings.

Harold's reservations vanished when he met Carmelita, a telephone operator at a local hotel. Though she had crooked teeth and was rather short, the shortstop was taken by her clear complexion and retiring manner. The two of them quickly became engaged in a stumbling conversation consisting of broken phrases and considerable body language.

Soon, however, fluency in Spanish became a moot issue.

* * *

The first one to awaken in the morning was Gypsy Joe. The stocky right-handed spit baller never slept soundly for more than a couple of hours. He was always waking up at night to observe the scene before allowing himself to resume his slumber. When the Texan opened his eyes he noted that Harold was snoring, but that Carmelita was gone. His watch had stopped so he tried to turn the shortstop's arm over. It was too difficult. A church bell struck. He guessed that they had overstayed their curfew. Time was of the essence.

The spitball pitcher quietly pulled on his pants and carried his shoes as he swiftly made his exit. If he played it right he might be able to return to the team bus undetected. Gypsy Joe's escape was discrete, but it did not go unnoticed. Maria had watched it all from her vantage point at the end of the hall in the back bedroom.

The waitress returned to Juice and awakened him with a nudge. The spray hitting, flamboyant fielding second baseman opened his eyes. In an instant he was alert.

"What passes?" he whispered in Spanish.

"Thy friend. The white man has just left."

"Bo?" Her face was expressionless. "The tall white man or the short one?"

"The short one with the wild eyes."

"That's Gypsy Joe. What's the matter? Did he take something?"

"No. I question only that he leaves like a thief, though I see he has taken nothing."

"What time is it?"

"We have no clock. The time we know by the church bells. When thy friend awoke, it was fifteen before the hour."

"What hour?"

"Ah, that I cannot say."

"We've got a curfew of three," began Juice in English as he rubbed his eyes with his hand, as if to clear his foggy head still full of drink.

"But we've probably missed that." Then in Spanish again, "We must get back to our baseball team. But a couple hours won't make much difference. We will be fined for being late, so why not enjoy the final hours."

"Thou must return at what time?"

"If we leave before eight we should have gotten enough rest for practice."

"Go to sleep, then. I will awaken thee."

Juice smiled and snuggled up to Maria's leg. There would be repercussions, but for now, he would relax in quiet slumber.

* * *

At nine o'clock the team gathered for a meeting. Joining the group late were Harold Law, Bo Mellan and Juice Johnson. Billy Beauchamp began to address his squad. He did not appear to pay any special attention to the latecomers. The first part of his speech dealt with some of the attitudes and behaviors he felt the team had been doing wrong in its Monterrey series. He outlined specific remedies he wished to institute and things to be practiced during their drill session.

The early morning sun seemed to brighten in a great glow that filled the heavens with an intense, vibrant show of illumination as the early haze, which always covers the city, was thinning just a little. The air was not clear, but there was freshness to the atmosphere that coaxed the reticent to continue his task.

"Finally, I'd like to impress a couple of points on you. First, this team may become something. I don't know. You have the potential for it. But you ain't there yet. You cannot be complacent. We make the reputation that we eat by. We've all got a lot at stake here. And we can't afford to ruin it by sloppy play. We're professionals. We have to put it on the line – every day. Remember that. Every day.

"That leads me to my second point. That's curfew. Now 3 a.m. is not too tough to make. You can do all the drinkin' and wenchin' you want until three. But you can't practice if you don't sleep. And you don't sleep when you come in here late. Now I says 1 a.m. on game days and 3 a.m. on off days is not too tough to make. Everything depends on you playing ball the way you can.

"I'm not a policeman. Anyone just missing curfew by an hour or so must pay a hundred dollar fine. Flagrant violations of more than that will cost you two hundred. And anyone missing practice or being late to a game may find himself off the squad without severance. I depend upon you, yourselves, to voluntarily report to me when you break a rule. I know who you are. I don't need no informers. Just the man hisself; he come forward and take his medicine."

Rainbow turned around and walked back to the bus. He said over his shoulder, "Practice in one hour."

The congregation broke up slowly. Bo, Harold and Juice, who were standing together, moved as a unit toward their manager. No one looked to see whether the other was coming. They just all moved together. Each man acting alone. All with one thought.

Gypsy Joe, who had climbed in an open window before anyone awoke and thus avoided detection, sat alone on a rock. He watched the band of three move away. He knew that even if they squealed, he would not be in any trouble because none of them could vouch for when he left. He watched the penitent ball players go toward their punishment. He walked over to a shady tree to get out of the sunlight. There the Texan squatted like a toad. From around his neck he grasped a little amulet that he always carried with him as a good luck charm. A former cellmate made it for him in the metal shop. Something about the abstractly shaped ornament calmed him. It had seen him through many incidents. His metal companion reassured him more than any person could. Gypsy Joe liked to stroke the shiny brass finish that never tarnished due to some protective coating that sealed out the natural elements. This coating was tough. Nothing could penetrate it. It was smooth so that dirt or grease didn't stick. But most of all he admired its shine as it appropriated the world around and displayed that beauty as if it were its own. Any image could be reflected by its surface depending upon where it faced. Just now, it captured the shade tree and the boulder next to which Gypsy Joe was squatting.

The stocky pitcher from southeast Texas remained where he was, slowly stroking the brass talisman as if he were performing an incantation that might reveal his horoscope and aid him in arriving at his end before any of his pursuers.

Chapter Seven

TWO THINGS STRIKE YOU IMMEDIATELY about Wrigley Field in April. First, the normal verdant lushness of the ivy covered walls and high infield turf is even more intense. This may be due to the rainy, cool weather or perhaps it is just the contrast to the oppressive winter that sometimes (around the ides of March) severely tests the spirit of hope.

Second, one notices directly that this edifice commonly known as "the friendly confines" is the coldest place in the city. The wind comes racing through the aging structure with greater force than in an aviation test tunnel. This means that while people on the street may be wearing light jackets, spectators in the ballpark don winter coats and lap blankets.

But Chicagoans are a hearty race. They consistently focus upon the positive characteristics of Wrigley Field in the springtime. For baseball represents summer. Summer means March is long way gone, and the Cubs signify baseball.

This latter claim must be made guardedly since the Chicago Cubs have not been one of the more successful teams since 1945. For starters, they have not won the National League Pennant since the end of World War II. For another, they have the nasty habit of focusing their meager successes either in the early part of a season and vainly raising fan hope, or in the month of September after a pitiful season that allows tongues to wag, yet again, the famous epithet (sic. epitaph) of Chicago sports teams, "Wait until next year!"

Things with this ball club have been so bad that at one time in the late 50s and early 60s their promotional advertisement read:

> Come to beautiful Wrigley Field. Bring a picnic lunch and meet friendly people. Enjoy the scenery and breathe in the fresh lake air and see a Major League baseball game besides!

Bo Mellan was sitting in the bullpen located down the left field line. As is typical in the spring, the wind was coming out of right field in gusts approaching thirty miles per hour. The field temperature of forty-seven degrees seemed like a lie intended to taunt lesser creatures. Surely some of the standing water in the outfield must have turned to ice as huge gusts of wind swept toward home plate with a ferocity that made hitting a rather unenviable occupation.

It is in the month of April that "the friendly confines" can inflate a pitcher's apparent worth and distort the true mettle of a ball club.

However, Bo was not getting such an opportunity. Since coming north with the team after spring training, he had not had one game appearance. Day after day through three full series he waited and watched the game from afar. He sat hunched over, cold and stiff.

Mellan didn't even get to pitch batting practice. His balls did not hit far enough. "You pitch a dead ball, fella. We need to get our men some confidence with their sticks," spat Bael as he pulled Bo out after a few practice pitches one day after they had opened the season in Pittsburgh. Bo had turned and walked out to left field to shag some flies, but that day everyone seemed to be hitting to center and to right.

"Just wait until we start this weekend series tomorrow," encouraged Sam. "He'll have to play you. This is our second home series and the fans will be wanting to see you after that spring you had."

"Had. That's about right. The people are going to forget all about me if I don't see some action."

"Don't know 'bout that, Bo. Why I remember when I was with them Giants. We were pretty well liked in San Fran. Even better than New York—least ways we were in the early sixties. We had Mays, McCovey, and Marichal. Shit. We was some hot operation. Nobody got no ink 'cept the front line.

"But come the late sixties and early seventies when we was losing more'an we won —and worse yet, gettin' pounded by the fuckin' Dodgers— Holy Shit! You'd think the team was made up of back-benchers and minor league prospects. Thems the ones the Chronicle wrote 'bout.

"Nope. I says this much: long as we're winning, you're probably nobody and Buddy'll use you and throw you away just as it suits him." Sam screwed up his green eyes and leaned over the Formica table top at the luncheonette where Sam was consuming both of their noonday meals. "But I'll tell you this—sure as I'm alive. This team won't play shit. Don't think they want to. Nothin' there. No heart—got what I'm sayin'?'"

Bo nodded and sipped the cup of coffee that he always drank dark and bitter.

"That team's got talent, but—" Sam interrupted himself by down-ing the last quarter of Bo's cold pastrami sandwich in a single bite. "They gonna fall apart," resumed the eyes with emerald intensity, "before All Star Break. Bet my life on it. You've gotta have it here to win in this league," he said, striking his sternum just a couple inches below his throat. "This team don't have it."

Bo stretched his thin lips into a semi-smile as he reached for the check that Sam let him take after a weak, but sincere, counter offer.

The two men got up without talking.

Bo left a couple bucks on a six-dollar lunch. Sam looked at the tip and then to the ceiling, and then put his arm on Bo's shoulder in a paternal fashion and whispered in his protégé's ear, "Say, that was no twenty dollar lunch there, son." He cleared his voice as if deliberating how to broach the subject further.

Bo turned his head and winked at his friend, "Tasted as good as one to me."

When they were outside Bo waved good-bye to Sam.

Bo was going to look at an apartment that he had seen in the paper. Sam was heading back to the stadium for a coaches' meeting. As the thin, former pitcher for the N.Y. and S.F. Giants opened his cab door, he turned and yelled to Bo, "Just you wait and see—el foldo by July 4th."

Bo forced a smile.

"I'm right, I tell you. You'll see," said the other as he slid into his cab. "If I last that long," replied the rookie pitcher softly as he waved to his friend.

* * *

Bo had to get to the South Side from the little cafe on Grand Street near State where they had had lunch. It was near the hotel where Bo had been rooming. Now, however, Bo was interested in more permanent lodgings. The place he found was in Hyde Park.

The left-handed pitcher walked up to a newsstand, bought a paper and asked directions for using the public transportation to take him to Hyde Park on the city's South Side.

A diminutive, crusty faced man with short, stiff white hair pointed a stubby finger out of a pair of cut-off jersey gloves toward a green railing only a block away. Bo was told to hop an "S" train and get off at Garfield Boulevard.

The station at Grand and State was dark. Several caged lighting fixtures looked as if they hadn't been replaced in years. They were forgotten derelicts of a system that was progressing toward obsolescence. The stairwell stank of urine.

Bo sat under one of the few beams of illumination still operating and opened the *Sun Times* newspaper. His eyes skipped past the lead front-page article about local politics under the ten-point banner: CITY COUNCIL WARS.

The pitcher was still having a hard time readjusting to his native land. It somehow seemed foreign to him. Even the ball club was not what he had expected. Rainbow had often talked with him about the Majors, but reality did not square with the picture his late mentor had painted.

"What the hell you think about that coon, Ice?"

Bo looked up at a very fat man dressed as a tradesman. He wore a grimy blue striped linen work suit with the name: 'ABC * Palchinski's Electric' on the back. In front he had his first name, John, stitched in an easy red script. Apparently he had been doing something near the switch where his work tools lay. It must be his break, thought Bo.

John continued, unperturbed by Bo's inattention.

"Him and his 'sweet sixteen' is ruining the council. Blockin' up the city's what them is doin'. All for themselves they is, too. No good lousy blackies."

Bo folded up his paper and walked up to the edge of the platform. There seemed to be no sign of the train. He wasn't even sure from which direction it would be coming. A rush of stale air told him something would be happening.

Meanwhile, the workman continued with his harangue, "I think Dailey and O'Neil oughta kick his black butt back to Africa or Alabama or some other foreign country."

The train arrived. Reluctantly, Bo began to read the front-page lead story. The article described how the mayor of Chicago, Eddy "Big Stick" Dailey and his men on the city council (called the "strong twenty-three"—meaning they had twenty-three of the fifty slots on the council) were in a battle with a Black group of councilmen called the "sweet sixteen," over reapportionment of the city wards. Wilson Ice, the spokesman for the "sweet sixteen," had called Sean Patrick O'Neil, Dailey's lieutenant and council chairman, a lot of printable insults while O'Neil and the Polish block headed by Adam Wojciuk claimed that Ice had cheated on his income taxes and ought to be thrown off the council. The whole event ended with an adjournment that no one could hear over the loud ruckus.

It was all a confusion to Bo. If this was the way politics worked in Chicago, Bo was not impressed.

Then there was sunshine, as the subway became the 'el.' The train rose dramatically above Cermack Road, past Chinatown into the light of the South Side.

* * *

Bo smiled for the first time since lunch and put down his paper. The faded blue eyes recognized nothing except Comiskey Park that loomed ahead on the right. He had been there over a decade ago. It had been a little walk from the hotel he had shared with Rainbow.

Seeing the old brickyard sitting atop its knoll reminded him that he had been in the same town as Angela for five days and he hadn't even thought to call. The green and white stadium with its one-time marvelous exploding scoreboard reminded Bo of a carnival ground before hours.

Bo didn't know Chicago, but Rainbow had talked about it plenty. He knew the city from his barnstorming days with the ABC's, Crawfords and Grays. Chicago had been one of the centers of the Negro Baseball Leagues. The Chicago American Giants were a perennial Midwest powerhouse. Only the Kansas City Monarchs could touch them (though the Cleveland Buckeyes occasionally gave them a run for it).

It was in Chicago that the Negro Leagues generally held their All Star game. "My, that was a special game," Rainbow used to say. He had played in four All Star Games. The first in 1934 was when he threw for the Crawfords. Gus Greenlee had paid him a hundred fifty dollar bonus for being selected and for pitching several scoreless innings against some of the finest hitters in the country. They played to 30,000 paid customers. It was a fine day. Many of his teammates, Oscar Charleston, Judy Johnson, Josh Gibson, Rap Dixon, Jimmie Crutchfield, Vic Harris, Satchel Paige and Cool Papa Bell were regular all stars. But something was special about that '34 team.

Robert Cole, owner of the Chicago American Giants, had thrown a giant party for them the night before. It lasted till almost game time the next day. There was music, women, whiskey, and a big-time crapshoot bankrolled by some of the high rollers in the league. '34 had brought in a lot of large gates even though it was in the midst of the Depression. Perhaps people needed entertainment more than ever.

"I came to Chi-town with eight hundred iron men resting in my clip, and I was hot to toss for more." Rainbow carefully rolled a cigarette. "Done lost over two hundred. Was damn lucky, too. Lot of ways a young man could lighten his pocket at that bash."

The young Rainbow Billy Beauchamp was only twenty-four at the time. But he was really younger than that since he hadn't played much ball while growing up in his hometown of Arkadelphia, Arkansas.

"Goddamn, how I hate farming. Not much else in Arkadelphia. But I will say this much for it: throwing hay builds up the shoulders and legs." The young Billy Beauchamp could hay all day long. "And I hated every minute of it.

"When the Little Rock Generals came by with a traveling team, I joined up and within the space of a year and a half —after a turn with the ABC's— I was up with Greenlee in Iron City.

"God, that was a grimy town. You needed a couple 'a good shots almost after breakfast to keep your wind level for the day." Rainbow's chocolate brown irises would shine and then he'd light another smoke. "That's probably why I took up these," motioning to the cigarette in his hand. "Got used to smoke in the lungs and didn't feel much natural without it.

"Anyway, Gus owned a bunch of joints. Prohibition was all over then, but just the same, they seemed a bit shady. I guess I had a pretty powerful thirst in those days. Kind of like you, Bo. But we played and played ragged: one to two hundred a month 'cept for the stars who renegotiated every few months.

"Everyone was changin' teams and going after the best bank roll. And Gus had the fattest roll. Some say he got it under the table and tried to wash it with his ball club. That way he could spend pretty much what he liked. But who knows?"

Rainbow stretched out his long legs so that the tops of his socks and about one inch of his leg showed out from the protective covering of his tan, brushed cotton trousers. It wasn't often that the former pitching star was quite so candid. Even when he was drunk, the man acted just the same as when he was sober: wary and watchful.

The smoke from Rainbow's cigarette curled and rose until it hit the ceiling and then flattened out and formed a band of haze that gradually descended upon the pair as they sat in the small, dark hotel room in Santo Domingo.

"Baseball ain't no money makin' operation from the owner's angle—lest you squeeze your players. But then sooner than naught, you'll lose your team—even if none of them jumps.

"No sir, old Gus could spread it around and we had good crowds in '34. Real fast. Best colored hotels and singing joints money could buy. But it didn't last. Nope, we caught it for an instant. We was full of the best players ever to put on a uniform—white or black. Tops. But we couldn't hold it.

"After '34 guys started changing. Judy and Vic were getting old and there was a general feeling of dissension. I remember in the '36 All Star Game the mood was so different I couldn't believe it.

"We had to get there on our own instead of playing our way over. No bonuses and no big party. Just get in and get back: pick-up the loot and skeedattle.

"No feeling to it. That's why I went to the Dominican Republic with Satchel in '37. No use staying with the Crawfords. They'd lost it. The management became the ones a playin' the games. The team decided that the owner's contest was more exciting than the ones we was playin'."

"Is that when you shifted to the Homestead Grays?"

"Nope. We had to play for Trujillo. Sounded like good money. Thirty-grand split ten ways—except for Satchel—who seemed to get the biggest part of it. He was the middle man, you know, and the middle man always takes his right off the top 'fore anybody else.

"We were lucky to get out of there. They had us in jail for a while. Remember that. Watch out for crazy guys down south. They play by different rules than they do in the old U.S. of A. Even today."

Bo nodded and stared at the smoke.

"A few of us got out on a boat at night run by a rum runner who was taking some stuff to Cuba. We paid him five hundred to take the three of us with him. So we played in Havana and along the northern coast there down to Cardenes for a few months to get a stake to take north. While we were there we hitched up with Buck Leonard's all-star team that was doing some traveling.

"There was one series we played Dizzy Dean's team of major league stars, and we cleaned them: eight games to one. 'Twas then I knowd that the Major Leagues was not any better than we was... deeper perhaps than most of the Negro teams 'cept the Crawfords, Grays, Cubans and Monarchs. But the stars of our league could play nose up with anything they had."

By now the smoke was descending and obscuring the face of Rainbow Billy. His wide hand gesturing, while holding his home-rolled smokes, only added to this effect. Outside, the light was beginning to fade. Neither man moved to turn on the bare light bulb that was centered on the dilapidated ceiling.

"Buck was a star with the Grays and told us the team was looking a bit short. So we headed up with him. Before the year was out the other two had left. But I stayed. Josh, Vic and Cool Papa came in the middle of the season. It was kinda like a reunion.

"Finished it up right there, except for a couple years at the end with the Chicago club."

"Did you like the Grays more than the Crawfords?"

"Not a question of that. Just different. That '34 Crawford team had more talent on it than any team in history. We lived like princes that year. And nothing makes quite such an impression on a young guy as having everything money can buy.

"But the effect doesn't last long. And the second time around it isn't quite the same. It's never the same. Trouble is that most guys spend their whole lives trying to get it back again. And you can't do it. Jist can't.

"That's why I started saving my stake for when the legs didn't give my arm the kind of power I needed to stay in the big time." The light outside was slowly fading away.

'The Grays were a real team. They didn't have the talent that the '34 Crawfords had, but they had something that we never did have on the Crawfords. It made everyone a better ball player, and it made me a pitcher."

"I know. I know," mumbled Bo, looking down and stepping on a roach.

"No, you don't."

Bo twisted his foot so that the back of the roach cracked audibly.

"You haven't really played ball until you get it. And you're not a ball player or even anything at all until—"

Bo made a clucking noise with his tongue as he lifted his foot. Remarkably, the roach was still alive. The freed insect scurried across the floor. Incredulous, Bo lifted his eyes to Rainbow, but the other was lost in a darkened, smoky haze.

GARFIELD—55th

The sign announced itself in block letters that somehow caught Bo's eye, though he had not been cognizant of the last few stops. Quickly he scrambled to the door and just missed being caught by the sliding panels that were in the process of closing.

The station overlooked Garfield Avenue. Bo got directions from the lady selling flowers and went east past the unhappy end of an even sorrier street to Washington Park, which stood on the western perimeter of Hyde Park.

Washington Park is a pleasant plot of urban greenery. It's cut in two by a street that meanders between the north and south sections. Once Bo got to Cottage Grove Avenue, he had to ask directions again. In ten minutes more he was standing in front of a four-flat brownstone with the name 'Deronda' chiseled into the stone above the door. Also, there was the figure of the waiting landlady. Her hair had a wild, unkempt look that was heightened by a face that wore too much powder and bright red lipstick. Even outside, Bo could detect the cheap cologne she wore to cover up her pungent nicotine habit. She was slight and appeared to be made of double gage copper wire.

"You're late," she said, even while Bo was introducing himself.

"I'm sorry. I'm new to the city."

"Half an hour. That's money, son. I demand my tenants be responsible. No one ever thinks of the landlord anymore. It's always 'we want this' and 'we want that'... I don't even know why I stay in business. There's no margin in it anymore. I'm just clearing taxes and heating on these buildings. And then there's upkeep. I don't know why I don't chuck the whole thing!"

"Could I see the apartment?" ventured Bo with even, well-modulated tones.

The feisty lady pivoted and opened the front door carefully with a key. Inside, a staircase rose immediately. A matted carpet that was now amalgamating with its pad led up two flights. On the first and third landings were two apartments. On the left side of the building were the two-bedroom flats and on the right were the one-bedroom apartments. Bo was considering a one bedroom.

The apartment itself was bathed in natural light. The bedroom that was just off the triple-locked doorway had a giant window that illuminated the room. And the combo living room/dining room was full of sun that visited through five bay windows.

The rooms were fashioned after a forgotten, older style with picture molding that ran along the old plaster walls 18" down from the ten-foot ceilings. There was a small kitchen with antiquated utilities and a walk-in pantry and larder. The condition of the plaster was not uniform, and the baseboards rarely met the rolling, tongue and grooved oak floor. Outside, a wooden fire escape covered with peeling blue oil paint descended to a dumpster which Miss Doolittle told Bo was emptied once a week from the adjacent alley.

"There's some work to be done, of course, but I'm proceeding according to a master plan for this whole structure that will take some time to complete. It may take me a little while, young man, but I keep my property, I'll tell you."

Bo nodded and allowed Miss Doolittle back to the living room. He liked those bay windows. Miss Doolittle fumbled about her worn, ill-fitting suit and with a sudden flourish produced a general apartment lease that crackled as the thin sheets and endless carbons straightened themselves out from their twisted posture.

"Do you want it?"

"Two-sixty-five a month?"

"First and last month's rent in advance. Thirty days notice in writing to vacate—even for job transfers."

"I'll take it."

The woman looked at him expectantly.

"I suppose you want something down?"

"I'd prefer the whole amount."

"I don't carry that kind of cash with me."

"A check will do."

He didn't tell her that he didn't have a checking account. "Here's fifty. I'll get you the rest tomorrow."

She snatched the money with one hand and made out a receipt with the other. Then suddenly she lifted her gaze and cocked her head. "You need furniture?"

"Maybe. What have you got?"

"Sofa, table and chairs, kitchen utensils, dresser and bed. You supply the linen. I've got 'em in three grades that go for 25, 35 and 45 a month extra."

"I'll take the middle grade."

"That'll be $309 a month plus $600 in deposits. You can pick up your key when you pay Adolph. He'll be by tomorrow at nine."

Bo found himself in the hall in front of his door. It certainly wasn't much. And undoubtedly he was overpaying for it, but he'd had much worse.

Then he heard the sound of creaking steps. Someone was ascending the stairs. Miss Doolittle? No, it was a young couple: a black man and a white woman. Their arms were full of grocery bags. When the man became aware of Bo standing at the top of the stairs, he stopped and stood motionless for an instant. Then he assumed an expression of defiance.

"What you doing here?" barked the man. He was a broad shouldered fellow who didn't appear to have an ounce of fat on his five-foot ten-inch two-hundred pound frame.

"Hi," returned Bo with a smile. "I'm your new neighbor. Bo Mellan's my name."

"Humph!" said the man with a scowl on his face as he pushed past Bo and into his flat. Bo looked at the woman who had a kinder expression on her face. She smiled a short smile that seemed to say, "I'm sorry, but that's the way he is—and he's the man of the house."

Bo gave a nod of his head and descended the stairs even as his neighbor's door slammed shut and the sounds of lock tumblers sharply engaging told a story of their own.

On the mailboxes at the bottom of the stairs Bo figured out that this couple was named Jenkins. L. Jenkins.

"How do you do, Mr. L. Jenkins?" asked Bo of the mailbox. "Nice to have you as a neighbor, Mr. Mellan," Bo answered for the box. "Are you new to the city, Mr. Mellan? You are, well, let me be the first to welcome you to Chicago. Let nobody ever say we are an unfriendly town."

"Much obliged." Bo returned to the box and opened the front door. He noticed there wasn't even a latch on the security lock that Miss Doolittle had pretended to open earlier with a key. "Yes sir, Mr. Mellan, welcome to Chicago."

Chapter Eight

THE NEXT MORNING AT 7:30, Bo Mellan planted himself on his suitcase outside of Deronda. His bag was a rugged metal-frame case covered with tan leather as was popular in the 1940s. The case was well worn and the corners had been reinforced with steel caps. If one looked twice, he could detect a seven inch rip on the broadside that had been sturdily sewn together.

Already people were bustling about. The hospital nearby was changing shifts and the university down the road was gearing up for another day.

The neighborhood was a rarity for Chicago. It was completely heterogeneous. There were doctors from the hospital who lived in a special residence across the street. University professors and lawyers who taught in the law school also trudged by from their Hyde Park condominiums. There were equal numbers of low income and unemployed people of all ages and colors who made their appearance as they marched on their way to somewhere.

Bo noted this mixture of people as he sat on his suitcase, arms outstretched, his hands resting on his knees. The pale blues were keen. He wanted to know all about his neighborhood. What better way than to watch people in their unguarded moments. And surely, who has the energy for pretenses at 7:30 a.m.?

A black mother with three kids emerged from Deronda. Bo introduced himself. The woman was cordial, but cold. She pulled her wide-eyed children along. The little people were dressed in new, cheap, ill-fitting clothes. The wide eyes didn't hide their curiosity nor their disappointment at losing a chance to gaze at this stranger.

Longhaired scraggly types also were making their way eastward, carrying thick tomes on organic chemistry and battered copies of English poetry. These were the students who added the final complement to the area.

Soon, a gold Cadillac Eldorado pulled up noisily and spun into the "no parking" zone marked off in front of Deronda. A tape player was blasting loud music to which the occupant seemed oblivious. Out hopped a twenty-three year old white male with dusty hair and a glowing complexion. He wore a khaki leisure jump suit. The fellow took a quick glance at his solid gold wrist watch and proceeded to the building as he jawed a wad of gum.

"You the new tenant?" he pointed a finger at Bo.

Bo nodded.

"You got the bread?" The man jangled over to Bo.

"You got the key?"

"Let's go upstairs."

Leisure suit was efficient. Within minutes Bo was pocketing his receipt and leaving his apartment. As he shut his door he saw his neighbor again. She seemed on the verge of meeting his glance now that the man of the house was absent. She paused for a brief instant and then hurried down the stairs—almost tripping on a place where the carpet had slid through its metal restraint and had flopped loosely about the step. The young lady slipped, but caught the handrail and honed agilely to the midfloor landing.

Bo decided to lock-up and get to the ball park.

It was an overcast day. Bo did a little running and stretching and took batting practice. Bo was a pretty good hitter for a pitcher, but he didn't have any power. He could spray the ball around and almost always made contact. He kept the ball in play.

Bo also liked to practice his bunting. Sometimes he would take almost his entire time in the cage working on various bunts. Today, a writer for *The Herald* came by and talked to the left-hander after he got finished.

"You bunt pretty well there. Most guys just try to make contact."

"Bunting's a tough order."

"Looked to me like you put a spin on some of those bunts. How'd you do it?"

Bo mimed an imaginary pitch and bunt to show the reporter.

"You made quite a hit in Sun City during spring training. Are you disappointed at not playing?" asked the reporter as Bo continued toward the bench.

"I'm not choosing to sit on the bench."

"Then you're pretty sore about your status now that we're three weeks into the season?"

Bo stooped. He didn't like the sound of the prospective story that was being written. "The Cubs pay me to do whatever they say. If I'm helping the team on the bench, then so be it."

The reporter, a youngish forty-five, laughed. "Who helps a team on the bench?"

Bo didn't reply, but tossed his bat into the rack and made his way into the clubhouse. Inside, he went over to his locker and took out a jar of yellowish brown ointment from his duffle. Bo took off his shirt and jersey and began rubbing the pungent, homemade concoction on his left arm and shoulder. It was a laborious process that he mechanically performed as he massaged muscles and ligaments in an ordered progression.

Most of his teammates were finally coming in when the reporter re-appeared.

Bo finished his massage and hurriedly stuffed the jar back into his duffle. In the process of packing, he ripped a piece of paper that contained the address of the restaurant for his eight o'clock appointment with Angela.

"What's in the *jar* there that you secreted away when you heard everyone come in?"

"What are you? My shadow?"

"I'm a man looking for a story. And believe me. You're a man who needs one just now."

"What makes you think so?"

"Rumor is that you're headed for Iowa before the week is out."

"That's life. I guess."

The reporter grunted and shook his head. "Well, if you change your mind, here's my card—I'll jot down a private number you can always reach me at on the back."

He handed Bo his card and left.

Bo folded the card in quarters with one hand and dropped it on the dressing room floor.

* * *

The Cubs were ahead by three runs when the game was called in the fourth inning because of rain. It was a cold, driving shower. The umpires didn't hesitate because the Thursday game could be made-up in a Saturday double header.

Bo walked slowly toward the dugout. The cold rain had cleared the diamond in a hurry. He was the last uniformed man on the field, save the ground crew. When Bo got to the dugout steps, he saw Sam Dowel standing alone in the corner, rubbing the back of his neck.

"This rain shoots our rotation," said the pitching coach to the thick mud forming along the cement curbing that separated the playing field from the home team's bench area. Then Sam turned to Bo, who had stopped on the steps. Sam screwed up his eyes and stared at his protégé, whose soaking wet uniform clung to his body revealing its true form. "You're our number one man in long relief Saturday. Can't use nobody else, especially if Willie gets into the game tomorrow. Nothing Buddy can do about it."

Bo nodded and walked into the clubhouse. Sam stayed behind and watched the mud grow thin.

* * *

It was four o'clock when Bo Mellan got on the 'el' that stood across the street from the ballpark. Four hours, he thought. Eight o'clock. He would see her again in four hours.

The train rumbled on.

In thirty minutes he was scaling the stairs of Deronda. Halfway up, he overheard some scuffling and muffled cries. It was from the two-bedroom.

Bo rushed up two stairs at a time. The old, creaking, wooden staircase noisily announced his arrival. The door to his neighbor's apartment was ajar. Bo knocked on the door jam. Again the cry. A staccato of heels across the floor.

The golden haired pitcher rushed in and saw two teenaged males rushing out toward the fire escape. Bo took after them, but they knew how to negotiate wooden fire escapes better than the southpaw hurler. By the time Bo made the first landing, the pair were already on the ground and off down the alley.

The curly haired pitcher returned to his neighbor's apartment. His intrusion had been just in time. The woman was lying on the floor crying. Her light brown hair was disheveled. She lay supine with her blue eyes closed and hands tied over her head to the leg of a chair. Her blouse was ripped in front, exposing a chest whose ribs had been beaten. Her skirt was raised and torn at the belt fastening. A pair of panty hose had been ripped off one leg and lay limp against the other.

Bo knelt down and covered her up with his chenille jacket. Then he untied her hands.

"They got away. I'm sorry. I was too slow."

The attractive twenty-four year old neighbor opened her eyes and focused on Bo. "They were going to... going to..."

"I know."

"But you got here. Stopped them. You stopped them before—"

"Don't talk now."

"Larry doesn't get here till seven when he's working. All I could think of was what he'd do to me when he found out."

"Do to you?"

"Oh, I feel so ashamed."

"Do you want me to call the police?"

"No!" she replied fervently as she sat upright. "You can't... you don't know what— " Then she became aware of her position and of Bo's jacket. She modestly pulled up the old, faded blue cloth that had lost most of its original shine.

"Perhaps I'd better go," said Bo, rising. "If I can do anything for you, just come over. I'll leave my door open."

His neighbor didn't respond, but watched him leave and shut the door behind him.

* * *

It was forty-five minutes before a faint knock could be heard at Bo's door. His neighbor had changed. She seemed strangely composed and even at ease.

"I brought your coat back."

"Come on in. I don't have any furniture yet, but I can get you a cup of water and some biscuits."

His neighbor hesitated.

"You don't have to come in—or if you do, feel free to leave the door open. I can understand how strangers might be frightening just now."

His neighbor looked down and walked forward. "I'm sorry," she said, walking down the short hallway to the living room. "You have been so nice. They had knives, you know, and you might have been hurt."

"Would you like that glass of water?"

"I can't stay, really. I just wanted to thank you and make a request that you don't tell Larry about what happened."

"Sure. But don't you think he'll notice there's been a break-in?"

"They came in through the back door. I had forgotten to lock it. I must have just gotten there when they—no, they had filled up a pillowcase, but put it down to go after me. All they got was about twenty dollars in my purse I had loose and a necklace I was wearing. They were nothing that Larry would notice. Please don't tell him." The woman walked over to the bay windows. "Larry's a good man. No one's a harder worker. But he's so funny sometimes and when he gets off, there's no stopping him."

"He's bound to notice your bruises."

"He hasn't inspected the merchandise for a long time. Too busy with his company. He's an electrical contractor, you know. She turned to Bo as she said this. Her eyes sparkled for an instant but just as quickly clouded again. "He can be—he's—you know, a tough man."

"He beats you?"

"It's really my fault, I guess. But you don't know what he might do to me."

Bo didn't respond. Then after a moment replied, "You don't have to worry." The two of them stood still, watching the other. "Would you like some help straightening up your place?"

There was no hesitation on her part. "Yes. But you've already been so kind."

"My pleasure, Mrs. Jenkins."

His neighbor blushed. She dropped her head. "I feel so bad about the way we've treated you. Please, my name's Mary Evans. People call me Cora. And Larry and I aren't married."

"'Well then, Cora. Can I help you put things in order?"

Bo helped Cora try to put things back the way they were. Her apartment was set out differently than Bo's. The door opened onto large living room/dining rooms off of which were the kitchen and a hallway that led to the bedrooms.

The place was decorated with pieces of cheap, ill matching furniture that had lost its youthful bloom. The colors and patterns contrasted with each other sharply. Even the white walls seemed to Bo to be too bright and brazen.

They were almost finished with their task when Larry called saying he'd be late.

"That might mean all night or possibly only midnight," explained Cora.

"What does Larry do as an electrical contractor?"

"He's in construction. He's an affiliate contractor with Advanced Building Contractors. You've probably heard of them."

Bo explained that he was new to the city and didn't know many of the local firms.

"Advanced Building Contractors is the largest employer of construction workers in the state. They do a lot of government projects like working for H.U.D. on re-habs of old, run down abandoned houses. H.U.D. takes these re-habs and re-sells them."

"Sounds like hard work."

"Oh he works hard all right, but they got a lot of frustration, too. Cause they used to get everything—you know, in the city—if you catch my meaning."

Bo analogized that he didn't, repeating his earlier plea.

"I thought they publicized the council squabbling all over the country."

"The city council?"

"Then you have heard of it."

"Not until I picked up a newspaper yesterday. Something about a 'sweet sixteen' or something like that."

"That's exactly it. See, there's always been a boss in this city. The present boss is the mayor, Eddy Dailey. They call him "big stick" because he clobbers anyone who opposes him.

"Dailey's group controls Advanced Builders and has given them all the city contracts. But then there comes along this Wilson Ice who has a cozy interest in an all-black company, Krakatoa—which I think means something like "Black is Best" in African. They want the business that Advanced has. And not just a little, either.

"Advanced will affiliate with anyone white or black or Mexican—so long as they do it by Advance's rules."

"Dailey's rules?"

"That's right. So what's so bad about that? Larry and a lot of other blacks in the city have been getting paychecks from Advanced long before Ice's outfit came along."

"And all this is part of the fights in the council?"

"This Ice and his sweet sixteen can almost block any proposal they want to. They don't give a damn about the blacks who've been working their butts off for years just to get a foothold."

"Like the people who work with Advanced."

"Yeah. Like Larry and hundreds of others. Those Krakatowa men want to destroy the city. Jessie Jefferson is trying to stop them, but now they're stronger than he is and he's been the spokesman for the black community in this city for thirty years!"

"Sounds like an unhappy situation."

"While those dudes fight down at City Hall, the real people of the city are going to garbage because no one can agree what to do."

Bo sympathized with Cora. There were many things, though, he didn't understand about all these political machinations she was describing.

Cora spoke so guilessly that Bo eagerly listened to her various ramblings without fully comprehending what she was saying. It seemed her words ingenuously created a panorama that made him want to sit back and observe. It was a spectacle that was filled with detail that belied careful scrutiny, but rather had to be viewed in its entirety. It was a picture that, as it unrolled, encircled Bo and offered a view in all directions: nothing was seen in precision, yet the illusion was generated of an entire being. He felt as if he had all of it before him, yet he couldn't have reproduced any of the details. Still, there was the phenomenon. And it captivated him. He had not had such a vision since—

Bo looked at the clock. "My God," he blurted out loud. "I have to go. I'm sorry, but I have to go now." The short cropped, golden head turned away in haste leaving a bewildered Cora.

It was nine o'clock.

CHAPTER NINE

"I WONDERED IF YOU WOULD SHOW." The air in the little back street establishment was stale. Bo Mellan continued to shuffle forward across the sawdust-covered floor without changing his pace.

"Yeah. Well, I'm a busy man."

"Not too busy to change your mind on seeing me, eh?"

Bo sat down and took the drink offered to him. He held the glass up to the light, staring through the foamy beer at his host. Then he took a long swig before the foam had a chance to settle.

"I wanted to hear what you had to say. You claimed you could help me. Perhaps I was a little hasty when you talked to me at the ball park."

Juan Cortez smiled. The baseball and entertainment entrepreneur got them some food and engaged in small talk before engaging his real subject.

"Look, boy. You Big League material. I think you could be some sort of star." Juan Cortez had a tendency to spit his words at you. The middle-aged promoter also had a habit of cleaning his fingernails with the thumbnail of his opposite hand. The right thumb ran around the left index finger from left to right; then around the middle finger from right to left; then made the circuit of the ring finger left to right again. There was a rhythm to his hands that imitated the staccato of his speech. All the while, Juan Cortez displayed his natural teeth—perfect except for an upper canine that was twisted.

"I don't know, Mr. Cortez," returned Bo as he sipped his beer and munched on some molé that he wiped up with a stiff tortilla.

"Yesterday was my best outing so far. I mean, I hadn't even had a complete game yet."

"Pah," spat Cortez. "I know talent. I got two traveling teams of my own, you know. We play first-rate baseball here in Mexico. You gringos think we just a bunch of grease balls, but believe me, we can really play." Cortez raised his toupee-clad head with pride.

"Oh, I didn't mean—"

"Of course you didn't. But most of you Yankees say that. We big time down here. Why, I believe the Caribbean Championship to be the a-uno test in all baseball. There are more real players down here than in your Major Leagues. A bunch of fat millionaires. That's what you have up north."

"I'm not sure I'd go that far," said Bo, dropping his eyes. He watched Juan methodically remove dirt from his nails and drop it wherever it happened to fall.

"No. No. I'm not bad-talking your teams. No, no. In fact, I firmly believe we gonna have Major League Baseball here in five years, tops. 100%. Yeah. You believe that." Juan's smile momentarily dilated.

"Well, you'd know a lot more about that, I guess," responded Bo, who dropped some molé that he was trying to eat. It fell on his pant leg.

"I believe you're Big League, Bo. Right now. You strike out seventeen good players. You got smoke."

Bo finished his molé and was into another beer.

"Why aren't you playing in the big time, Bo?"

"The big time?" Bo looked up. Juan's grin infected the young man.

"Major Leagues. Yeah. Here or up north. You make a truck load of pesos, believe it."

Bo smiled. He couldn't get his eyes off Juan's teeth. They almost seemed to sparkle. "Maybe. Someday. Maybe. I don't know. Someday... perhaps. I've got to get better."

"You a-uno now. You don't get better." Juan paused as his grin dilated and relaxed once more. "But maybe you get—worse."

"Worse?" Bo lifted his eyes to Juan's. The young man couldn't hold the gaze.

"Sure. Lot of times. You got it only so long," Juan gestured dramatically. "You got so many pitches in that arm. How many? Maybe a thousand? Maybe a million?" Juan resumed his project of working his thumb through all the dirt he could. "All this time your bossman is makin' a mint off of you. He take you for all you're worth and then pick up another arm."

"You don't know Rainbow."

"I know bossman. He's all alike. Oh, I know what you think. This Rainbow; he different; he really cares." The smile dilated once again. "But why then don't he do what is best for you? If he care, why not give you a Major League tryout? You good enough."

"Well, I—"

"Pah. If he care, he want what best for *you*, not *him*. If he let you go, he lose money. You a big drawing card for him. 100%. Believe me."

Bo didn't respond. He tried once more to look into Juan's eyes but couldn't. This time, the young man's eyes skipped instead to Juan's hairpiece. The hair was arranged to one side with a part that only went half-way. Along the part was a row of sewn threads that was raised about an eighth of an inch. If you looked carefully, you could see each stitch in clear relief.

Bo only saw the general arrangement of synthetic strands as they lay in their tailored confinement. He missed the raised stitching.

"You think about it, Bo. See if I'm right. Think about you future. Only so many innings, then no more. If that bossman like you so much, why don't he help you out?"

There was nothing more to say. Juan gave Bo his card and then departed. He left quickly before Bo could discover the raised stitching.

*   *   *

Later that night, Rainbow called Bo over to talk with him. They had just finished dinner. The team had one day and two nights left in Mexico City before moving on.

"I heard you was talking to Juan Cortez after the game," began Rainbow directly.

"What? You've got spies out or something?"

"That man is poison, Bo."

"He didn't seem so bad to me."

"He wants to ruin our team."

Bo was silent.

"What did he do? Make you an offer to come with him?"

"That shows how much you know," said Bo with emotion. "He just wanted to compliment me on a good game. Something more than I ever get from you."

"A compliment is a lot like a good woman. It means a lot more when she don't go whoring around with everyone."

"What do you mean by that?"

"I mean that I don't want you or anyone else on this team talking to that no good son-of-a-bitch sleaze. He's out to ruin us because he thinks we're cutting into his territory. I've been getting his messages since we got to this city. And some of them weren't too polite."

Bo turned and walked away. Tonight, he would be like José Morales and go off by himself.

*   *   *

The next day they had two games. The first match was a late afternoon contest with a factory team for small money but big exposure (most of the co-workers hung around to watch the seven inning exhibition). It was a low-key game accented by some clowning by Juice and Harold. The crowd loved it.

In the evening they played one of the league teams that had a free day. The league season ended in October so that a late August contest was a little gravy for a team already out of its division race.

Bo pitched the game of his life against a good hitting team. He struck out fourteen and tossed a five hit shutout. The Elite Giants won 5-zip. It was a big payday. There were fourteen thousand that came to see this traveling all-star team that had been playing so well. This night's performance did not diminish the Elite Giant's reputation.

*   *   *

Bo walked back to the bus and glared at Rainbow. The aging owner did not respond, but drove them to their park for dinner. After a short meeting, they ate canned stew.

It was the last night in town. Juice and Harold were slicking up for Maria and Carmelita. Gypsy Joe, Ramon Jimmerez, the catcher, and Roy Carnes, the first baseman were also grooming themselves for a party that Maria was throwing. They were going to make a real night of it. Rainbow rewarded the team for a fine showing in Mexico City by lifting curfew. Spirits were high.

"Are you coming with us?" Juice asked Bo as the second baseman prepared to leave.

"I think I'll pass."

"Suit yourself. Great pitching today."

The group left. Another cluster stayed behind to play cards and get drunk. Sam Huxall and Candy Laro (another pitcher) were figuring to augment their wages, which they had just received.

José left by himself, and Bo sat alone in the rear of the bus.

The lights were off and the curly haired hurler could see Rainbow and the others engaging in one of Bo's favorite pastimes. He took out Juan Cortez's card and began turning it over in his hand. It was a long ways from Milwaukee. However, in time he'd only been gone four months. Cortez's card was printed in raised letters. It was too dark to see anything clearly, so Bo merely rotated the card around and around and around as he ran an index finger over the prominent characters.

"You all right, boy?" It was Rainbow.

"Why don't you get me a Major League tryout?"

Rainbow lowered himself into a seat across the aisle from Bo and swiveled around so he could put his charge in full view. "So that's it, is it?"

"I pitched a damn good game out there today."

"You got a shut out. Struck out more than a dozen. That's not bad."

"Not bad!" Bo exclaimed, slapping his knees with both hands as he tried to turn his seat toward Rainbow. The release lever on his seat was stuck. Rainbow lit up a smoke while he watched Bo struggle. In the darkened bus Rainbow's face was suddenly illuminated and then disappeared again.

Bo finally managed the lever and swiveled his seat around. "I was Big League."

"I never said you didn't have an arm." The lighted cigarette was a solitary beacon.

"Then why won't you get me a tryout? Juan Cortez said—"

"You've been talkin' to him again?"

"What if I have? You can't muzzle us. What about free speech and all that?"

"I'm the manager. I make the rules. We in Mexico now, boy. They don't do things the same as in the States. You get what you can take down here." Then there was a pause.

"Now, I want to know. Did you go back to Cortez?"

"What's it to you?"

"Just that I made a rule, and a team lives and dies by its rules."

Bo sat shaking his head.

"I'll tell you about your Juan Cortez. He almost had your show-case game shut down tonight. He told some Interior Ministry men we didn't have the right paperwork when, of course, we did."

"So you showed them, and that was that. What's the big deal?"

"Wrong. Down here, officials looking into anything always got their palms out—whether you're right or wrong. All the same. I tell you, son, this kinda stuff happens back home, but they're usually a little less obvious. 'La Mordida' they call it. 'The bite.' It came outta tonight's gate. I pay or we don't play. And what I pay them is money I don't have for paying you."

"What does that got to do with getting me a tryout? Can you swing it or not?"

"Sure I could. I'm sure I could get you into the Instructional League in Puerto Rico. They don't pay too well, but you might get a Big League tryout in the spring. Or maybe one of the Mexican League teams might need a young arm. Getting a tryout isn't hard to arrange. But you'd be a damn fool to do it."

"Oh yeah?"

Bo looked eagerly over to the beacon as it burned slowly and evenly.

"You go up now and you'll get eaten alive. You a young man, Bo. Eighteen. Scared as shit to leave Milwaukee. Mooning over my granddaughter, Angela—who's head over heels about that good-for-nothing DuRon Garvey. You just a boy. Sure you got an arm. And you can bring it, too. But you ain't no pitcher yet. You can throw hard and have a middling curve, but it takes more than that.

"A pitcher's got to have it up here and here." The beacon rose and fell from the old man's head to his chest. "The head you get from experience at a level you can learn on. You don't learn nothing starting too high or too low.

"The heart. Well, I can't say how you get a soul, boy. But I know it comes out of blood and sorrow. That's what makes you a man."

There was a considerable break in which nothing was said. The beacon was fading when Bo asked, "But what if I lose it before I finish my so-called training? Then where will I be?"

"You gotta take that chance. A person doesn't get many chances in life. When they come you gotta be ready to play 'em as best you can. You can get your tryout anytime, but don't you think it's better to have yourself ready so that when the time comes you can make the most of it? You probably won't get no second chance."

* * *

The Pan-Am Elite Giants arrived late that afternoon in Yautepec, which Rainbow had just setup the day before. The game was scheduled for three and an evening game set in Cuernavaca at eight. The crowds would be small, but they had to keep playing on their way west to Chilpancingo, then north to Guadalajara.

On the bus, Juice Johnson and Harold Law were alive and in high form from the previous evening. Roy Carnes, the slow, muscular first baseman, was relating the events of the party to the poker playing cook and third baseman, Pedro Gonzales. But before the slow speaking, big hitting ball player and former auto mechanic could get through more than two sentences, Juice would give it a twist, Harold would put a cap on it and Juice, in turn, would send it a-twirling.

"Let him tell his story. C'mon now. Be serious," intoned Gonzales.

Juice and Harold and Ramon, who had also been cutting-up, became very somber with pious expressions of attention.

"Well, about this hat," started Roy again, trying to repair his tale.

"It was the largest goddamn sombre-eo, somber-eo—how do you say that, Ramon?"

"We know what you mean, Roy," replied Ramon.

"It was a hat," put Harold.

"Say 'hat,' Roy," added Juice. "H-A-T. Rhymes with 'bat,' something you know how to handle."

"Well, it was all red with this white stichin' on the side and little tassels floatin' around the brim." The native Texan auto mechanic cum gopher ball slugger wanted a more vivid device to complete his picture.

"Show us, Roy," encouraged Juice.

"What did you do with the hat, Roy? Tell us that."

Roy fluttered his stubby fingers in the air to show how the tassels hung. The action was just right. He broke into his infectious, good-natured grin.

"What you doing, Roy? Making snow?"

"Gotta go in the mountains for that, Roy. No snow in old enchilada land."

"I think Roy's seeing things."

"How much you drink out of that hat, Roy?"

"Them's the tassels," laughed Roy, explaining his moving fingers. "And I tell you I drank a gutful. Why, I could a put all three of you runts in that sombrero and still had room for spare change."

This time Pedro Gonzales laughed as Big Roy had finally put one over on his tormentors.

"Like the man said," Roy added, "takes a whole lot of half-pints to fill a ten gallon hat!"

Candy Laro, their young right-handed hurler, set out one imaginary point for Roy. "Chalk one up for The Hulk."

When they got to Yautepec they looked up their local contact. The small time entrepreneur looked disturbed. Someone, it seemed, had dumped three truckloads of gravel on the field they had planned on using.

"What an unfortunate mistake," said the local man.

"I don't know about that," was Pedro's free translation of Rainbow's reply, "but if you've got a vacant lot we can play the game. We've got lawnmowers."

So the Elite Giants took out scythes and three mowers and made their own diamond. It was a lot of work for the hundred bucks that the little crowd brought them. But for Rainbow, it would have been worth it even if they hadn't cleared a centavo.

They had to beat Juan Cortez and his dirty tricks.

* * *

During the next three weeks, the Pan American Elite Giants were besieged with "bad breaks." Games that they scheduled were mysteriously cancelled. Dates were set through local promoters who didn't exist. And every so often, the evil Mordida would descend upon them to suck away their meager earnings.

Everyone was edgy. They had not been able to break into a routine. The players were tired and wound-up. They breathed the name 'Juan Cortez,' though his name was not uttered aloud. How could he so successfully sabotage their operation? He had such exact information on what they were doing. How else could he get their secrets, *unless*—the inference was almost unthinkable.

No one wanted to discuss this possibility, but it was there clearly in everybody's mind. Suspicions began forming. Pedro always did the calling for the team because after Rainbow, he was the oldest and he was fluent in Spanish, being a former Mexican citizen. Could he be turning in his comrades for his native countrymen or José Morales? He always went off by himself—what could this be for? What did he have to hide? It seemed that almost everyone had some quirk about him that made him seem suspicious.

So it was that they pulled up to a field near Zacoalco for a nine-inning contest. Even though it was late afternoon, it was still very hot and the humidity was high. The field was located next to a lake and a lone, narrow stand of trees that bordered a wild, undeveloped area on the outside of town.

The thickness of the air and their run of "luck" lately made everyone on the team a bit testy.

The team they were playing was from a local stone quarry. These local rock cutters wanted everything played straight: no clowning. The field was easily the best they had played on since Chipancingo, though there were no bleachers for the spectators. Rainbow planned to pass the hat in the third inning and again after a homerun or spectacular play.

Candy, the scheduled starter, warmed up with Bo. The young right-hander motioned to their opposition. "Those guys look like gorillas. Rainbow said they fancied themselves to be hot shots. But they got as much finesse as a bunch of apes."

Bo laughed, too. He had been scheduled to start, but had a little shoulder stiffness and so begged off. Of their eleven-man roster, three were pitching specialists and two could throw in a pinch or to rest other arms when they played easy opposition.

"Looks like they really think they're hot shit. See them go through group calisthenics. Ain't they pretty?" Candy laughed a little too loudly and couldn't help mimicking their version of deep knee bends. The squad of synchronized locals didn't seem to notice. They moved and breathed as a unit with machine-like precision in their exercises. This exhibition had a different effect upon Rainbow, who came running over to Candy.

"Put a lid on it, boy," intoned Rainbow guardedly. "There's something about them I don't much like."

Candy clucked his tongue at the over-anxious manager. These guys would be nothing. The Giants would lay them out one-two-three. Why, the Elite Giants had only lost one game in three weeks! At 35 and 1 they could afford to be confident.

It was time to begin. Rainbow called his men together. Candy and Ramon were still cutting-up about their muscle-bound opposition.

"Shut up," barked the manager. "Listen, these guys ain't no brick-layers. You can take 'em, but we've got to be careful. They look like a mean lot to me. And those policemen over there are wearing guns with live ammo."

"What are you trying to say?" drawled Roy. "We should be afraid of these quarry cutters?"

"Not afraid—just careful. Play everything conservative. We don't have to be aggressive to beat these guys. And keep it close for at least three innings. That's when we pass the hat."

"They're muscle-bound from carrying too many rocks," said Harold.

"Rocks in the head," put in Juice as he tried to restrain a laugh.

"I'd like to see what kind of rocks they have," said Roy with a sneer.

"Solid granite by the looks of it," said Sam Nuxall, the right fielder.

"Bust their nuts just the same if they push me."

"Let's get going. Juice, you're up to bat," said Rainbow, anxious to defuse their spirited cockiness.

The game was uneventful for the first three frames. Then, in the fourth, Juice bunted his way onto first and Harold executed a perfect hit-and-run as Juice bolted to second. The second baseman went to cover for the steal as Harold squirted a ground ball through the space that the fielder had just vacated. On the play, Juice went to third.

The Elite Giants had runners at first and third with none out. Mellow Carmello Muenoz was up. Their catcher called a pitch-out but nobody was going. The pitcher tossed over to hold the runner. Their first bagger put a hard tag on Harold: slapping him in the chest. Then a couple more throws over. This time the mitt came thudding on Harold's head.

Then to the plate. The pitch bounced five feet too soon and went over the catcher's shoulder. Juice raced toward home. The pitcher broke off the mound and busted Juice with a shoulder block as the speeding infielder crossed the plate. The blow sent Juice sprawling and brought the Giants' bench to its feet. But Rainbow got them to sit down again.

Then the umpire called Juice 'out.'

The impartial arbitrator ruled that the pitcher busted Juice before he touched home. While the 125-pound second baseman was sprawled out on the dirt, the catcher had approached and put on another heavy tag.

Rainbow and Pedro came out together to argue the decision. But one look at the umpire caused the manager to back down. The local police had their nightsticks out and were smiling as they slapped them against their open palms. Rainbow didn't miss a detail.

"Let's go back, Pedro. We ain't going to get anywhere by arguing."

The pair retreated to an accompaniment of jeers and catcalls. When they got back to their bench Rainbow said, "Bo, go and try to collect our share of the money. Gypsy Joe, you're going in to pitch next inning. I want someone with experience out there. Candy, quietly load our stuff into the bus and be ready to start her up in an emergency. I've got a bad taste about this."

Carmello struck out, but big Roy brought home Harold with a four-bagger. The score after three and a half innings was two-zip.

In the bottom of the fifth, the hometown team got a runner home on a ball that clearly was foul but was ruled to be fair and resulted in a triple. The triple was converted with a sacrifice fly.

In the sixth, Carmello hit a line drive in the gap. It looked like a triple for sure, or possibly an inside-the-parker, but Mellow was tripped when he rounded second. He scrambled back to the bag, but his ankle was hurting.

Next up was Roy, who had homered last time at bat. The first pitch was a fastball that was aimed directly at the big man's skull. Roy flopped backward into the dust.

Even as he was getting up and hurling curses at the pitcher for sending a projectile nearly eighty miles an hour at his head, Rainbow and Pedro were out of their coaching boxes to restrain the slugger.

The visiting bench was also up and quickly armed themselves with baseball bats.

Rainbow and Pedro got to Roy just as he had made it to his feet. "Hold back, boy. We can't win this one. They've got us out numbered twenty-to-one. They even got the police on their side. Let it be."

"That goddamn son-of-a-bitch is going to start singing soprano before I get finished with his mother fuckin goddamn fuckin—" Roy was searching to find the appropriate word to end his threat. Rainbow and Pedro were telling him he had to hold back, but Roy was confused and full of rage.

"—Shit!" Roy finally finished.

Big Roy allowed himself to be checked by Rainbow. Pedro asked the umpire to warn the other bench about throwing at the head. But the ump said it was just a brush back pitch and if the visiting "profess-ion-ales" were really that good, they shouldn't act like a bunch of pansies. Rainbow turned. He eyed the police. They seemed to be content to lie back in the grass and drink beer.

Then Rainbow felt a sting on the side of his face. Someone had thrown a metal slug at him. A sharp burr on the dull metal disk sliced a three-inch message in the coach's cheek. The manager gave the crowd a long look. The quarry men were roaring with laughter. Then the manager fixed his gaze on something. Rainbow paused and slowly bent down to pick up the slug. He examined the evidence carefully and placed it in his pocket. Then he signaled Carmello in from second base.

"Damned if I'm going to let them kill us. Let's go."

Carmello broke into a trot toward the bench. The crowd was suddenly silent. No one moved except the aging manager, who slowly walked from the third base line to their bench across the diamond, and Mellow who was jogging in from second base.

When Carmello passed the stone cutter's first baseman, the latter swung his gloved hand at Mellow and decked the young man with a single blow.

In an instant there was chaos.

Roy Carnes ran up the line and slammed his bat into the ribs of the offending first baseman. Then Big Roy turned and swung a full blow at another cutter, but missed.

"Look out, Roy," cried Mellow, scrambling to his feet just in time to warn the first baseman of a bat-swinging stone cutter. The adversary had his forty-ounce weapon heading towards Roy's skull when the big Texan pivoted and in one motion intercepted the other's swing with his own bat.

The collision of heavy wooden bats swung with full force split the scene with a shattering CRACK!

Wood splinters flew,	Carmello threw	Bo, who
sending Roy's attacker	a punch to the stomach;	failed to collect
reeling backwards when	the stone cutter crumbled.	their money,
Roy was taken down as	The Giants	now became aware that
he lost his balance	all rallied to confront	he was cut-off;
trying to break the jaw of	the other team.	isolated from
the nearest stonecutter.	But Rainbow ordered	his way to freedom.
A group of three grabbed	his men	His only choice:
the fallen ballplayer,	to retreat	away from
raised clubs but	as the Giants made	the angry crowd
fell away as	a beeline	when a cutter drew

a skillfully maneuvered blade

slashed an escape route

for Roy, who hobbled away

in a vain effort.

The blade returned

amidst heavier weapons

to help Mellow while

pushing him toward

safety.

one more time

around falling bodies

to the bus.

The doors just closed

as the angry mob

hurled rocks

and tried to tip the bus.

Candy gunned

the bus that rolled with

The blade returned,

the trouble

a zip gun

and fired at Bo

when the pitcher

ran at full speed

toward the woods

where there were no people

His escape depended upon

speed and instinct

determined progress through the mob.

passed him by

The local police arrested Roy and Carmello just as they neared the departing bus.

*   *   *

Candy made the old bus race. There weren't any other motor vehicles at the site. Everyone had walked or bicycled. Even the police had come on foot. In less than a minute, they were safe.

"I thought they'd blow our tires," said Pedro when Rainbow requested an assessment of personnel and their condition.

Rainbow picked up a few pieces of glass and tossed them into their garbage can. "What's the body count, Pedro?" The manager appeared to be strangely detached. "Should have put plexi-glass in them windows."

"Ramon lost a couple of teeth and his left eye's shut. Sam got a gash on his throwing hand—" The third baseman-cook-second in command stopped and took Rainbow by the arm and sat him down. The manager continued to retrieve glass, but he wasn't being careful. His hand began to bleed. Pedro, who himself had a gash in his scalp, put his hand on the manager's shoulder and gently opened the clenched hand that held the jagged pieces of blood stained glass. The whole team watched in silence as the third baseman tossed the sharp fragments away and then returned to the man who had always seemed to take everything in stride.

"The police got Roy and Carmello just as we were leaving. José and Bo are missing."

Rainbow continued to stare ahead. Did he hear what Pedro was saying? The old man's expression didn't change.

"Rainbow?" prompted Pedro again. "They got Roy and—"

"It was a set-up."

"How'd you—"

"I saw one of Cortez's men in the crowd. The guy who was with him when he first came to me in Mexico City." Rainbow stood and turned to his team. "The whole riot was fixed. They were waiting for us."

"But how could they?' There wasn't enough time for them to arrange it. We didn't even set the date till—" Pedro stopped.

Everyone on the bus knew the only way this could have happened. They had felt the retribution of Juan Cortez for almost three weeks. But the inevitable conclusion of how their enemy had been able to deliver his timely attacks had been unspeakable—until now.

Rainbow stared into the eyes of his team. "There's only one explanation: somebody on this team has sold us out."

CHAPTER TEN

THERE WAS A POUNDING. Thump. Thump. Thump. The sound of the guard's night stick as he walked down the aisle of the all night movie theatre. Thump. Thump. Thump. There was a rhythm to it. In three-four time he waltzed up and down, patrolling the decaying movie palace. Thump. Thump. Thump. Steady. Only interrupted when someone's hand or limb hung over the aisle armrest. Then the crisp metronome seemed to miss a beat. Flesh does not resonate like metal. Thump. Thump, uuh. A submissive groan.

When the guard thought you were asleep, he gave you a poke. The second time, you were on the street.

"This ain't no hotel, bud," the mild Irish accent would proclaim. As the guard rousted one of the patrons out of the house of illusion, the shadowy figure docilely allowed himself to be led away from the tacky, foul smelling cinema into the light.

"Out the door with you, now," sang the mild brogue to Bo Mellan as the pitcher was thrust into the crisp spring morning near Washington and Clark.

It was very bright. Bo shut his eyes and pressed his hand to his head. The liquor still made it spin. He wanted another. The young left-hander started to walk. His legs were weak.

Bo saw a bar through his squinting blues, but found it closed when he got there. Another. Same result. The time? His watch had stopped. Then the bus station. The sun was now at his back.

He slid onto a stool and started drinking coffee. Dark and bitter.

In the swirling deep blackness he saw another illusion being played. This time the characters were familiar. They were in Milwaukee on Medford Avenue. Medford is an unusual street. It doesn't run north-south nor east-west. It is set on a northwest-southeast diagonal that makes finding one's direction almost impossible.

Bo lived in an upper duplex on Medford Avenue with his mother, Mary. They rented their two-bedroom flat from Willie and Corrine Robinson. Corrine was Rainbow's daughter.

The house was very ordinary by Milwaukee standards. It was converted to a duplex with a side entrance and a separate staircase for the upper. Two full dormers with wood siding stood atop the dull, red brick structure that had been constructed in the early thirties. There was a small backyard and a cement patio that stood in front of the two-car garage. The Robinsons had a vegetable garden like most folks in their neighborhood. Every August when the tomatoes, greens, and onions were ripe, Rainbow would roll out the old oil drum, caked on the outside with rust, and do up a pile of ribs that he barbecued slow and tasty, with fresh ingredients and boiled greens.

It was not to be compared.

Bo's mother, Mary, was a hard working woman, but her health was never very good. Mary Mellan worked with Corrine Robinson at the Fifty-third Street School in the lunchroom. There wasn't a lot of racial tension on the North side. All the fuss occurred south of the freeway. Father Groppi and all the marches could have taken place in Racine for all they knew. Things were quiet on Medford Avenue.

Ever since they moved in, Rainbow Billy Beauchamp had befriended Bo. The older man owned a dry cleaning business. He liked talking to men more than to women. His only child, Corrine, had but a single child, Angela.

Bo and Rainbow had a rapport from the start. The young twelve year old admired the tight-lipped older man. Bo remembered looking up at Rainbow and marveling at the texture of the other's skin. It seemed so smooth from a distance. But really it was rough and irregular with large pores. Perhaps the illusion arose because everything on the old man was pulled together so tightly.

They often sat together on the small cement patio in front of the garage. On a still day, Bo could smell the older man's body. It was a heavy, thick odor mixed with smoke and Pabst Blue Ribbon beer. The combination transported him to exotic places as Rainbow spun his yarns.

No one else listened to the stories of Rainbow Billy Beauchamp.

Corrine was a stranger to her father. But still, she remained at the family homestead with him. Willie, her husband, did not take care of their money well, so they never had enough to buy a place of their own. They had a child and expenses. Rainbow didn't charge them rent, so why move? All they were expected to do was the maintenance.

But maintenance was difficult. The status quo did not maintain itself on an even level. There was constant fighting between Willie and Rainbow. So that when Bo's mother died, it seemed natural that his friend should move upstairs to take care of Bo.

For a time the fighting subsided.

Bo was coached and coddled by the Milwaukee dry cleaner. Often, the two of them would walk over to Dineen Park, talking baseball all the way. When they got there, Rainbow would work with his young charge on the mechanics of pitching, hitting and fielding.

"You've got to learn it all because you don't know if you'll always be a pitcher. At your age, every good player is either a pitcher or a shortstop. Not many end up there."

The lanky, black dry cleaner went to all of Bo's high school games in the spring and then in the summer to the Legion and Langsdorf League contests. Bo put in his hours with those teams and extra practice with Rainbow. But the favorite time for Bo was when his friend would sit with him at twilight on a summer evening. It was then that Bo would hear tales of their baseball's machinations at their highest level.

"A pitcher has gotta know hisself. When he don't got it, he can't go challenging them hitters or he'll get bombed. Why, I remember back in '43 when I thought I was about washed up. The year before we had a pretty good season, but then we were cleaned by the KC Monarchs in the series: four straight—though we protested the last game because the Monarchs picked up three starters from the Newark Eagles—just for the series! 'Twas 'gainst the rules. But what could we do? Satch was hot and so were the Monarchs. I pitched the second game as was she-lacked. That sort of thing had been happening quite a bit. Thought I had lost it.

"Then in Mexico that winter I was playing with Smokey Joe Williams. You know, Smokey Joe pitched until he had a head of gray hair. Once he one-hit the Monarchs over twelve innings striking out twenty-seven. Best pitching performance in history. Bar none. Twenty-seven!

"Well, Smokey Joe gave me a thin, kaki-colored metal case once after I'd gotten him out of jail in Puebla. Damned if he hadn't bought some hot Aztec silver statues. Says he didn't know they was stolen—which wouldn't have bothered the locals except he couldn't pay enough to smooth it over.

"Inside the metal case were a pair of thick glasses.

"I don't need glasses, Smoke.'

"'Maybe they help you see your way to another couple-a-years pitching, Rainbow.'

"Well, I thought several months about them glasses 'till I finally figured out what to do with them. We were back up in Pennsylvania to start the season with the Grays— there was no spring training in our league; you played you self into shape. Suddenly I had it! I spread the rumor around that what was bothering me were bad eyes and that I'd licked the problem by purchasing a pair of specs— which I didn't want to wear too much, being as I was too proud.

"It made pretty good press—even got into the white folks' papers. They slated me for opening day against the New York Cubans.

"In warm-up before the game I put on these glasses and looked just fine. I was giving it a little more heat than I usually do for a warm-up. Then when old Crawdad Fletcher steps up to lead-off, I take off the specs and send the first pitch as hard as I can over his head to the backstop.

"This bothers old Crawdad a bit because I could still bring it about eighty five miles per hour to the plate and he thinks I don't see him too good.

"The next pitch I send right toward his elbow. He bails out before the ball was halfway there. There was a little commotion so I takes out my glasses, you see, not hurrying or nothing. Oh, I put those wire rims on just pretending to get a better view of what was happening. Then I takes them off and gives them a cleaning and then put them back on again.

"Crawdad is lying flat on his back, screaming at the ump to make me wear my glasses. Says I'll kill him.

"The Cubans' manager is out asking for a warning—but how can you warn a guy who can't see? And how can you tell him what to wear?

"It was something; I tell you. They brush off old Crawdad and set him up again in the box and so I toss a curve that begins at his head. The poor guy is on his back again while the umpire calls, 'Strike one.'

"That's all I needed. Didn't have to run through the routine more than a couple times after that. Word got around that this Rainbow Billy Beauchamp is liable to kill you every time you step up to bat—no protective headgear in those days, son.

"Guys would walk to the plate waiting for me to bowl them over. They saw me as a half blind buzzard throwing a pretty fast zinger. Trouble is that anyone could hit my zinger so I only throwd it wild. I struck 'em out with my curve, change-up and drop. Turned the fastball into my 'wild man's' pitch."

The dry cleaner laughed. "Yes indeed. Them glasses were my edge. Put me into my last all-star game, they did. And put five more years on my career.

"You got to get them batters thinkin', Bo. They can't think and hit at the same time, so you solve their dilemma for them and take that bat outta their hands."

Bo leaned back on the patio bench and smiled. He looked up to his teacher. It was getting dark, but Rainbow's image was sharp and clear.

* * *

When the black fluid was gone, Bo refilled it again and again. Gradually his head was beginning to clear. As it did, the arteries in his skull constricted in response. The rookie pitcher had a giant hangover.

Between episodes of pain, Bo put together the events of the previous evening—after he left Cora. He had taken a cab in a vain attempt to keep his date with Angela, but, of course, she had gone. He tried calling her house, but it was of no use. He had blown his chance. Bo knew Angela. She was a woman with spirit. She had her father Willie's, temper. Bo never knew anyone who could cross her. No one, that is, except DuRon Garvey.

DuRon met Angela just after she left home to attend UWM. Bo was a junior in high school and had high hopes. Angela wanted to try life on the "East Side." So she got a place on Downer with three other girls. Her job and government loans allowed her to be completely self-sufficient. The only times Bo saw her were when he hopped the Capitol Drive bus that took him to the University.

In Milwaukee, the East Side passes as a citadel of culture. From this bastion of education and the arts the entire surrounding area is supposed to be fortified. It is said that in northern Milwaukee there are East Side and West Side personalities. An East Sider transcends his midwestern locale. It is almost as if he might reside in one of the great and distant metropolitan strongholds of our country such as San Francisco, Los Angeles, Boston or New York—perhaps even Chicago!

It seemed to Bo that after Angela left for school to take up accounting, her personality also changed. Her easygoing, non-pretentious manner became cluttered with ornamentation of all description. She dropped references to people and places that Bo had never heard of—yet wished somehow he had—or maybe it was simply that he felt ashamed he hadn't.

Something was different about Angela. Rainbow said it was DuRon Garvey. DuRon was studying engineering and worked as an intern at General Electric in Milwaukee. Bo questioned privately whether DuRon would ever finish his degree. DuRon had been a student for five years. When Angela moved in with DuRon, Bo knew his rival would never make it. Bo was not around long enough to find out. The final fight between Rainbow and Willie sent them packing for points south.

*   *   *

After more coffee, Bo discovered he had a half-pint with a couple of shots of whiskey left in it. Bo dropped the contents into his coffee and bought a tin of aspirin.

Soon, the pain was manageable and the golden haired hurler bought a "number four" breakfast and a newspaper. The chewy eggs and soggy toast gave him a little strength, but it was not enough. He had to move slowly. First, he made his way to the general services desk and put down the last money he had to send some flowers and a note to Angela.

Then he started on a trek north. It was about four miles to the ballpark and the station clock registered 8:45.

*   *   *

Practice always started at ten. The players got loose and then they had a few meetings, after which was batting practice and the game at 1:20.

At a normal pace, Bo could usually perambulate city real estate at the rate of four miles an hour. However, today, things weren't normal.

Bo had not walked this route before. He didn't know the various neighborhoods nor the most direct path. It felt good to keep moving, but he was in slow motion. His mind did not focus, but seemed to be fully occupied with the mechanics of his perambulation. Occasionally he stopped and asked directions. When the replies came back in Spanish, he knew he was almost there.

It was 10:35 when the rookie left-hander checked into the locker room. Sam drifted over to the latecomer.

"A silly way to lose fifty dollars, Bo."

"I'm a silly guy."

"We've got a pitching meeting in ten minutes."

"Oke."

The chenille-jacketed athlete shuffled over to his locker and solved his combination on the third try. The contents were still damp and smelt a little musty. Bo slumped on the bench and shut his eyes. In his hands he held a sodden athletic supporter.

A partially dressed Bo Mellan came late to the pitching meeting. Sam was going over the way that they would be pitching the opposition. Bo stared at the ripples in the thin carpet that covered the locker room floor. He casually wondered whether these could be stretched out again to create a smooth surface or whether the job required another carpet altogether.

As the meeting broke up, Bo lifted his eyes and noticed the manager's office door was open. Staring straight at him was a smirking Buddy Bael.

*   *   *

The wind was blowing in. It was a much warmer day. The thermometer had soared to fifty-five degrees at game time. They were playing the Reds, the most powerful hitting team in baseball.

The Reds jumped to a three run lead in the first and added two more in the fourth and one in the sixth on a Wayland Avenue home run right into the wind. There was one out.

Then the call came for Bo to get up and throw.

So many times Bo had been ready to give them his best, but was never called. And now—now he hadn't even warmed up properly. Now Bael would have nothing to prevent his sending Bo down. Bo reached into his duffle and took a pinch of a dried herbal concoction that he slipped into his mouth. He chewed slowly as he went quickly through his warm-up routine.

If it had been ninety degrees, his shoulder might not have been so tight. But in fifty-five degrees with a cool breeze off the lake, it would not respond. Some things could not be hurried. He needed help.

A base hit was followed by a walk. Bo's shoulder was not loosening. Another walk. The call came down. Bo was in the game: his first Major League appearance. How could he—he'd be bombed. He didn't have his good stuff. The Cubs were down 6-2; another run would be a disaster.

The golden haired pitcher hesitated. Then he walked back to pick-up his warm-up jacket. He needed help. Bo looked up at the crowd. What did they want with him? Then he stared down to their dugout and imagined he saw Bael smiling confidently. Bo wasn't at his best and he knew it. Then he reached into his duffle and took out an old, battered metal eyeglasses case. Bo held the metal case and stroked it slowly with his thumb. The faded blues turned back to the field.

Bo was ready to pitch.

Chapter Eleven

"WHAT DID I TELL YOU?" said Sam as he tossed down his third rob roy and ordered another. "It was only a matter of time."

Bo smiled and sipped his coffee.

"We haven't had much opportunity to talk; your new place being on the south side and all—"

"Now we're traveling in Cal-i-fornia."

"Yeah. And warm. San Diego. LA and San Fran. Not a bad trip this time of year."

"They're pretty strong clubs."

"With you in our starting rotation we shouldn't do too bad. What a beginning you've had. Three wins in less than two weeks."

"The first one was really cheap."

"Not on your life," replied Sam as he sat back and lit a smoke. "If I didn't know you better, I'd have said you were totally wrecked. It seemed like you were walking one off—but you don't even drink!" Bo fidgeted in the black naugahide covered booth. They were sitting in a rather large lounge that occupied more than two thirds of the restaurant.

The only light came from behind the bar and from small squat candles set out around the tables randomly, one to three per table, with a glass centerpiece that absorbed rather than reflected their light. The lounge was on three levels that rose and descended around the semi-circular bar.

"Bael thought he had you all right. He had already made out papers to send you down to Iowa the day before, so that when he saw you so wasted, I'm sure he felt he had the cincher."

Bo smiled and took a handful of nuts to chew on.

"And that routine with the glasses made you the lead article in all three Chicago papers. You were even picked up along the wire services. I tell you, three wins and already you're a national celebrity."

"And you should be my press agent."

"No shit, Bo. We had NBC call us to see if you'd be pitching this Saturday. They want you for their 'Game of the Week.'" Bo dropped a couple nuts on the floor. It was true that he had gotten an inordinate amount of attention from his face-saving antic. He was being billed as a great showman and the 'last of the old-style pitchers.' Even his escalator performance contract had been discovered. 'A throwback to an earlier era,' they were saying. Bo smiled. What would Gus Greenlee have said?

He thought of Juice and Harold and what had happened in Venezuela. The money and excitement were not new to him. He preferred the soft flickering of the votive candles inside the rolling grotto where he was now. The gentle light warmed the darkness as semi-melodic strains were repetitiously reverberating in the space about them. It was a solemn sanctuary in which indistinguishable words floated about as people ordered Bloody Marys and confessed their souls to the bartender.

And though Bo was only drinking coffee, he felt a part of this communion.

"Your daughter lives somewhere around here, doesn't she?"

Sam rubbed the back of his neck and grunted.

"Didn't you say she lived in Los Angeles?"

"Downey."

"Is that close?"

"Right next to Inglewood. We'll be staying only twenty minutes or so from her house, I guess. It's been several years. . ."

"I'd like to meet her."

The pitching coach cocked his head and screwed up his green eyes. In the flickering light they seemed almost iridescent.

"What are you asking?"

"I'd like to meet you daughter. Roberta, isn't it?"

"Bobbi. Only her mother calls her Roberta. I can't stand 'Roberta.' Besides, she isn't a 'Roberta.'"

"How old is she, again? In high school?"

"Oh no, Bobbi's only in—why she was only thirteen when—" Sam set his drink down and pushed it some distance from him. "I guess she might be sixteen. What grade is that?"

"Sophomore or junior, generally."

"Well then, there you are. What else would you like to know?"

"I don't know. You've told me bits and pieces about her. I thought I'd like to see for myself." Bo paused and laid the contents of his hand out on the table. "What about you, Sam? Wouldn't you like to see her?"

Sam reached out for his glass and looked at Bo through the scotch and vermouth. The uneven candlelight emphasized the lines of separation that demarcated these two spirits. As they floated about randomly, Sam tried to understand why this swirling emulsion would never mix.

"Kind of disgusting, isn't it. Don't even know the grade your kid is in."

"You've led a traveling life."

"I've always led that kind of life, but I always kept in touch. I love my family. It was never my idea to—" Sam set down the glass again. He could not abide the separation.

"Why don't we get Bobbi a ticket for the game Saturday? I'll bet she'd love to go."

"I don't know, Bo. That might not be a very good idea."

"Why not? Everyone loves a ballgame."

Sam snatched his drink and downed it at once. But it was not all gone. Some of the fluid clung to the sides of the glass and dripped down, slowly, separately. "Don't you understand? It's not that I don't want to see her, or her to see me. It's just that goddamned Bael. My divorce. And Linda, my wife—my ex-wife, that is. Didn't you ever hear…" Sam's voice drifted away.

"I don't understand. What are you trying to say?"

But Sam had turned away to signal the waitress. It was time to break bread.

*   *   *

"Adultery. Fornication and every kind of abomination. That is what I am talking about. Take the youth today. Look at them. Why, they're nothing but a bunch of pampered sissies. Do you want to trust the future of this great land to a bunch of drug taking faggots?"

The crowd of Westwood Rotarians murmured anxiety. Behind the portable podium and loudspeaker unit stood a pot-bellied man in a bright plaid sports coat. It was the manager of the Chicago Cubs, Buddy Bael. His tie seemed too tight around his neck, but the popular baseball man did not reveal any obvious discomfort. He looked about his audience of jovial businessmen and smiled. Then he returned to his text.

"What's wrong with this country is that we're filled with god-damn defeatists! A country is a lot like a ball team. You've gotta make 'em believe they are winners.

"You can have the best team in the world, but without a strong driving force behind the scenes, you won't get anywhere. We need leadership. And we need it badly.

"Oh, I know some people will tell us that there is something dreadfully wrong with the American people. Our President even gets on TV and tells us to our face that we are losers!

"Now I ask you. How far do you think I'd get with a ball club if I told them in spring training that they were a bunch of losers? Baseball is just like life. That's why it's the national pastime. It ain't just no symbol of life; it *is* life. And you know it.

"The battles on the diamond are the battles of the boardroom. The winning team has the right kind of leadership! Your salesmen and factory workers and my players: they are the raw material with which we have to work. But it's the leaders who make the difference." Bael looked up again at the group. He wiped his brow deliberately with a handkerchief and then fixed his beady eyes on the elite of West Los Angeles.

"That's why I'm touring the country trying to drum up support for leadership initiatives, like your own project for future Rotarians. If we could create a dialogue between various groups, like the Lions and Jaycees and so forth, we could do a lot to renew this great land of ours. The Chicago Sun is creating a clearinghouse to do just that. A loose affiliation between these various groups so we can turn the tide.

"Will you help me to revitalize these programs to bring back the kind of leaders we used to have, the land of people who made our country great? Will you help me build that clearinghouse so we can save America? Will you help?"

There was a mumbling of assent among the luncheon crowd. The charismatic evangelist for strong leadership smiled as he watched his collection plates fill with folding money.

* * *

"Listen, I know what I'm talking about," the high-pitched voice declared firmly.

"I've never questioned that, Mr. Cakos. It's just that I want the line-up we put together to be—how shall I put it—reliable."

Buddy Bael sat in his hotel room clenching the phone receiver with his right hand. Beads of sweat were forming on his bald crown.

"This is very important, Bael. I've got a feeling that Ice is gaining support. We need a massive PR effort to carry the day or Krakatowa is going to get some of this action." The long distance line was very clear.

"I don't think that will every happen, Mr. Cakos. You've got Jesse in your pocket, surely—"

"You don't know anything, Bael. You're a child. Do you hear me? An unthinking child." The voice of the team's owner was getting shrill. Bael knew the progression only too well. Beads of sweat rolled down his oily scalp.

"I'm sorry, sir. Of course you know best. I'll certainly get Big Train Lincoln for you and Leon Baines. They can appeal to all their soul brothers." Buddy let out a chuckle, but immediately tried to suppress it; without effect. "But, if I might make a suggestion—"

"Of c-c-course you can't."

Stuttering was the final stage, but Bael had to let his boss, who was also the silent owner of Advanced Builders, know his mind. "But don't you think a more suitable white athlete might be Sammy Tempo, our shortstop? Sammy is very articulate—"

"D-d-damn it all B-B-Bael. Do what you're told. I want a trio of athletes to help sell the Loop Development p-p-project. Lincoln and Baines are fine, but I w-w-want that kid, Mellan. The kid's a star."

"But sir—"

"Get me M-M-Mellan. I want that boy."

Buddy Bael put down the phone. The general manager and field boss for the Chicago Cubs was a wealthy and powerful man in his own right. He remained in baseball, he told himself, only because of Ruppert Cakos. And though Bael controlled many lives, he was still under the Mogul who owned a major Chicago newspaper (the Sun), TV and radio station (WDRT), Major League Baseball team (the Cubs), the largest construction firm in the state of Illinois (Advanced) and extensive land holdings in Chicago. Even at 75, Ruppert Cakos was a man to be feared. In a city run by influence and infiltrated by organized crime, there was only one person that nobody pushed around.

Buddy would have no choice but to search and capture the golden haired, left-handed rookie, Bo Mellan.

CHAPTER TWELVE

BO AVOIDED CAPTURE. He streaked for the woods to be out of sight. All the fracas was occurring in the other direction. The undergrowth was thin, but there were bushes and tall grass that guarded the entrance to the sylvan sanctuary. Bo crouched low. The lake was twenty yards to his left, and to his right were twenty more yards of trees that followed the contour between the lake and the dirt road all the way to the town some two miles away.

Directly in front of Bo were the bushes and grasses that bordered the baseball field. Many of the spectators to the game had fled immediately upon the outbreak of trouble. Those who remained were largely standing around or helping fallen comrades. A few of the quarry workers were fighting amongst themselves.

Bo saw the bus pull away. There was a cluster of people around Roy, but they fell back and Roy limped pitifully toward the departing bus. The police, who were standing back all this time, corralled the weakened Texan and put handcuffs on him.

Bo saw someone on the ground. It was Mellow. A group of four cutters were giving him a beating. Suddenly, from out of the debris that had moments before surrounded Roy, Bo saw the figure of José Morales slash his way towards Carmello. The speedy centerfielder cut a path as he inflicted wounds with his six-inch blade and intimidated many more.

Carmello made it to his feet. The police, following close behind, were ready for him, too. It was only then that José lit out for the very haven that was protecting Bo. The silent ballplayer was quick, but he had suffered a number of wounds himself. The crowd, who moments before had been spellbound by his reckless intensity, was suddenly filled with a passion for this man. They united against him.

The distance between Bo and José couldn't have been more than twenty yards when the mob caught the centerfielder. Perhaps it was merely his imagination, but Bo thought for an instant the centerfielder saw him. Those dark, penetrating eyes seemed to look right into his soul.

The young left-hander ducked down. There were thirty or forty people in the mob. There was nothing that Bo could do, he told himself. If he went to José's aid, they would both be torn apart. What purpose would that serve?

Still, Bo had seen those eyes. They had recognized him. They didn't plead. Nothing was said, but Bo could not get the vision of them out of his mind, even later that night as he made his way back toward the town along the dusty road.

It had been for only a few minutes that the crowd had surrounded José. The police were finally taking control. But not before the outsider had his switchblade secreted from him and pointedly returned into his abdomen.

Bo saw none of this. He was trying not to make any noise. So intent was he on becoming a part of the natural flora that he did not even hear the moans of his fallen teammate.

All of it had happened so quickly. It was coming back to Bo in strange ways. His mouth was dry, but when he finally summoned up some saliva, it merely mixed with the dirt on his lips and in between his teeth, forming an ill tasting mud that immediately caused his mouth to become dry again.

He had been aware of that taste when he tried collecting money for the game. The promoter was stalling. The taste had made Bo impatient and anxious.

* * *

Now Bo was nowhere. Walking. Nowhere. He was a conspicuous figure as he made his way towards somewhere wearing his tattered baseball uniform. Roads always led to places. If he kept going he was sure to find something-but what? The team? The quarry? The town?

Bo didn't have to wait long for his answer. Before him stretched a residential area of what appeared to be the town. It was dark. There was a dampness in the air. Those eyes. The pitcher shivered from the damp that rose and mixed with the air to form a heavy smell. It was an odor full of unidentifiable particulates; each so innocuously minute, but together, they cut short your breath.

The smell had been present even when the team had arrived for the game. But Bo had not noticed it then. Now it was strong. Perhaps there had been faint hints of it earlier, Bo told himself. Especially when Rainbow had told Candy and Roy to stop joking around.

There were few lights, but it was easy to walk because of a bright night sky. Bo decided on a cautious approach to the village. By going away from the lake he could skirt the houses and get an idea of where the jail might be—if indeed this was even the same town that held Carmello, Roy, and José.

The wind was gusting. The leaves rustled. The same noises Bo had heard when he lay on his stomach while José was being captured. What had happened to him? Had he been beaten before he was taken? Why did the Venezuelan come back for Roy and Carmello? What was the reason? Those eyes. Bo had responded by hiding. But what good could he have done? The breeze caused Bo to shiver.

It wasn't hard to circumnavigate the town. Not many people were out and about. Bo was able to move unobserved in the darkness. Soon, he saw what looked like a town square and a building that had lights inside. It was a jail.

Bo hurried, but found all the cell windows were ten feet from the ground. There was nothing that could be done from the outside. A lower window revealed three policemen and a fourth man who was well dressed. Bo recognized the man. It was Lopez, who worked for Juan Cortez. Surely there was hope! Lopez was a reasonable man. Bo could appeal to him for the release of his teammates. The whole episode was based upon a mistake.

Lopez and the police thought it was a mistake when Bo opened the door to the jail. He didn't need an introduction. His bright blue eyes announced his presence.

"And who art thou?" asked the police captain in a Spanish that had been well lubricated with tequila.

Bo knew enough Spanish to answer, but told them he had reached his limit in language comprehension.

"Perhaps I can intercede," said Lopez in Spanish to the captain. "I speak English fluently." Then turning to Bo he said, "Don't I know you?"

"Of course you do, Mr. Lopez. I'm Bo Mellan."

"Mellan? Mellan? The name sounds familiar, truly."

"You came with Mr. Cortez once to see me after a game. I pitch for the Pan-Am Elite Giants."

"Oh yes, of course." He reached out and shook Bo's hand. "What seems to be your trouble?" Lopez was about 5'8" and had dark, stringy hair. He wore a two button, navy suit with trousers that displayed double creases and were a little too long. This forced Lopez to regularly hike them up again.

"Some of our players were put in jail this afternoon."

"Jail? What did they do?"

"Nothing. It was strange. All of a sudden a fight broke out."

"And your teammates were innocent victims in this melee?"

"Yes, that's right."

"Well, permit us to see what we can do." Then, Lopez said something to the captain, who accompanied Lopez and Bo to the jail cells. The building had seven cells, two of which were vacant. Three were filled with Mexicans unknown to Bo.

The captain led the way, with Lopez and Bo coming from behind. When they approached the last cell that held Roy and Mellow, the captain pivoted a bit too sharply and almost lost his balance. Lopez put his arm around Bo's shoulder and brought him to his teammates.

In the small 6' x 7' cell were two figures seated on the floor, leaning back against the wall. There was no furniture in the cell, only a small drainage hole in the back corner of the enclosure that stunk of excrement and attracted flies. The only illumination came from the light in the passageway that radiated dimly through the thick iron bars.

"Are these your comrades, my friend?" said Lopez.

"Roy. Mellow. It's me, Bo."

Slowly the faces of the weary figures turned upward. Bo waved. But even as he did so, Lopez guided Bo back to the office saying in

Spanish, "You've kept to your bargain, now we'll keep to ours; but we mustn't let them get suspicious."

"We'll get you out, fellas. Don't worry," yelled the golden haired hurler over his shoulder.

Bo was seated in a wooden chair whose joints were very loose. Lopez sat on the corner of the captain's desk while the policeman got himself another drink. In the corner, on a bench, slept two officers completely oblivious to the proceedings.

"The captain tells me your friends started a riot."

"Oh no. That's a mistake. There were some hot tempers—it just seemed to start by itself. I wasn't looking. I was supposed to collect the money."

"And did you get it?" Lopez's eyes opened wide.

"No. They kept stalling and then there was the fight. I guess if you were to arrest anyone remotely responsible, you'd have to lock-up most of the other team as well."

Lopez smiled and said something to the captain in Spanish. The other replied with a gesture of indifference.

"When was the last time you saw Cortez?"

Bo was surprised. He wanted to get his friends out of jail. "I don't understand. A few weeks ago I guess—what has that to do with—"

"—And did he make you an offer?"

"What are you up to?"

"I'm prepared to give you five hundred dollars a month and the release of your comrades in return for a pitching contract on one of Mr. Cortez's teams."

"Five hundred? Why that's almost half of what I get now—"

"If it's a question of money..."

"It's a question of nothing. I don't know what you're talking about. You said you could get my teammates out of this garbage dump. Why are talking about contracts and nonsense like that?"

"Because that's the only way you'll get your comrades out of jail." Bo looked hard at the Mexican and his stringy hair. Lopez smiled and ran a finger along the false crease in his pants.

"I don't understand," replied Bo incredulously.

"It isn't very complicated. Either you sign on with us, on our terms, or your friends rot in jail. It's that simple."

"You can go to hell," replied Bo, jumping to his feet.

"Porjillo, Hernandez, right now!" commanded the man in the navy suit. The two sleeping gendarmes jumped up and grabbed the golden haired hurler.

Bo tried to struggle, but to no avail. He was no match for his adversaries. Lopez walked over to Bo and grabbed his face with one hand and gripped it tightly.

"One more chance, gringo, what will it be? Baseball or jail?"

The soldiers applied steady pressure as they twisted Bo's arms behind him. Lopez was holding Bo's face so tightly he could barely move his jaw, but the hurler was able to summon enough control to spit mud at his vicious interrogator.

Lopez took a step back and cleaned his face with a handkerchief that he folded and returned to his coat pocket. Then he pulled up his pants and sneered, "Put him with the Venezuelan."

* * *

It was the first cell. Bo hadn't noticed it before. Lying in the center was the limp body of José Morales.

The left-handed hurler looked on the battered figure with terror. His clothes were torn and ripped. His chest was brown with dried, flaking blood. His face was misshapen and puffy from broken facial bones. Bo knelt down and looked at the face through the harsh shadows that were cast by the heavy iron bars.

"José?" Bo said softly.

The eyes remained shut. His breathing was labored.

"José?"

But there was no response. Bo put his left hand on the other's forehead and smoothed the thin hair off his brow. Morales had never been a man to communicate much. His face did not reveal what kind of man he might be. It was a face that could fit many different and contradictory personalities, and Bo had always wondered whether there might have been several people who lived beneath that facade.

There was so much Bo wanted to say. Those eyes—that penetrating look had revealed so much—about both of them.

Bo suddenly became aware of his own unkempt, long curly hair and tried to brush it back with his right hand. "José. I'm sorry. I was in the woods. You needed me. You were calling me to help—just as you had helped. But it seemed so hopeless and I was so afraid.

"I've never been—" Bo stopped. He didn't know how to say it. He propped up José's head with his uniform shirt rolled into a bundle, and then he ripped off a strip of his jersey to try to wash the centerfielder's face. There was no water and Bo's saliva was dirty. He could not make it clean. So Bo held the other's head in his left hand and tenderly stroked his face. "José? Can you hear anything I'm saying? I was wrong, José. But if I had gone out to help—we'd both be lying on the floor right now. Would I have made any difference? You're good at fighting, but I don't know knives and guns. Even my fists are not very—

"But I could have tried..."

José moved slightly and started bleeding again from his side. The effusive liquid was hot and sticky. Bo made another rip in his jersey for a bandage that he tied without effect around the centerfielder's waist.

The blood continued to flow through the bandage. Bo tried applying pressure to the deep wound and seemed to be having some success. Then José opened his eyes.

"José? Oh don't die, José. Lord Jesus, don't die."

The eyes were not harsh. They didn't judge Bo. They showed pain, but this wasn't the principal focus. The eyes were looking into Bo.

"Do you understand what I've been saying? Who are you, anyway? Why do you go and let yourself be cut up for a bunch of guys you've only known a couple months? A bunch of guys that are practically strangers?"

A faint smile appeared on José's lips. Then his abdomen writhed in a convulsion. He had lost control of his bladder and wet himself. His chest heaved twice and then his eyes opened even wider, but in an instant, without notice, the stare became inanimate.

Bo let up his pressure. Some more blood came out, but without force. Bo listened for a heart beat. But there was none. He reached again for the outfielder's face, but it felt different: thick and doughy.

"José..." Bo started to say, but the sound caught in his throat. "What have I done?" The words were whispered: light but not without substance.

"Have I—" Bo shut José's eyelids and moved the body so that José's head lay on Bo's lap. The young pitcher shivered as the night breeze blew in the window atop the cell. It smelled heavy and noxious.

Forsaken, Bo stared out the window at the world. Next to him lay a man whose blood had been spilled. But it was the pitcher who felt poured out like water with all his bones out of joint. His mouth was dusty and dry.

The young man sat watching, waiting. He felt like a worm. His heart was like wax, and his body felt out of joint. His blue eyes faded as the darkness waned and dawn entered into his prison.

Chapter Thirteen

IT WAS ANOTHER DAY BEFORE RAINBOW managed to buy his players' freedom. He had to exceed the bribe that had been left by Cortez's agent and convince the locals that a quick solution would be in everyone's best interests. José's body was taken up to Guadalajara for burial. Rainbow didn't want to pollute the corpse by burying it near the murderous village.

Roy was basically all right. Mellow suffered from internal injuries and had to heal. Bo was untouched. No one acted normally as they rode to their next stop. The team was scheduled to play seven games in Guadalajara and then make a loop of the neighboring areas, and then return for a dozen more games in two weeks.

Guadalajara is one of the best baseball cities in Mexico. It is comprised of four areas: Libertad, Refonma, Joarez and Hidalgo. In all but the last area, there are many local teams and partisan followers. There is also a Mexican League team plus a couple semi-pro leagues. Except for Sunday, which is reserved for bullfights, every afternoon and night features many games around the city.

The Pan-Am Elite Giants pulled into the city and proceeded immediately to a game that was followed by the burial of José Morales. The team was very flat and was soundly beaten two games straight. Most everyone was banged up from the fight, but that was not the problem.

Nobody seemed to want to talk. There was a troubled silence that was not interrupted except through convoluted innuendo. This would not do. The team was short-handed. At full strength they had

been eleven. Now, with José gone, they were ten. Further, because
Carmello was banged up, only nine could play. This meant that
two-thirds of their outfield would not be there. Bo was moved into
left and Gypsy Joe into center. Candy pitched or spelled either of
the other two.

Rainbow was on the lookout for another player, but couldn't
make a move immediately because the team was short of cash.
Juan's dirty tricks had held down their purses, and the remainder
of the Mexico City gate had gone to bailing out his players. The
shortness of cash caused Rainbow to call a team meeting after they
had just dropped their fourth of six games.

"You guys looked pretty awful out there today. I don't have to
tell you that when you play like that, no one will want to see us.
And when people don't show, we don't eat." They were sitting in
their bus. Most of the players slumped low in their seats. Rainbow
stood in the aisle. It was late afternoon and overcast.

"We are living on what we're doing right now. There ain't no
yesterday 'cause yesterday's done been used up. And unless you
guys turn it around out there, we gonna start drawing smaller 'an
smaller crowds.

"Already the people ain't coming out the way they did in Mexico
City. That shouldn't be. They nuts about baseball here. We should
not be clearing only our expenses, but be building up another cushion for the road.

"I'll tell you what I think is wrong: you all look sluggish out there.
It's like you don't feel for playing ball. Too much trouble for you.
Well, I'll tell you that anyone can go out and do his job when he feels
great and the world's on his side. But it takes a man to go out there
when he feels like shit and no one's with him. A man with guts
don't pay no heed. When he goes out between them foul lines, he's
a baseball player. Period. He does a professional job no matter how
he feels, because he's got pride and because he likes to eat. Each
one of us are no more than a week or so 'tween making a wage and
pumping gas for our dinner."

Several eyes looked over to Roy, who used to do just that. But
Roy was staring straight ahead. The overcast day could make you
sleepy or edgy, depending on how you were stimulated. Just now,
no one was sleepy.

"Let me tell you a story that Rube Foster told an old manager of mine, Judy Johnson. The way Rube told it, there was once this donkey and an ox who worked on a farm. Now farm work ain't easy. I should know. I was raised on one back in Arkansas. Damned inconvenient to work sunrise to sunset just to break even. Damned little incentive, I tell you. And insects or the weather could take it away from you at any time. Nothing you could do about it, 'cept plant again 'an eat a little less in the winter.

"Well, that's what you do on a farm. Hard work. And one day the ox got tired of it all and didn't go to work in the morning. That evening the donkey comes back to the barn and the ox asks, 'What did the boss say 'bout me not being out there?'

"'Didn't say nothin,' replies the donkey.

"The next morning the donkey gets up and asks the ox if he's going out to the field, but the ox says he's still too tired and has to relax while he sleeps and eats all day. So that evening the ox again asks the donkey, 'What did the boss say 'bout me not being out there?'

"'Didn't say nothin,' replies the donkey, 'but he visited the butcher.'

"The next day the ox went out bright and early and got into his traces. The farmer comes out and says, 'What you doing there, ox?'

"'Just getting ready to work. I'm all rested up and set to go.'

"'You might as well go back to your stall and sleep some more.'

"'Oh no, I'm ready to work today,' says the ox.

"'I'm telling ya, you might as well stay,' says the farmer, 'because yesterday I done sold you to the butcher.'"

Rainbow stopped and looked around at his team. Players were looking down and starting to fidget.

"I think I've said enough. We got to go out there and do a job. We can't be thinking about them quarry cutters or Juan Cortez."

"—What about José?" asked Mellow. "He saved my life."

"And mine," added Roy.

"I don't see what—" started Pedro, the third baseman and second in command as he tried to smooth things over.

"Somebody's been selling us out," put Ramon Jimmerez, the quiet catcher, "and we've got to find out who."

The others mumbled their assent.

"What do we know?" asked Pedro, standing up and turning to his teammates. Rainbow lit a cigarette and sat down. "How can we find out anything? We don't want no witch hunt here."

"I don't know," said Gypsy Joe, "but it seems mighty queer that Bo, here, got out of everything without a scratch."

The curly haired pitcher turned his tired and fading blues toward Gypsy Joe, but didn't say anything.

"Yes, tell us," put Ramon, "how you got out of it so light?"

Bo was silent.

"You see? And what about the feller you was telling about, Mellow?" added Gypsy Joe.

"Lopez?"

"Yeah, Lopez. Carmello said the two of them were pretty thick in the jail," added Gypsy Joe.

"Did you say Lopez?" asked Rainbow.

"Yeah, that's right," replied Gypsy Joe. "Who's he?"

"He works for Cortez. I saw him at the game with the quarry cutters."

"Do you see what I mean? And Carmello was telling me—"

"—Why don't you let Carmello tell his own story," said Pedro to the stocky right-handed hurler.

"Be my guest," put Gypsy Joe. "Tell them, Mellow."

Every eye turned to the quiet left fielder whose physical condition was still not very good. "Well, Roy and I were in one of those little cells. We weren't doing too good. I was out cold for a time. It was very dark."

"Get to it, Mellow."

"Leave him be, Joe."

The teenage ballplayer looked down at his socks and spoke in soft but audible tones. "One time when I was awake, this man they called Lopez came by with Bo. Bo was very friendly with us."

"—And friendly with Lopez, too. That guy had his arm around him," added Roy through clenched teeth.

"Yes, they seemed to be on good terms," said Mellow, looking up.

"Tell them what Lopez said to Bo when they left us," prompted Roy.

"Why don't you tell us?" put Pedro.

"I don't know Spanish that well," argued the first baseman.

"He said that their deal had worked out well and that Bo would be compensated for it," said Mellow in a stronger voice.

"See there? What did I tell you?" declared Gypsy Joe. "If you want the traitor you don't have to look no farther." The stocky pitcher pointed a finger at Bo.

There was total silence.

Bo looked around at his teammates. Then he stood and got his duffle from above the seat and slung his jacket over his shoulder. "I guess you've got everything all figured out, eh? It doesn't matter what I say, so I won't say anything, except adios. That's how you say it in *Spanish*, isn't it?" These last words were delivered to Mellow, who, along with the rest of the team were on the edges of their seats. A spell of amazement held back their almost universal desire to tear the traitor apart. Then Bo was gone.

As the young left-hander walked out the door, Rainbow Billy Beauchamp pivoted his parlor seat around and watched his charge walk away as the ash on his cigarette slowly began to curl.

Chapter Fourteen

BO MELLAN PARKED in front of the Dowel family residence in a borrowed Chevy. He had slipped the Dodgers' equipment man $10 for "gas." Bo was puzzled by drivers in the Los Angeles area. Everyone was in such a hurry and generally they seemed to be bad tempered. But this did not bother the rookie left-hander. He just followed his route and marveled at how one gets a different perspective of the topography when driving.

It was May and one of the more pleasant months to be in southern California. The heavy inversion layers of July and August had not formed and the weather had a degree of unpredictability about it.

The house in Downey was a rather plain, frame, ranch two bedroom with white vinyl siding and a two-car garage that sat at the end of a driveway which divided a very small yard. The surroundings were equally unpretentious. This neighborhood was populated by those generally older and generally white—though there were a few younger families sprinkled in (generally Mexican Americans).

Bo pulled up the Chevy and put on the brake. He hadn't called ahead. It was possible that no one would be home.

"Yes?" answered a voice from behind the front door. Only part of an eye was visible through a parabolic peephole.

"I want to see Bobbi Dowel," replied Bo to the eye.

"What do you want with her?" demanded the voice.

"I'm a friend of her father, Sam. I'm a ballplayer. I just wanted to have a few words with her."

There was a pause, then a turning of bolts and latches.

"I suppose you won't do any harm. You can come on in."

Bo was shown a seat in the living/dining room. The pitcher sat on a worn, woolen "sculpted" carpet that had faded from green to light brown. The walls were still green.

Linda was an attractive woman in her late thirties with blonde hair that was short and coiffed into a contrived "casualness." Her skin was youthful except around her eyes that wore makeup to hide the ravages of a life that hadn't gone just the way she had wanted. On the floor was a nearly empty liter of gin and a glass that held only melting ice cubes.

"So, how is old Sam? Just the same as ever, I suppose?"

"I don't know. I've only known him a couple of months."

"Only a couple of months? Already you're running his errands? What's the matter? Couldn't he face the old lady?"

"Pardon?"

"Don't be dumb. You know the score as well as I do. Sam is gutless. He couldn't stand up to baseball when they were pushing his nose in shit and making him eat it. I did everything I could to make him…" She took out the last cigarette from the pack and then set it down without lighting it.

"A big nothing. He's a nothing and he always will be. I'm glad to be rid of him. That no good; groveling—" she struggled for the appropriate epithet: "woman," she finally managed.

"You've got it all wrong," said Bo, sitting with rigid posture on the front of an under-stuffed cushion. "Sam's our pitching coach and he's got meetings all afternoon for our game tonight. We're opening against the Dodgers, you know."

"I wouldn't know, nor do I care. I think baseball is the most corrupt and lousy thing I've ever heard of. Why, if you only knew what it did to—" Linda turned and went over to a small grandfather clock that was housed in a rich black mahogany cabinet. "So much pressure *to be the best*. Always the best. As if it made any goddamn difference how fast a grown man can throw a little leather covered baseball." Linda looked at Bo again. "Can you imagine, adult men devoting their whole lives to a silly little game? Letting it completely control them and becoming more important than any other fucking thing in their goddamned fuckless lives!"

Linda began pacing in front of the clock. Again, she was drawn to the pendulum's slow, steady motion. Bo thought the clock looked quite old. "I'll bet he's talked about me to you, plenty. Men do that with their chums. They talk about the bitches who haul away their paychecks in goddamned lousy alimony: sucking their blood." Linda was still looking at the clock, but her gaze had risen to the face.

"You've got that wrong, Mrs. Dowel. Sam hasn't ever said a word against you to me."

The blonde haired woman spun around on her heel saying, "I'll bet he hasn't. You see! That only proves my point! He's too gutless to say anything. No balls. Do you understand? After what I did to him any real man would have beat me within an inch of my life and put the goddamned fucking lover I had six feet under the ground." Linda's gaze was fiery and accusatory. She held it for only a moment before going over to the coffee table and lighting that cigarette. She sat down but only remained there for enough time to take a single puff.

Then she was up to look out the window.

"I suppose he didn't even tell you that much, that son-of-a-bitch. Just a little song and dance about a life he left behind. That'd be just like him." Then again to Bo. "When is he going to realize that he has to accept responsibility for his actions? He's just a little boy in a man's body. A little boy whose life is centered on a childhood game. Oh goddamned hell." This time Linda fell into her sofa. With practiced hands she poured gin into the tumbler and downed it straight.

Then Bobbi came home. She looked at Bo with mild apprehension, which the pitcher attempted to allay with a quick introduction. He offered her the tickets without moving more than a step from the Queen Anne armchair. The teenager seemed uninterested, but nevertheless accepted the offer.

* * *

The traffic on the Pasadena and Hollywood Freeways near the ballpark was as thick as rush hour. Sunset Boulevard and Stadium Way were bumper to bumper. There would be a full house to welcome the left-handed rookie pitcher of the Cubs. His fastball moved so much, it was rumored that even Mellan couldn't control it. He just reared back and hurled the pill between 93 and 98 miles per hour toward the general area of the plate. They also said his pitch was uncontrollable because he could barely see what he was throwing at. Bo Mellan had been quoted as telling the catcher not to bother holding up his mitt as a target because Bo couldn't see it anyway. They were reported to be working on an alternate system of signals for the shortsighted pitcher.

Bo denied this story saying that he only knew how to throw a fastball so that there weren't any need for signs, anyway.

Such is the stuff of sports page headlines. And Bo was a sports page headline.

Saturday's game was a pitcher's duel throughout. Bo didn't have control of his fastball, but struck out countless hitters with his change-up and curve. In the eighth, there was still no score when Bo came up to the plate. There was one out and a runner on second. Bael had decided to let Bo hit instead of lifting him for a pinch hitter.

Mellan got up and telegraphed a bunt that brought the first and third basemen charging toward the plate while the shortstop ran to cover third. Bo quickly pulled the bat back and punched a bouncing ball into the vacant left side of the infield. The runner scored and Bo held the home team in the last two frames for a 1-0 victory.

The Cubs had won before a packed house and a national television audience. It was an important win for Bo Mellan and the Chicago Cubs.

After the game Bo was besieged by reporters, but on this day, Bo was intent on hurrying away. He had Bobbi waiting. Before the game, Bo had told Sam that he planned on taking Bobbi to Alfredo's, a favorite dessert place just off Alameda and Firestone. Sam had described it as a place that he had liked to take his daughter after they had moved south from the Bay City.

But Sam had been somewhat negative about coming along. And now, when Bo was hurrying to get away, he kept an eye out for the pitching coach in order to argue his case again. But Sam was nowhere.

Bo pushed through the group and told the reporters they ought to interview Bael on his decision to leave Bo in the game to hit in the eighth.

How does it feel to be 4-0? Did you lay off the fastball because it wasn't working for you today? Was that fake bunt a ploy the team worked on in spring training? Where are you from? What minor league teams did you play for? What's your favorite color? Can the Cubs win the pennant?

Then he was with Bobbi.

"Where's Sam?" asked the freckle-faced girl with light brown curls that seemed to bounce on her shoulders.

"He's tied up in an important meeting. I told him where we were going. Perhaps he'll come later," added Bo optimistically. But neither of them believed it.

Bo got a cab and, after a little prompting, found Bobbi to be a very talkative young lady. He heard about her favorite subjects in school, a few boys that she found attractive, and that she played the viola.

When they had slid into their booth at Alfredo's, Bo felt like he knew Bobbi Dowel. At Bo's suggestion Bobbi ordered for both of them. Then it was her turn to do the questioning.

"You met Mother yesterday."

"Yes." Bo looked directly at Sam's perky little girl.

"What did she say about Sam?"

"Oh nothing much, I guess."

"That's a lie. She's always talking against Daddy."

"Well, she was a little hard on him. Why is that?"

"She's always been mad at him. There are two types of people: pushers and watchers. She's a pusher and daddy's a watcher."

"I see." Bo was seated at the back of the booth and could view the front of the restaurant. It was bright and lively with ragtime music and cheerful waiters.

"No you don't. Mother has always had it in her mind to change Daddy. As far back as I can remember. And when things started getting bad in San Francisco, she did everything to try to change Daddy, including having an affair with the manager."

"The manager?"

"Yes. You know him. It was Buddy Bael."

"With Bael? But he was the one who made Sam quit."

"Exactly. Mother tried everything to make Daddy into a 'doer' but nothing ever worked."

"So she had an affair with his enemy?"

"I know it sounds screwy, but that's what happened."

"So they got divorced?"

"Oh no. If Daddy had played the injured husband routine, I think everything would have been fine. But he didn't. He moved us to L.A. and tried to work things out. That was the last straw for Mother. It's not that she didn't love Daddy. She did—still does, I think. It's just that she didn't respect him. Too weak for her. She hates weak people-including me, sometimes. She says 'you've got to take control.' Well, she did all right.

"She filed for divorce and ever since, we've been living on alimony and a little something from a trust left by her parents."

"Sounds tough."

"Oh I don't know. Most of the kids at school seem to have divorced parents. I think it's becoming the norm rather than the exception."

"Still, it's hard being raised by only one parent. There are times that... Don't you ever feel that... " Bo's eyes became blurred. The brightly lit atmosphere and happy faces seemed only to make things worse.

Then the ice cream came. The deserts were huge. Bo had never seen so much ice cream. Each variety of dessert had its own special name: the zoo, the galaxy and so forth. There must have been three gallons of ice cream staring at him, thought Bo.

"You've got to be kidding," said Bo, looking at the dish.

"They give you a badge if you can eat it all."

"But you'd get sick."

"That's why they call it a 'pig trough.'"

"I see. But isn't there a lot of waste?"

"Well, they can't very well recycle it, can they?"

Bo was about to mumble something else about his pig trough when he spotted Sam Dowel coming through the door. Bo stood up and signaled. Soon the Cubs' pitching coach was sitting next to his daughter and eating Bo's pig trough.

Bo sat and listened to the two of them talk for a few minutes. The pair were so occupied that they did not notice Bo's slipping out of the booth, paying the bill, and leaving the restaurant. The faded blue eyes almost sparkled as Bo walked alone in the sunshine down Firestone Boulevard to the team hotel.

Chapter Fifteen

IT SEEMED LIKE A VERY LONG WALK BACK. Bo trudged the final mile and a half by foot. The team plane had arrived into O'Hare at 2 a.m. and Bo had taken a bus to the Loop and a subway to Garfield/55th. From there he had walked.

It was 4:15 a.m. by the time he pushed open the front door at Deronda. The road trip had been a mixed success. Bo split two decisions and the team was one game below .500. The crowds were coming out in large numbers to see Bo pitch. If this continued, Bo's escalator clauses would make him rich because his contract gave him a percentage over the average attendance as well as performance bonuses.

It was 4:18. Bo needed several tries to get his door unlocked. The left-handed pitcher walked in and switched on the light. Everything was different. Before, his apartment had consisted of his few pieces of rented furniture set down in almost the exact places that Adolph, the custodian, had placed them. Now, not only had the furniture been rearranged, but also there were rugs on the floor and pictures on the walls. Everything had been cleaned. Drapes hung in the windows and three small tables sported lamps. The only explanation was Cora.

Bo had given her a key to his place and asked her to keep an eye on things and to collect the mail. He had also left twenty dollars in case of an emergency. But twenty dollars would not have bought all this! The furnishings were used, but appeared to be in good repair. He would have to look more closely in the morning.

As the rookie pitcher made his way back down the hall to his bedroom, he fumbled through his mail: two pieces caught his attention. One was a note from Cora and the other was a letter from Angela. It was late, but one of the epistles could not be set aside.

The pitcher stretched out in bed without disrobing and eagerly opened up Angela's message. It was very brief, thanking Bo for the flowers, and inviting him to a small party if he were back in town. The date for the party was tomorrow—today, really. He would be seeing Angela later this very day.

Bo set down the page of light blue stationery, and then retrieved it again to reconfirm what seemed like impossibly good news. It was 4:30 a.m., but Bo was a long ways from sleeping.

*   *   *

Angela lived in the South Shore area, which was once a grand neighborhood, but now was in some decline. She rented the top floor of a three-flat that was relatively modern for the district.

Bo was the last guest to arrive.

"Hello, Phil," said Angela casually, as if ten years had only been yesterday.

Bo forced a smile. Angela was the only person who addressed him by the name on his birth certificate. She hadn't changed much except that her hair was cut short, close to her head. She wore a flowery, pastel shift that went to the floor.

"Please take off your shoes. It's a custom of the house," she said in the same easy tone. "Let me introduce you to my other guests." Angela led Bo into her living area. Everything was focused upon the wooden floor. There was no furniture. Cushions supported the guests and small tallow lamps provided the light.

On the floor was seated a man in a stiff brown cotton robe and a couple in brightly colored dashikis. The man, al Sulami, looked like an Arab and the couple were ebony-skinned blacks with prominent features.

"We are Ethiopian," said the husband. "My family name of Razi is an old and honorable lineage."

Bo nodded. He wasn't all together sure exactly where Ethiopia was. It sounded like Africa, but beyond that he was at a loss.

"We bring a proud heritage to our work," continued Razi.

Bo looked over to the wife, but she immediately dropped her vision in such a way that the pitcher felt like he had done something wrong.

"...and along with Sunda, our Indonesian brother in Islam, we have formed Krakatowa: an explosive entry into the Chicago business community."

"I see," responded Bo.

"You have heard of us, no doubt."

"I'm sure I have, but I'm really a newcomer to the city."

"But surely we are known all around the country for our courage in attacking corrupt power structures which have infested this rotting edifice of influence and deceit that has robbed Afro-Americans of economic well-being for so long."

"You'll have to forgive me, Mr. Razi. I'm not sure I understand everything you're saying. I never went to college, you see."

"College has nothing to do with the issues at hand. Krakatowa is rightly winning renown far and wide for its visionary championing of the Afro-American cause."

"Phil has been out of the country recently. Perhaps the news doesn't travel so far," put Angela.

Razi looked troubled, but then declared in his sonorous voice, "Out of the country? Traveling? Were you on a vacation, I suppose? In Europe, I shouldn't wonder. What was your itinerary?"

"I'm sorry. I don't understand that word," replied Bo.

"What word? 'Europe'? It's where your fair skinned ancestors came from. The ice and snow took all the color out of their skins." Razi laughed loudly, but Angela immediately put in, "Don't be so hard on Phil. He doesn't understand your sense of humor."

Mrs. Razi continued to look down and al Sulami quietly observed everything from the shadows.

"Who's joking? I merely wanted to know what outposts had not heard the stories of the people's war in Chicago." This was said to Angela. Then Razi turned to Bo and leaned forward. "Well, my colorless friend?"

"My name is Bo Mellan. Angela here calls me Phil, because she's known me a long time. I really prefer being called by my name."

"Called by name; not name-calling." The bony shoulders of Razi shrugged indifference. "That's agreeable with me. But what part of Europe were you in?"

"Veracruz, Guadalajara, Chihuahua, Monterrey—all over really—most recently Caracas." The last name was mumbled. And then he added almost by rote, "I lived there ten years."

"Lived? Worked? South and Central America? Are you an oil company manager?"

"I'm a baseball player."

"Oh my. What exotic friends you have, Angela."

Angela smiled and then got up to serve the food. Bo immediately joined her.

"I wasn't prepared for that," said Bo, once they were in the kitchen.

Angela deftly placed some flat pancakes onto a stoneware platter and arranged various bowls filled with sauces around the edge. "I wanted you to meet my friends. We can talk when they leave."

"Just tell me. What is Krakatowa?"

"You really don't know? Don't you read the newspapers? City Council Wars?"

"You mean Ice and the City Council?"

"That's right. You see, there's this big Federal contract called the Loop Redevelopment Project. It's really for the whole city and is it huge! Ten billion dollars according to the papers—city bonds, state and federal money. It's going to give the whole town a face-lift. Revitalize targeted areas over fifteen years. Do you understand what that will mean?"

"Those numbers are too high for me."

"They're too high for me too, and I'm an accountant—or was until yesterday, but more on that later. I've got to get this food out. Anyway, it just seemed as if Advanced Builders were going to get all of it by default. That's why Krakatowa was started. They wanted minority businesses to get an even break on some of the money."

"But doesn't Advanced hire blacks?"

"Sure they do, but only if they work for the City Machine. It's all so cozy. The blacks who take that money are either crooks or Oreos—because no self-respecting Afro-American would work for Dailey."

The food was served, and Angela and Razi gave Bo a lesson in Chicago Politics. They emphasized the feudal power structure of the city. Beneath Dailey were his four lieutenants: Adam Wojciuk, Tony Ballestrieri, Sean Patrick O'Neil, and Jesse Jefferson. They controlled the Polish, Italian, Irish, and black voting wards respectively. O'Neil was Council president and Ballestrieri headed Advanced Builders as well as being the mob liaison with the ruling Acardo Family. Jesse Jefferson and Adam Wojciuk also had indirect ties to Advanced Builders.

Everything was very convenient—too convenient for Razi, Sunda, and Wilson Ice. Together, they began uniting what had been left of the Black Power factions of the sixties into a new coalition that aimed to topple existing power structures.

Bo listened attentively so that by the time the other guests left, he was no longer the object of Razi's pointed barbs.

"I think you were a success tonight," said Angela as she slid over next to Bo.

"With your guests?"

"Razi doesn't like many whites. He's a Black Muslim, you know. To him you are a devil."

"A devil? Me?"

Angela laughed. "Don't worry. Al Salumi wouldn't have let anything happen to you. He's an orthodox Muslim and has a strong sense of fair play."

"He'd need more than that to take care of me."

"Al Salumi's very powerful, even though he's a mystic."

"Is that why he's so quiet?"

"You are terrible."

The candles were burning low. There was so much Bo wanted to talk about: questions that had festered since they had parted last in Milwaukee.

Bo had written a score of letters that had never been answered. The only news he'd received was a single note sent to Rainbow when she broke-up with DuRon Garvey. Angela had followed DuRon to Chicago after living with him for three years in beer town.

But DuRon had other plans. So Angela got a job as an accountant for a greeting card company and settled into the South Shore. This much Bo knew before he came. When he left that evening, he knew no more.

They didn't talk about people and places. Instead, they mumbled abstract garble that Bo did not understand, but felt. Talking with Angela was not the same as conversing with anyone else.

Everything in Angela's apartment was close to the floor. There was a starkness to it all that appealed to Bo. It was overtly informal, according to contemporary standards, and yet beyond this immediate presentation it was formidable and remote. One could feel immediately at ease, but then, once settled, he felt how totally alienated he was from these surroundings. They were apart and unto themselves. The intruder was isolated: totally alone.

Bo took his leave before the last of the candles had extinguished itself. Two things were on his mind as he hopped on the bus. First, Angela was out of a job for the first time in her life. She acted sanguine, but Bo could sense her underlying anxiety. He had been away for some time, but some things remained always and unchanged.

Second, Angela was coming to the game tomorrow and afterwards they were having dinner. The bus doors closed. Bo watched through the greasy window as the city came to him while motoring home on the nearly empty south side route.

Chapter Sixteen

"I WAS WONDERING HOW LONG IT'D TAKE YOU," snapped the bald headed, pot bellied man behind the desk.

"I had to get dressed," replied Bo Mellan as he sat on the functional metal chair.

"We've got a few things to talk over."

"I'm listening."

"Your contract. For starters. I have to confess that when we signed you, everyone thought it was quite a joke." Bael chuckled behind an oversized grin.

Bo looked right through his boss.

Bael's smile disappeared. "Why, it's ridiculous to pay the minimum salary. You're worth more than twenty-five grand. The club doesn't want to take advantage of you, boy." The baldhead and rounded shoulders leaned over his desk.

"I'm satisfied," responded Bo in even tones.

"Yes, yes." He chuckled again. "I'm sure you are. But Mr. Cakos and the Sun Company don't work that way. Fair play. That's what they stand for. Oh, I told 'em that they shouldn't turn a young man's head with fat renegotiations, but they were as insistent on doing the right thing by you, boy." Bael nodded his bald head as if he were answering himself. Then he opened a drawer and removed a multiple carbon document with his stubby fingers. "So if you'll just sign this paper here, we're willing to triple your salary." Bael slid the paper over to Bo and took out a gold pen and laid it atop. "You sign right there at the bottom; I've marked the place with an 'X.'" Bo took the pen and fiddled with the mechanism momentarily until he finally got the point to retract. Then he leaned over and set the pen in the shirt pocket of his superior. "I guess Mr. Cakos will just have to be disappointed. As I told you before: I'm satisfied."

Bo got up and walked toward the door.

"Get back here."

Bo stopped and turned. His movements were easy and unhurried. "Is there something else?"

"You bet there's something else. Who do you think you are? Some no good bush leaguer trying to act like the big time? I can send you down to the minors anytime I like. Do you understand me? Anytime I want!"

Bo looked back just as before.

Bael slammed the top of his metal desk with his fist. Then he looked up with different eyes. The edges of the reef had disappeared under the waves of tranquility. "This is the big time, boy. You're going to need a few friends or you're sunk. You can count on it. Trouble makers don't last."

Bo nodded. "Is that all?"

Bael didn't respond at first. Then he said in a different voice. "We have a public relations appearance in three weeks. I'll give you the details. June 10th. Keep it open."

Bo nodded. "Is that all?"

Bael opened his drawer and stuffed his cheek with tobacco.

*　*　*

Bo walked back to his locker. His arm was a little stiff and needed some attention. On the way he met Sam.

"What happened in there? I could hear Buddy yelling from the other end of the locker room."

"Wanted me to re-negotiate my contract."

"What did they make you give up?"

"Nothin'. They wanted me to give up my performance escalators, but I wouldn't do it."

"What?" Sam hit his fist into his hand. Then in a low tone, "Do you know who's behind Bael—they've got muscle."

"Bael mentioned a Ruppert Cakos. But I don't know Ruppert Cakos from a pig's ass. What's he going to do, kill me? I'm not going to worry about Bael or Cakos or anybody else. I don't even know who this Ruppert Cakos is."

"Ruppert Cakos is the most powerful man in the city. He runs everything he wants: the paper, the ball club, the TV station—even the Acardo family steps out of his way." Angela reached for a cigarette, but then remembered she was quitting again. She sipped a Manhattan instead.

"The mob?"

"You got it. They got a pawn in Tony Ballestrieri. He represents their interest on the City Council. Cakos has that man in his pocket."

"I see," responded Bo. They were at the Black Hawk on Wabash and Randolph. It was a restaurant with political ears. Angela ordered another Manhattan while Bo stayed with his soft drink. "Didn't you say Ballestrieri owned Advanced Builders?"

"He's the President, but not the owner. No one knows who pulls the strings, but you could make a good guess. What is all this, anyway?"

"Nothing. Just trying to get Chicago through my thick skull. It isn't easy. Chicago's a lot different from Milwaukee."

Angela laughed. "You got that right. Milwaukee is a small town even though it's bigger than Boston. Chicago is a city proper—or improper—whatever."

Bo smiled. It often seemed to him that Angela was making some quip that he should be recognizing, but wasn't. It didn't matter.

"What about your employment? You promised to tell me the whole story." Bo slid back in his seat. The Black Hawk is a well-lit restaurant. Fluorescent tubes near the ceiling brought to light countless portraits of prominent political and sports figures in the city. There were no shadows in this establishment.

"Not much to say," replied Angela as she played with her drink. Bo stared at Angela. He saw smooth skin and softly rounded features. The rookie pitcher thought she had an intelligent look to her. There was also something else which he couldn't put to words.

Angela looked up. Just above Bo's head, on the back wall, was a larger than life portrait of Eddy "Big Stick" Dailey. Her eyes returned to Bo.

"Things are depressed on the south side. Things are depressed all over, for that matter. And you can bet that they hit us the hardest. My company had to cut back. Pure and simple. Last hired…"

Bo shook his head. "And there probably won't be many openings elsewhere if things are as bad as you say."

"You got that right, Phil."

Bo turned the conversation to old times at Marshall High. Those were days that he remembered with nostalgia. Angela didn't have the same fondness for high school. She had always been waiting to get on to college. For her, high school was a time of meaningless stagnation while she was ready to move ahead.

But they did share many memories about Medford Avenue and the classic fights between Willie and Corrine. It had never been a quiet house, even when Bo's mother had still been alive.

As dinner progressed they moved into the present. Today Bo had pitched another victory for the Cubs. But Angela was not much interested in sports. Finally, over dessert, Bo suddenly exclaimed, "I've got it! A way to solve everything."

"What are you talking about?"

"Your job, the bad economic conditions in the city, the racial climate: everything!"

"I think you were out in the sun too long today."

"No, I'm serious. It's so simple. We will form a non-profit corporation or company—whatever they're called—to revitalize the city."

"And I suppose you'll put up the ten billion?" Angela could barely restrain her laughter.

"Oh, I don't mean the whole city—like the Loop Redevelopment Project. That's not what I mean. Something simple. Aimed at the people who really need the money: the working poor in the city. There might be a lot of businesses, like the card company you were working for, who might need a little cash to get them over a hump—or a new business that could get financing through banks and all if they were given some seed money to start. We might even be able to subsidize some job training or something like that."

Bo's eyes flashed as if a hint of brightness had returned.

"That sounds real good, Bo. But money is what talks."

"I have a little. And if I keep pitching like I did today, I'll have a whole lot more. I've got a performance-based contract."

Angela stopped laughing.

"I'd be willing to give it all to something worthwhile. And with that as a start we could hit the bricks to raise more. A baseball player is a kind of celebrity, you know."

Angela slid forward in her seat. "How much money do you have, Phil?"

"Not that much right now. At payday I should have twenty thousand or so—I hope. But by All Star break I could have a couple hundred thousand and double or triple that by the end of the year."

"A half million?"

"Unless somebody shoots me," returned Bo with a smile.

"Do you know this isn't as stupid as it sounds?"

"Thank you, I think."

"No. Listen," began Angela, talking to her open hands that rested on the table. "If we can get institutional status as a non-profit lending institution, we can lend out 80% of our holdings five times and quadruple your half-million into two-million. Then there's matching grants we could apply for, and community support that could bring us up to four million or so. That's three or four full-time staff. Not bad, really." She looked up at Bo who sat across from her. "How did you think up something like that, Phil?"

Bo frowned.

"No. I mean it's such a good idea. If you could really get the cash..."

"We can start in June. You'll be the first paid employee."

"No. At first everyone is volunteer. I'll draw unemployment for a couple of months. We've got to get a broad base of good will. Maybe I could talk with Razi."

Bo shook his head. "I'd rather not, Angela. His company is such a hot item in local politics. Why don't we put ourselves above that sort of thing? I don't mind supporting individual subcontractors, whoever they are—Krakatowa or Advanced—but I'm not for getting into those kinds of battles. Let's be content with the small time. There's plenty to be done there."

Angela pouted for a moment, but quickly agreed. She was full of ideas about how they'd start their *Chicago People's Project* (a name she coined). Occasionally she interrupted her chatter with, "It's a great idea, Phil."

Bo tried to listen, but he did not understand money very well. At one point he interrupted Angela. "I think if we go through with this, you had better call me what everyone else does, Angela. I really prefer 'Bo' to 'Phil,' you know."

The left-handed pitcher delivered these words with a thick, halting voice. His eyes were fixed only on Angela. But she didn't respond. Her defiant gaze was set squarely upon the larger than life portrait of Eddy "Big Stick" Dailey that was spying on them from the opposite wall.

Chapter Seventeen

THERE ARE TIMES WHEN THE BODY'S most fervent desire is simply to let it stretch out in quiet contentment. The tumultuous crises of life are no longer considered due to the body's urgent need for somnolent relief.

Bo Mellan lay on his stomach with his head covered by a pillow. It was seven forty-five. Though it had been a warm night, Bo still covered himself with a blanket. The neighborhood was really not overly quiet on a weekday morning, but the pitcher did not wake up from the noise even as a key opened his apartment door.

"Hello," called Cora from the doorway.

There was no reply.

Cora stepped inside and looked into the bedroom. On the floor were shirts, socks and pants that seemed to be resting exactly where they had been removed.

"Bo?"

A slight stirring.

Cora came in and started picking up clothes. "I know you're an early riser or I wouldn't have come. But the morning waits for no one, right?"

A moan could be heard from under the pillow.

"I haven't had a chance to see you since you got back from the Coast. I heard you come in, of course. But I didn't want to disturb you." Cora opened the small closet and began hanging things up. The sun shone brightly through the window while Bo vainly held the pillow over his head.

"How do you like the way I fixed things up for you? I even brought in a few groceries; did you see?" Cora had finished straightening up and stood near the foot of the hurler's bed. Her hands were on her hips, and a smile was on her face.

Another moan from under the pillow.

Cora laughed. "Oh Bo, you lazy head. I'm going to get you some breakfast. I want to hear all about your trip."

Slowly the grip on the pillow loosened as it became clear that the pattering feet were not going home. His body moved deliberately, in stages, resting in the intervals, even as strains of singing could be heard from the kitchen.

The mirror revealed a puffy face, the eyes barely flickering. Another groan and lots of cold water.

* * *

"Oh Bo, you don't know how proud I was to see you on television when you pitched in Los Angeles. You were super!"

Bo began drinking coffee.

"I just knew you were going to win. They couldn't touch you. And I listened to the San Francisco game on the radio. You should've won that one too. You really brought the team back when they were down. I was so mad at Big Train Lincoln for that throwing error that cost you the win. It was so unfair after you had come all that way back."

"Baseball isn't fair."

"You can say that. I tell you I was so mad." Cora sat down next to Bo at the table. She looked at her neighbor with beaming eyes.

Bo was slumped over his coffee. He stared blankly into the blackness.

"I can't begin to tell you how thankful I am to you for all you've done for me, Bo."

The pitcher remained as he was.

"Your advice to me. Those conversations. They've really helped."

Bo squinted. Then he turned his head to Cora. "What are you talking about?"

Cora laughed. "That's just like you, Bo. You're always so modest about your achievements."

"What am I supposed to have done?"

"Why help me, of course. You gave me self confidence."

"But you only came over here a couple times since—the intrusion."

"It seems like more than that to me. The things you said. Your whole way. It made a deep impression, believe me."

Bo turned his head to the window that overlooked the back alley. He held his head in his right hand and sipped his coffee. It was luke warm.

"And so many things have been happening to me in the last ten days. I can't believe it."

Bo looked at the decrepit fire escapes: rotting wood partially covered with peeling blue paint. In case of emergency, this was the structure people would depend upon.

"You were right, of course, about Larry. He was shacking up with a bitch named Jeanie. Can you stand it. The two-timer. Well, I told him where to go. I did. I really did."

"What happened?"

"He left. Packed up in one case and said he'd be back for the rest. Said he didn't need that kinda shit from me. Said I was a ball buster. Can you believe it? When I think of what I gave that man. He came back and got the rest. Took some of my stuff, too. But it's worth it to be rid of him."

"I never told you to break with Larry," said Bo, still looking out of the window.

"Oh I know. You only talked about general things. It is not so much what someone says that you hear, but something else. You let me see how things were."

"I'm sorry if I caused you to lose or whatever...."

"Sorry? That jerk beat me. I let him punch me out because I was too dependent on him. I let that man be everything. It's true. Really."

Bo watched as a rather long, thin brown cockroach ran along the window sash. It pushed hard against the glass as if it were trying to escape. The hurler turned to Cora.

"So he's left—for good?"

"That's right. And I've been happier than I can say. At first I wasn't sure how'd I'd react. I've always been the sort of girl that people dumped on. No more. I'll tell you. Believe me." She smiled. "And I owe it all to you."

"But I didn't do anything."

"Not much you didn't. I've learned so much since knowing you. When my boss kept treating me like shit, I finally stood up to him. And it worked."

"He's treating you better?"

"No. I got fired."

"Got fired?"

"But it's not bad. The job was no good, anyway. I got thirty days notice. Then unemployment. I'll get something else. The hours were short, but now I'm gonna need more money anyway; with Larry gone and all."

"A lot of good I've brought you: you've broken up with your man, and you've lost your job."

"And I'm happy!" Cora smiled. Her eyes moved around taking in all of Bo Mellan.

Bo fidgeted. "I want to pay you for the furniture you bought. It must have cost you some money."

"No. I got it at my sister's aunt's building. They had a big sale there. Barely over the twenty you left."

"Would fifty more cover it?"

"It was only fifteen more or so. But I don't want it. It was my idea. I did it on my own."

"Just the same, without a job you'll be finding yourself short of cash." Bo pushed the money towards Cora.

"Let me do something for you. You've done so much for me. Please." Cora's eyes were entreating. She didn't touch the money.

"You really shouldn't be spending your money like that."

"I've got two more paychecks. Don't worry about me." She got up and went to Bo giving him a warm hug and a kiss on the cheek. "You're a dear," she said. "Do you know that?"

Bo looked back at the window. The roach had found a crack in the sash that was just big enough for its escape. Bo thought that the insect paused a moment, almost in defiant mockery, before effecting its exit. Cora gave Bo another tight embrace.

CHAPTER EIGHTEEN

THEY CALLED IT "A COCKROACH'S MOTHER." It tasted like mud. But Bo Mellan was downing them in rapid succession.

The little bar in which he was drinking was in the bawdy Libertad district of Guadalajara. This was the old part of the city where the main marketplace was located and where the hotels and women went very cheap. It had been a couple of weeks since Bo left the team. It seemed much longer to the young man.

At first Bo had stayed at the two-star Americana, but the rates drove him to cheaper accommodations in less than a week. A few friendly card games lightened his wallet further, so that as things stood, he was sitting with five hundred pesos in his pocket drinking a foul tasting concoction that was going for twenty pesos a shot. With room and food requiring two hundred pesos a day, he was two days from being flat broke.

Over and over he replayed the scenes in his mind. His two meetings with Cortez in which the toupee-clad entrepreneur had seemed so ingratiating. Then he visualized Lopez at the jail. Lopez was two different men. The smiling, friendly Cortez lieutenant and then....

A fly landed in Bo's drink, but the hurler didn't bother removing it. Instead, he set down his greasy glass and put his hand to his head. The young man could not focus very well. He would have to get a job, but as a foreigner who could not speak the language, this would not be easy. Perhaps he could contact someone in the sizeable-American community that resided in Hidalgo. There, speaking English might be an advantage. Easy job. Big money.

The air was heavy. Bo had to get outside. He was going to be sick. Steps unsteady. Going toward the door. A hand on his arm. Then falling. Wretching. Rolling over. More hands. Then sleep.

*   *   *

Bo awoke. His back was sore. His head was lulled by continuous, dull insensibility. The young man sat up. It was dark. A single light shown in the back alley where he was lying in garbage. His left sleeve was stiff with dried vomit. Money: gone. Body: sore from laying in tumbled refuse. Minute insects crawled in his hair and about his skin. It was night and all he wanted to do was become unconscious.

As he examined himself, a pain began to grow at the base of his skull. The hurler tried to lift himself up, but slipped down again and began to cry. He made no attempt to check himself. It had been three years since his mother had left him. How safe he used to feel in her arms when the whole world seemed set against him. He longed to call her name. But his mother was dust. She could no longer comfort him.

The alley light was faint, but it was sufficient to show him where he was. Behind him was the bar where he had been. In front of him, decaying matter corrupting into its elemental components. The crying stopped. His eyes focused upon the sharp edges of a metal lid bent back; still on the can. His paling eyes stared at the edges made jagged by a can opener. The discarded metal disks that lay in the dump were sharp. They could slice right through a man's skin.

The edges seemed to sparkle before Bo's eyes. "'I want... my mother... I...'" the sounds were barely audible. His fixed expression did not alter even as a rat ran over his leg. Bo reached toward the can, slowly, tentatively.

Out of the metal receptacle shot a giant cockroach. It scurried up Bo's arm. He spat at it and missed, but the motion caused the roach to fall and run for safety under the trash heap. Bo looked up at the light; faint as it was, it still made him squint. His head was beginning to throb. It was time to get up and move on.

Within an hour he had a job at his hotel doing dishes, mopping and sweeping up. He worked five hours a day for lodging and one meal. He'd need more, but this would do for now. The job gave him time. And Bo needed time. Time to sort things out.

After a few days, Bo heard that the Elite Giants were coming to play a series in Libertad. The young man hocked his pitcher's glove for seventy-five pesos so he could afford the twenty-five pesos admission price. He'd be sure to be unrecognized in the crowd. His face was drawn; skin yellow cast and his hair shorn close to get rid of the lice. No one would recognize him even if they happened to pick him out in the crowd, he told himself.

It was a different man who came late to the game and watched from afar. He was not the bright eyed, temperamental boy who had shown flashes of brilliance as a pitcher sometimes overpowering the other team with raw talent (at other times being pounded out early). That cocky, inconsistent pitcher, who could only pitch well when he was ahead and things were going right for him, was gone. In his place sat a pale-eyed dishwasher/janitor with only a handful of centavos to his name, fighting for survival.

The Elite Giants still had but nine players. No extras were on the bench. Mellow was back in left and Candy was on the mound. The team looked tired, but managed to win the game 8-7 on an eighth inning home run by Roy Carnes.

The big crowd began to disperse. Bo headed over to a park three blocks away. He wanted time to sit and think. It wasn't easy sitting in the stands while people were playing baseball. Bo needed time to examine the confusion.

Bo sat in the twilight staring at the street ahead. Then he thought he saw a familiar form pass under the street lamp. Could it be? It looked like a former team member. Something in the walk, perhaps, or maybe it was the confusion in his own mind, compelled Bo to get up and follow this figure from the shadows to whatever was his destination.

After awhile the figure ducked into a bar and quickly emerged with an envelope. It was dark by now, but the form moved under the street lamp. Bo saw that he had been right. It was Gypsy Joe Grandy. The stocky pitcher had an envelope in his hand that he eagerly opened. The contents were removed and the envelope fell. There was money and a note. Gypsy pocketed the money and read the note. Then he took out a match and set the paper on fire and tossed it towards the grate. In another moment he was gone.

Bo stood mesmerized for a moment. Then he ran for the grate where he found the envelope and the charred remains of the message that had been completely burned except for one word that had survived its incinerated fate. One word stood out on the remaining fragment.

That word was 'BOMB.'

Chapter Nineteen

BO DIDN'T HESITATE. He knew he had to warn Rainbow, but how could he do it? He dare not show his face, and there was no telephone service. The only alternative was a messenger. He had fifty pesos in his pocket. It was plenty of money for a private courier, but at this time of night none was available.

The young man with closely cropped hair went back to the hotel and bought a few sheets of stationery to write his message. Quickly, he departed again and inquired after the team's whereabouts from two taxi drivers.

In an hour Bo was at the site. He saw Pedro, Ramon and Rainbow sitting around a table playing cards and smoking cigars. Their faces glowed in the dimly lit park.

Bo determined to sneak up to the bus and drop the message through the window onto Rainbow's seat. But the young dishwasher was not adept at stealth and stepped upon a small, dry branch that cracked loudly. Bo froze. His mind tried to race through various actions, but he was not up to rapid calculation.

Finally, he turned to retreat. But his way was blocked. Standing in front of him was Rainbow Billy Beauchamp. Bo stood staring at the partially lit figure.

"Well?" Rainbow's tone was steady but slightly impatient.

Bo bit his lip and then thrust his note into the other's hand before disappearing into the darkness.

The young man ran. His legs had never been tested at any distance for some time and soon they began to knot up in cramps. Where he was he couldn't say. Why had he run? What would happen to the team? Would Gypsy succeed? How was he going to do it? Would Rainbow believe his note?

Bo gathered himself and wandered back to his hotel.

* * *

Rainbow put the note into his pocket and returned to his game. He played his hand cagily, smoked his cigars and waited.

* * *

The next day the Elite Giants were scheduled for an early afternoon game, a clowning exhibition and an evening contest. It was almost noon when the team bus pulled up to the same diamond they'd played the night before.

The sun was high in a cloudless sky. Heat radiated everywhere as people strolled around for a seven-inning contest that many could see on an extended lunch break. Everywhere, brown skin absorbed the purifying rays of the sun. And the smell of perspiration mixed freely with the dust that was brought up by the wind.

There was a moderate amount of grumbling as the Elite Giants bus rumbled up to the playing field. The players knew their schedule for the day and the other days they'd spend playing in Guadalajara.

Much of the crowd clamored around the bus as it pulled in. There was something different about a traveling team that made their attraction almost magnetic. Here were a bunch of guys who had no guaranteed salaries or schedules to rely upon. They were always a few steps from disaster. Everything was bet upon their abilities and their consistent power to carry them through. Within such a traveling team the spectator can see, at the same time, a wandering freedom wed to a dogged adherence to a rigid style of play that brought them and kept them where they were.

As the Elite Giants made their way to the field there was one set of eyes that carefully monitored the progress of the Pan American professionales. It was eleven forty-five by the chimes of the church bells. All the ballplayers, save one, had set their duffels on the bench and were going through their effects to get what they needed for the warm-up and game. It was a methodical procedure that became even more deliberate under the influence of the scorching mid-day heat.

Rainbow, who had been talking briefly to the promoter, came back to his team's bench. The bench area was ground level and fenced in with chain link to form a rectangular box around the players. Rainbow leaned against a post that stood at the entrance/exit of the bench area. He was smoking a short stub of a cigarette with a long ash that curled down.

"Gypsy Joe." The manager's voice was even, but there was something slightly unnatural to it. It was this flavor that marked it out. Everyone stopped and looked first at their manager and then at the ash that seemed at any moment ready to fall. Every eye, except those of the stocky pitcher who was tying his shoes, was fixed on the ash. Rainbow watched with more than dispassionate interest as the hard throwing pitcher finished his laces and flipped over the tongue of his shoe, kicked his cleats on the bench and pulled up his pants. Gypsy Joe Grandy was ready. He turned and saw everyone looking at him. The stocky Texan looked down the line of players to Rainbow standing at the end. No one said a word.

"What's up? Do I gotta pitch all three games today?" The Texan laughed and started forward.

"Where's your equipment bag?" asked Rainbow dropping the ash, but holding the stub tightly between his fingers.

"In the bus, I guess. Didn't think I'd need it."

"Get it."

"Later. I've got warm-up for the game." The stocky right-hander moved forward. Rainbow didn't budge. He was blocking the way. No one could get out without walking over the wiry manager.

Gypsy Joe stopped. He squinted at Rainbow. "What is this? Some kinda joke?"

"No joke."

"What goddamn difference does it make if I have some friggin' duffle bag or not?"

"Just get your bag."

"Tell somebody else to get it. It's almost twelve and I've got a game to throw."

The stocky Texan moved forward again to push his way free. "Get out of my way, old man. I don't need this."

But the end of his sentence echoed dully as the Texan froze just where he was: defiantly postured with one hand on Rainbow's shoulder. He stopped where he was—transfixed. The rest of the team moved their eyes from Gypsy to the apparition that stood before him. It was Bo Mellan holding Gypsy Joe's duffle.

"But maybe you need this, Joe," said Bo in evenly measured tones. His thin lips turned up slightly at the corners. The dishwasher then tossed the bag at its rightful owner.

The stocky Texan grabbed the bag that was tossed at his face and held it with tensed hands for a moment as his eyes shifted back to the team bench and again toward his exit route. Then the church bells struck twelve. Gypsy Joe hurriedly tossed the duffle to the other end of the bench and pushed Rainbow aside. The Texan frantically rushed forward into the fist of the nineteen year-old dishwasher.

In an instant Joe Grandy was down on the ground. Roy Carnes pounced on top of him. The first baseman gripped the stocky pitcher by the arms and shook him.

"You goddamned lousy traitor. It was you who's been doing this to us. It was you all along. You're responsible for José. Why you— you'll be begging me to break your neck by the time—"

Rainbow and his team gathered around and restrained Roy. The manager of the Pan-Am Elite Giants leaned over Gypsy Joe. The pitcher was gasping. "The bomb. There's a bomb in my duffle. It'll go off any second."

Rainbow Billy Beauchamp reached back and slapped Joe Grandy hard across his face.

"There is a bomb in there all right, but Roy defused it this morning while you were washing up. There's no chance of it going off. But a trick like that makes Roy pretty mad. And you know how hard it is to contain Roy. Remember Zacoalco?"

The first baseman grunted convincingly.

"I didn't know they'd start a fight. Lopez never told me."

"That may be, but Roy here is a hard man to persuade."

Roy twisted the other's shoulder until the humerus was almost out of joint.

The stocky Texan writhed. "I'll do anything you want. They made me do it. Just get him off me."

Rainbow restrained Roy and had Gypsy Joe sign a statement confessing to his activity with Lopez and Juan Cortez. Then the manager reached took Gypsy Joe's wallet from him. Rainbow took out fifty dollars and handed it to the stocky Texan. Then he put the wallet with its ill-gotten gains into his own pocket.

"Get out of my sight, boy. If I ever see you again it's going to be your last day on earth."

Gypsy Joe took his money and spat in the direction of his former teammates. Then he turned and walked away.

*   *   *

"You knew about this, Roy?" asked Ramon in an anxious tone. "Why wasn't I told?"

"Why didn't somebody tell me?" echoed forth.

"So it was Joe all along. What about Bo?"

"He tipped us off about the bomb," put Pedro.

"You mean he saved our skins after the way we...."

"Where is Bo anyway? We've gotta make it up; we've gotta—"

But Bo was not to be seen. After he decked Joe, Bo had vanished. The church bells struck 12:15. It was time to play baseball, but they only had eight players! There was only one solution: Rainbow Billy Beauchamp would have to don a glove for the first time in twenty-two years. The boss of the Pan Am Elite Giants had become a player-manager.

CHAPTER TWENTY

CANDY LARO PITCHED THE FIRST GAME against a weak team. But Candy's arm was tired from pitching the night before in a very tight contest. He was through for the day on the mound. In their clown game Sam Nuxall threw. He had nothing on his pitches, but the competition was very weak. Besides, in that game the antics of Juice and Harold were the principal attraction. That evening was a different story. The Elite Giants were pitted against tough competition.

Mellow started the game but gave up six straight hits. The reputation of the team was at stake. The early afternoon fracas had stirred up interest in the game and a good crowd of nearly eight thousand had showed up for the contest. If the Giants fell flat now, they might have to write off this entire baseball region for quite awhile.

A change was needed. Into the game came Rainbow Billy Beauchamp. Sixty plus years of experience against young men who could be his grandsons. The bases were loaded with nobody out and three runs in.

The spectators jeered the old man as he took the hill. Ramon threw back the ball and Rainbow dropped it. The crowd howled. Insults flew as the aged pitcher knelt over and instead of picking up the ball stepped on it and fell on his seat. Refuse started flying onto the field. The wiry player-manager picked up the ball from his seated posture. The leather sphere had a long slice in it where he had stepped on it. The old man smiled and got to his feet.

As soon as the field was cleared off he tossed a slow curve that was outside and low, but the batter jumped at it and grounded into a home to first double play. Two outs; runners on second and third.

This time a high curve, inside. Wack. The batter creamed a long fly ball that seemed to hang up in the air even though it sounded like a sure round-tripper when it left the bat. Mellow pounded the glove and took it on the run. Two pitches, three outs. The catcalls stopped as Rainbow went out to congratulate Mellow on his catch.

"That last one should've gone five hundred feet," smiled the manager as he greeted his outfielder, patting him on the shoulder and quietly switching baseballs for their half of the inning.

Because the day had been hot and dry, the air was buoyant and the scores were high. Rainbow Billy Beauchamp had gone through his arm and all his tricks to keep his team in the game. It was 8-6 in favor of the Giants in the bottom of the seventh when Rainbow's arm died.

There was one out and a runner at first. The other team's power hitter was up. Ramon came out to the mound.

"Nothin' in the strike zone. I don't know how much longer I'll be able to throw."

"You've got to hold out, Rainbow. We ain't got no one else."

"Jist don't let nothin' get by you."

The count was one and one when the husky batter belted a long drive that just curved foul at the last minute. Another conference.

"He's hitting 'em even when they ain't strikes. Listen, we're going to pretend to walk 'em. On ball four, set-up outside—'cept I'll send one down the middle. We've got to try it."

It worked. The foul ball seemed to shake-up the pitcher, who obviously had used up his stock of tricks for the night. The walk seemed like a logical move. The batter waited with his bat resting on his shoulder even as the last pitch came by—right over the plate. Strike three. Two outs.

This time the crowd was jeering the home team. The pitching performance of this hurler, who had little speed and no stuff, had won a grudging admiration from the spectators so that even though they cheered when the next two batters doubled; they still felt a twinge of sadness for this aging hurler who really knew his pitching.

Rainbow stood on the mound with his glove under his arm. Everything was over. He couldn't pitch anymore. He turned to face his ball players in order to select the best replacement. But he knew none of them could get by this team. They'd never get an out. The aging man shook his head. Here was twenty years in the dry cleaning business. Lost. Forever.

Then heads began to turn. From out of left field came a figure trotting in. He wore baseball shoes, but was not in uniform. The figure was a young man with a sprightly, confident stride. It was Bo Mellan.

As the man in his tee shirt and jeans came through the infield, Pedro met him and swatted him on the butt. Rainbow strode off the hill and handed the baseball to the returning stray.

"Where's your glove, boy?"

"Done put it in hock to watch you play."

"Here, use mine. You been watching?"

Bo nodded.

The manager gave Bo his uniform shirt and then strode slowly to the bench. The crowd cheered wildly. They had seen something, and they knew it.

The opposition scored twice more before the inning was over, but Bo was able to hold them during the eighth. Unfortunately, the Elite Giants were only able to manage one more run and ended up losing the game 10-9.

"You looked pretty good out there, boy."

"I lost the game."

"That may be, but you came out of it a winner."

"I just couldn't let that performance of yours be wasted. I mean I learned more watching you pitch those seven innings than I ever had before."

"Shit boy. I'm washed up and I knowd it. I just used what I got."

"You sure know just how to do it, though."

"Soul, boy. Like what I told you before. When you got it, you're always a winner."

"I believe you."

"I know that, boy. And you got a dose of your own out there tonight. Yes sir, boy. I think you're going to be a pitcher."

Chapter Twenty-one

AFTER THE GAME THERE WAS ONE PIECE of unfinished business: a meeting with Juan Cortez's agent, Lopez. Their man was not difficult to find. Indeed, it is a promoter's aim to be highly accessible for ongoing business deals.

It was around midnight when Rainbow Billy Beauchamp, Bo Mellan, Pedro Gonzalas and Roy Carnes came calling at the hotel suite of one Signor Lopez. The short man with his stringy, plastered hair had nothing to say when he opened the door to this quartet of visitors.

"Won't you invite us in?" put Pedro in proper Spanish as the four pushed their way inside.

It was a fancy room with a red sofa and plush carpeting. The room was well lit. The flashing lights of the hotel's restaurant and casino formed a gaudy pattern on the sheer curtains. Bo and Roy took Lopez by the arms and walked him back to the sofa. Against the wall were two suitcases. Rainbow looked at the cases and opened one up. It was packed.

"Going somewhere?" asked Rainbow.

"I'm sorry, I ne habla bueno English."

Roy gave the man's arm a severe twist. "Cut the bullshit, greaseball."

"Ah-yee!" shouted Lopez. "Let me alone. I will punish you for—"

The words were cut short by Roy's forearm which slammed into the other's throat.

"—I don't think you are in a position to be making threats," put Pedro.

"—Tell them, Bo," coughed the powerful henchman, "don't let them do this to me." The man eyed the left-hander who was holding the promoter's other arm.

"What should I tell them, Signor Lopez? Should I tell them how you tried to frame me? Or should I tell them how you were responsible for killing one of our team members? Or maybe you'd like me to add how you have been engaging in a string of sabotage tactics that almost ended in mass murder this afternoon?"

Lopez's eyes widened. His forehead glistened more brightly than his plastered hair. "You have no proof. It's all lies."

"That's where you're wrong, amigo," said Rainbow with a smile. "We've got a statement from Gypsy Joe Grandy detailing everything."

"Pah! That would never stand-up in a court of law. I promise you, if you don't let me go I'll have the lot of you in jail."

"I don't think so. You see, the best place we could take this is not the law courts where you could bribe your way right out, but to the newspapers. It'd make a great story, you know. There's no way you could keep that out. And the publicity from that might be just enough to destroy you. Entertainment is a business, you know, where a good press means everything."

Lopez's breath became short. Roy and Bo dropped their hold as Pedro removed a small revolver from the man's wrinkled navy blue suit coat. The swaggering man of Zocoalco slumped back. His mouth was open; his hands grasped his double creased pants.

"I don't suppose Juan Cortez would take kindly to that, would he?"

Lopez continued to gape while his hands indiscriminately clutched at the false and true trouser creases.

"At the very best you might be out of a job. At worst... ?"

Lopez turned to Rainbow. "I might be dead." The words were ingenuously pronounced in almost childlike tones.

"I knew you'd understand. Just keep your boss out of our way and everything is jake, got me?"

"Jake?" The words caught on his lips.

"You got it. Now good-bye." Rainbow started to lead his band out. Then he stopped and walked back to Lopez, who was coming out of his trance. "Just one more thing I forgot." Rainbow sent a short left to the saboteur's solar plexus. It was a compact blow, but it doubled the other man over.

"That was for José."

Then the star pitcher for the Homestead Grays delivered a blow to the chin that sent the promoter reeling backwards and into the wall behind him.

"That's to remember me by."

The next morning Rainbow Billy Beauchamp took the balance of Gypsy Joe Grandy's money and sent it off as a money order to the mother of José Morales. When the manager returned, he had to instruct his team on how they were to perform with nine players. A special rotation had to be established for the balance of the competitive games. However, most of their games, once they left Guadalajara, would be against small town teams until they reached Cindad Judrez and El Paso. That would give them a month or so to brush up on their fancy entertainment show before hitting another competitive series. By that time, perhaps, they could add one or two men to their squad.

* * *

It was on this road trip that the team began to establish patterns that would characterize them for most of the next decade. It was almost as if the Elite Giants were two different teams: one that played serious games against all comers including Mexican League clubs and All-Star teams in the Caribbean, and another that put on a show in small towns against home grown talent. Within a year or two Rainbow had a list of the better small town draws that were most agreeable. For these people, the Elite Giants would roll into town and hold a parade as they handed out flyers to promote their game. Then, as often as not, the businesses would close early for the baseball game. Everyone would come. It was an event with gambling, cockfights, and general high spirits. After the game the town often organized a fiesta around the team's arrival into town. This might include a large dinner for everyone served on the main street of town. Then there would be music, dancing and booze until the wee hours. After a short sleep, the team would be gone again at dawn en route to their next engagement.

The comic routines developed spontaneously. Most often they revolved around Harold and Juice. For example, Harold might toss a double play ball from between his legs to Juice. If a call went against them the diminutive pair would approach a much taller umpire and the ump would pretend not to see them until one climbed upon the other's shoulders—but then, of course, they could not see the umpire!

Other gags included Roy Carnes batting while holding the bat in only one hand, or Bo driving in a nail with his fastball, or Candy Laro starting off each game with no fielders behind him. He'd pretend comic panic at discovering his situation after the first pitch. Then after some impassioned persuasion, the fielders would reluctantly take their positions.

Sometimes Harold would take a ground ball and run it out of his mitt along his arm and shoulders—like a slide—to his hand before taking the ball and throwing the runner out.

Trick ball handling became an art. Mellow could stage a fall in the outfield and catch the ball sitting down. From his right field position Sam Nuxall would feign sleep. When the ball came, he miraculously arose to make the play.

Everything, from the fancy warm-up drills to the gags during the game, were aimed at pleasing the small town and rural audiences who often got no other outside entertainment during the year. Their joy and appreciation made these portions of their schedule the most rewarding even though it was also the most fatiguing.

The people would look forward to the return of these showmen-athletes. Their routines were mimicked by the small children in their play. These lighthearted antics would temporarily ease the oppressive struggle and poverty that dominated the villagers' lives.

Rainbow gradually established three "circuits" for team travel. Each began and ended in Mexico City, which became the team's home. He scheduled in several large baseball centers within each loop to keep them sharp and to change the pace. So after eating the dust of scorching Durango (where, incidentally a white scorpion once found its way into the ball bag) they would get some rest in Chihuahua. A few days in a hotel and a higher grade of "straight baseball" went a long way toward renewing the spirit.

When the team finished a circuit Rainbow would give them three or four weeks off in Mexico City before proceeding to the next loop. The Pan Am Elite Giants ran two Mexican circuits and one in the

Caribbean just after the regional championship when baseball interest was high. The team played in the Dominican Republic, Puerto Rico, Panama, Trinidad and Venezuela (but never Colombia). This territory was the easiest of all. The team often played before crowds of fifteen thousand or more. Then they'd feast on Grundy or Callaloo or Carne de Cerdo and dash out to the ocean for a jibara beach party where the sweet fruit of guava and mango were as plentiful as the beautiful women, who they pursued after dinner.

It was a fast life that took its toll on some, so that many players came and left the squad. Of the original group, only Mellow, Harold, Juice, Bo and Roy remained after two years on the road. Ramon and Pedro saved their stakes and went back home to their wives and children. And Sam Nuxall wore himself out: too many women, too much booze, too many parties and too little sleep. He left with only the severance pay that Rainbow sometimes paid for work well done.

New replacements came and learned how to work the portable lights, lawn mower and scythes, but they only became Elite Giants when they caught the spirit of the regulars. It was this spirit that was nurtured in the hot lowlands, the sub-tropics, and high desert of rural Mexico—when they slept on the bus or in people's homes only to hit the road again at dawn. The many miles of dreary driving on dirt roads were punctuated by long games of poker in which much of the creative evolution of new gags and routines took shape. The trappings varied, but certain structures remained fixed: Rainbow's thin cigars; Bo's good natured, but inept gambling; Harold and Juice's comic genius; and Mellow and Roy, the pair who resembled Laurel and Hardy formed a close, protective friendship.

This was the life that etched a certain character upon each. It created a team that could play to small towns and big cities alike. It created an ineffable substance that nurtured each of them and helped them grow alone and together.

Chapter Twenty-Two

IT WAS 8 P.M., BUT STILL VERY LIGHT on the longest day of the year. Bo Mellan was making the trek from the 'El' to his apartment. He'd just crossed Klog Drive and was cutting through Washington Park when he saw a couple of men come into his vision. The hurler scarcely took notice until they started coming towards him.

Bo looked around. It was perfectly light, but at that time of night the park was deserted. The lazy lagoon that sat in the center of the park was completely calm. The children's playground at the far end was closed. A ring of trees along the perimeter of the park concealed all interior activity.

Then the men were alongside Bo. They wore ill-fitting suits that smelled of sweat mixed with cologne and garlic.

Bo thought about bolting for the street, but didn't.

"Mr. Mellan?" said the taller of the two muscular assailants. Bo glanced at him. The man had a box-like jaw and a raised scar that ran vertically along his temple.

"What do you want?"

"We want to talk with you, Mr. Mellan," repeated the scarfaced goon.

Bo kept walking.

"You wasn't too smart at that press conference last week."

"What are you talking about?" asked Bo to scarface.

The little man gave Bo an elbow to the ribs. Bo shot a glance at his escort. The husky fellow had fat baby cheeks and a little mouth with lips that seemed permanently pursed.

"You shouldn't outta interrupt," said the little man in a high, off key voice.

"Where are you taking me? What do you want?"

"You know Mr. Balestrieri is a very generous man. He's willing to give a guy a second chance. Anybody can screw up once."

"Yeah, anyone," echoed the cherub.

"And he wants to send a message telling you there's no hard feelings."

"He wants to be your pal," added the cherub as the pair grasped Bo's shoulders and waist respectively.

"Sure. When you get on the tube and tell everyone how Advanced Builders are good for the city, he'll be right there shaking your hand. Real friendly." Scarface was all smiles. "You know how to be friendly, don't you, Mr. Mellan?"

"Sounds great," began Bo. His escorts were bobbing and nodding their heads at his response. "Except for one thing… ."

His companions didn't like this. They stopped Bo's progress. They were right behind the massive WPA statue of Father Time that stands before the Midway leading to the Lake. Scarface put Bo's neck in an arm lock.

"What was you saying?" There was concern in Scarface's visage.

"I wouldn't back Advanced Builders if my life depended upon it."

The cherub sent a sharp punch to the pitcher's kidney. The blow would have felled the pitcher except for the arm lock.

Bo groaned.

Snap. A long blade appeared. "I'm not a doctor or nuthin' but I guess it's be pretty hard to pitch if you was to have an accident that cut up your muscle tendons."

Bo tried to wrestle Scarface to the ground, but the muscle-bound gorilla was the better fighter. He spun Bo around and, with a kick to the groin, sent him to the ground.

In an instant the cherub was atop the hurler waving the knife around his chest. The cherub suddenly stopped. From behind the statue came two Black youths who dispatched the Italian messengers with a combination of martial art-style kicks and punches. Bo scrambled to his feet to effect an escape, but before he had gotten his bearings, the gorillas and their antagonists had gone. It all happened so quickly that Bo was somewhat unsure just what had happened.

The hurler for the Chicago Cubs stumbled past the place he had been held and walked around to the front of Father Time. The message of the Thirties was awkward and heavy, but somehow the statue seemed appropriately to rule majestically over the Midway. As Bo's eyes descended, he saw a figure sitting at the base of the monument. The pitcher squinted to make sure he really saw someone. The figure was dressed in brown and seemed to blend in with Father Time.

It was al Sulami.

Bo approached the seated figure. "What... did you know... ."

"You are a marked man, my friend. You've taken on a very powerful organization."

"You mean Advanced?"

"More than Advanced. You attack the most powerful man in the city, Ruppert Cakos."

"Cakos? He owns Advanced?"

The slender man nodded. He was seated akimbo at the base of the statue in his robe. There was a quietness to his manner.

"But why should it make such a difference? I'm a nobody. How could I be that important?"

"The Loop Redevelopment Project will bring Cakos over a billion dollars in commissions and kickbacks. That's a powerful incentive."

"But what have I got to do with it?"

"You are a celebrity. As a sports player you excite the public's imagination. Also, word is getting around about your Chicago People's Project. Everyone trusts a man who will give away most of his own money for charity as you are doing."

"But surely I wouldn't make that big of a difference."

"Maybe. Maybe not. That isn't important. What is important is that Ruppert Cakos thinks you will make a difference. And he's a man used to getting his own way."

"I wanted to steer clear of political involvements: Advanced or Krakatowa."

"That, I'm afraid is a course that will lead to disaster."

"But why can't I stay uninvolved?"

al Sulami smiled.

"All right. So I'm involved. Can't I be neutral?"

"If you aren't with me, you're against me."

"So everyone hates me?"

"Advanced represents the ruling power structure. All those who are a part of that structure will see you as an enemy: the ethnic whites and many blacks and Latinos. The main opposition to the present structure is represented by Krakatowa. These people will also try to woo you. When they are rebuffed, they, too, will view you with hostility. These are the militant blacks and Latinos. What is left you will have."

"But that's nothing."

"Politics is not mathematical. I may describe 70% of the voters in one way and 30% in another and still not have characterized the whole."

"I'm not sure I understand."

al Sulami smiled as he arose. He walked to Bo and put his hand on the rookie pitcher's shoulder. "You are a wild beauty; an uncultivated flower: a messenger from Allah. In a natural environment you would grow strong. The prophet Mohammed was illiterate and yet he wrote the Quran because of his wild beauty. But in this unnatural domesticated cultivation, only hideous hybrids survive. They kill the natural beauty because they have unnatural ends. But if the day ever comes when they succeed in their designs, that will mark the end of our species. Our only hope is in Allah's messengers. They uphold the five pillars upon which everything is based."

Bo tilted his head. The Iman patted the pitcher's shoulder. "If I can help you, you need only shout out my name. I will have eyes watching over you."

"Then it was you," began Bo as he dropped his gaze for a moment. "Your men saved me—I want to thank you for—" He lifted his gaze but the mysterious holy man had vanished. Bo's words were heard only by Father Time.

Chapter Twenty-three

IT WAS A FOUR-BLOCK WALK back to Deronda. Bo trudged up the stairs toward his apartment. On the top landing Cora stood waiting for the rookie pitcher.

"You look awful. What happened?"

Bo sighed and fumbled for his key. "I had an accident going through the park."

"Are you hurt? Let me clean your face. You've been bruised."

"I'll be all right. Just a little rest." Bo opened his door. Cora pushed him in and sat him down on the couch. The pitcher remained as a damaged statue while his neighbor went about washing his face and neck.

"I started work today at your People's Project. I think the whole thing is very exciting. You know that friend of yours, Angela, is really a talented worker. She's been at this only a month you said, but already she's filed grant applications everywhere. Why to hear her talk, you'd think she was head of the Illinois Department of Public Aid or something."

Bo sat back and thought about Ruppert Cakos. This man was the owner of Advanced Building Contractors, Radio, Television, Newspapers, a ruling factor in the Mob and City Council, and worst of all: Bo's boss. How could he fight back? Could he get something on Cakos as Rainbow had with Juan

Cortez? Cortez was a considerably less formidable opponent, but the same principle ought to hold. The rookie pitcher thought the idea was plausible. But how would he begin? He could not for the life of him come up with an answer.

"There. Don't you feel better," cooed Cora as she applied the cool cloth to the pitcher's forehead and tenderly washed his face. "We can't have the star of the Chicago Cubs looking like a barroom brawler, now, can we? I'll bet you picked up some of this in the game today after they put you in as a pinch runner. The radioman said it was a risky move to insert the ace pitcher as a pinch runner— especially after you had that hard slide to break-up the double play—, but Buddy Bael must have had his reasons. He's been around baseball a long time, he knows what can happen out there."

Bo grunted as Cora cleaned up his bruised face and got him something to eat. But the left-hander was not paying much attention to Cora's questions about his pitching or about the new team spirit that everyone was talking about. Instead, he thought about the time he was a dishwasher in Guadalajara. The lure of fame in the Major Leagues and all the glitter of Juan Cortez had been so appealing. But what was it all? The hot water made your skin crinkle and crack while the lye soap burned those very fissures. Gypsy Joe Grandy. Promises of money, promises of... Zocoalco.

They all led to Zocoalco. Later in Venezuela with Grandcourt. The others hadn't learned the lesson. Promises lured the soul into a cramped jail cell while a human soul expired in agony.

"The radio announcer said you might be the best pitcher in baseball."

Bo got up and called a cab. He had to see Angela.

*   *   *

"I don't know where you found that girl you sent me. She doesn't seem to have a brain in her head." Angela had set up her apartment like an office. Everywhere were scattered piles of papers. As Bo moved through the clutter he was constantly being admonished to watch this foot or mind this or that stack of letters. Angela had purchased some file cabinets and a used photocopying machine, but still they could not contain the mountains of paper work.

"Don't you think a larger place would help?" asked Bo.

"A waste of money. Foundations give money to groups that have low overhead. We've got to impress those sons-of-bitches that we mean business." Angela poured herself a cup of coffee. "By the way, do you think you can come up with a little more money? There's a matching grant proposal that we almost qualify for. For every dollar you put in, they contribute two."

"When do you need it?"

"As soon as possible so we can process the forms."

"Well, I get paid every two weeks. I hand over everything to you except eight hundred or so. We'll have to see how the bonuses go."

Angela put down the coffee. "I'm sorry, Phil. It's just that I'm so tied up in this. We'll be ready to begin giving out money in another month—if I can get everything together. There are just so many details."

"Another month. That's way ahead of schedule."

"It's all so exciting. We could really be something. But we've got to be on guard. Things could fall apart at any moment."

"At least you have my money."

"But we can get so much more. This might become one of the largest charitable organizations in the city."

"Angela," said Bo, coming over to her and sitting on the edge of her desk. "You've got to slow down. Here it is eleven o'clock at night and you're still going like it's mid-morning. You can't do us any good if you become a physical wreck."

Angela looked up at Bo. He reached out and touched her cheek. She put her hand on his arm and held it. Bo leaned toward her and kissed her on the lips. The director of the People's Project stiffened. She let the ballplayer kiss her, but her lips were non-resilient. Her eyes scanned the pile of papers on her desk that Bo was disturbing.

The pitcher got up and walked toward the window. Angela followed and stood next to him and put her hand around his waist. Bo started when she touched his sore kidney area.

"What's the matter? Tender muscles from pitching?"

"Yeah. Pitching. Dangerous occupation. You really have to know what you're doing."

"I wouldn't know," replied Angela, dropping her hand. "I never followed sports much."

"No."

"I don't know why; too many other things to do."

Bo looked out into the darkness. He thought he saw somebody watching him from the street. Was it someone from Cakos or one of al Sulami's men?

"If you were to ask me what we really need, I'd have to say someone to go out into the community and sell our program to the general public." Angela walked back toward her desk. Bo remained staring out of the window.

"These community visits would inform those who could use our services and also prompt grass roots financial support. The way I see things now, with a little luck, we could reach our start-up goal in a few weeks.

"What with that matching grant, and maybe a few more plugs from you on local radio and TV—oh Phil, isn't all this so thrilling?" Angela rose high on her toes as she stretched her hands to the ceiling. The man outside disappeared. Was it only his imagination? Bo turned to Angela.

"Phil?"

"Call me Bo."

"I'm sorry." She laughed. "Old habits—Bo. We're going to need somebody to do community relations." She moved toward him again.

Bo nodded. "It's late, Angela. I'll see you later."

The pitcher walked directly to the bus stop and waited.

Chapter Twenty-four

"BO, I'VE BEEN MEANING TO TALK WITH YOU."

"What's up, Sam?" replied the veteran of many Mexican campaigns as he applied his secret balm to his pitching arm. It was only eight-thirty and not many ball players had arrived yet. The locker room was musty, but without the added smell of twenty-five bodies, it resembled more a vacant basement where mold, insects and powerful chemicals resided in a tentative co-existence.

"How's the arm?"

"The same as ever. As long as I take care of it… ." Bo kneaded the muscles with firm, steady pressure.

"You're set against Hernandez tomorrow. He's their best arm this year."

"Well, let's hope I'm up to it. I got hit pretty hard last time out."

"The team could use a lift. Four out of six losses at home. That means a shake-up."

"Anybody pressuring you, Sam?" Bo finished rubbing his salve.

"I don't know. Nothing particular." Sam, who had been hitting his left fist into his right palm while standing, now sat down next to Bo. The gray hair on his temples was spreading so that two thirds of his head had been transformed from dark brown to a colorless opacity.

Bo opened his locker and stuffed the liniment into his duffle and took out a thin jersey.

"You know Bobbi's in town."

"Really?" Bo turned to Sam. The pitching coach was staring at the uneven cement floor that was steeply slanted toward ancient, rusting drains.

"Yeah. She's been writing me regular and I've called up a few times." Sam's eyes were riveted on a long rust stain that ran towards the relic floor grate. "So many things, you know, that you miss and don't even realize." Then Sam looked up at Bo. "Sometimes all I want to do is be with my kid. She so pure, Bo." The pitching coach spat towards the drain, but missed.

"Have you got a full weekend planned?"

"I was a fool to ever leave them. It's just that—" Sam began rubbing the back of his neck. "—Circumstances. Sometimes you just can't do what you want to."

Bo stared into the wide set green eyes. "I think we almost always do what we want to, Sam. Trouble is we never consider what we really want. We think one thing is going to deliver it, but instead it turns us away from what we were looking for all along."

"And then you end up hating yourself."

"You can always turn it around, Sam. Even if you're lying knee-deep in garbage you can always get the hell out." The pitching coach screwed up his eyes and started to breathe heavily; forcing the air out of his nostrils with audible bursts.

Then Sam stood up and hit his fist against a locker. Bo started lacing up his shoes.

"Damn it all, Bo. Who are you, anyway? You just don't seem to understand the way things are. Too much of that Mexican sun, I'll bet. Done things to your brain." Sam's voice was on edge. "In this world you've got to survive. Do what it takes. Understand me?"

Bo finished with his cleats and stood up. "I understand you're upset."

"Upset?!?" Sam opened his arms incuriously as if he were being asked to accept gravity working in reverse. "Do you realize what you're doing?"

"What are you talking about?" Bo stood face to face with Sam Dowel.

"Everything. Right from the start Bael has been out to crucify you. Don't you understand that?"

Bo's pale blue eyes did not blink.

"Most of it is Bael. I know that. The guy wants to control you. Don't you remember when he wrote that message on the board during spring training, 'You are my Players. I own You.' Damn it, he means it, Bo. The guy gets something on you and that's the end. He takes over lives. Look what he's done to me—to everyone. Don't you see? We may be a losing team, but he's got us. We're his."

"Why are you telling me this, Sam?"

The pitching coach began rubbing his neck again.

"Don't you see—it's bad enough you're fighting him right out in the open. But when your fight starts affecting other people... ."

"Has he been pressuring you about me, Sam?"

"Raked me over the coals during that damned public relations event last week."

"The one with Advanced Builders?"

"You walked right out. That's about the worst thing you could have done."

"No one told me what the affair was about. 'Community Appearance' was all I was told. But when I saw what it was... I can't support a group like Advanced, Sam."

"Why the hell not? Who do you think you are? A man's got to make compromises."

"That may be, but Advanced can't be one of mine, Sam."

Bo started to leave, but Sam stepped in front of him. Bo stopped, surprised. "You really don't give a shit, do you? Who the god-damned hell you might hurt with your little demonstration of—I don't know what."

Bo paused and examined Sam's face. It was distorted by ridges of skin that rose high and pulsed from arteries beneath.

"It's very simple, Sam. If he's on you about me, support him. Simple as that. I'll understand." Bo walked around Sam for the door.

"I'll lose my job, damn it."

Bo stopped as he grabbed the doorknob. "I told you, Sam. I'll understand. Do what you have to do."

Sam watched the heavy metal door as it slowly closed shut.

Out on the field Bo was going through exercises for his legs. Rainbow used to say that you aim with your arm, but you pitch with your legs. As long as they're strong, and you've taken care of your shoulder and elbow, you can play a long time.

It was a bright day with a high sky. That always made it difficult on the outfielders to pick up the trajectory of fly balls. Bo hoped that the warm weather would hold through the weekend. They were finishing up a home stand. Bo was due tomorrow. In his last three starts he had two "no decisions" and a loss. His record was 10-5. It was important to him that he throw the ball well tomorrow against the Giants.

As he finished his calisthenics he noticed Joe Beezy, the youngish looking reporter for *The Herald* sitting back in the stands sipping a can of diet soda.

Joe had a habit of turning up at the oddest times. Ever since he had pressed Bo for a story early in the year, the sports columnist had sat back and watched the curly haired hurler from afar. To his credit, Joe did write some credible pieces, but he also loved engaging in speculation. His column: "The Day After" was widely read in the city.

Bo eyed the writer for a moment. But then it was time to finish the last set of wind sprints and loosen his arm. Batting practice would start soon and the field would become crowded.

"I'd like to see you, Mellan. Right away." The sound was the gruff voice of Buddy Bael. When Bo walked inside the manager's office he was not offered a chair.

"We've got a few things to discuss, Mellan."

Bo stared right into the manager's eyes.

"For starters, it's important for you to remember that you have a personal services clause in your contract."

"Yes sir." The pale blues were blank.

"I don't know whether you understand what that means or not, but let me enlighten you. When we send you out to represent the team at a social or public function, you are expected to do just that. Do you understand? You don't excuse yourself and leave." The man's baldhead revealed one raised, twisting blood vessel that was distinguishing itself even as the general manager and field boss spoke.

"Yes sir," echoed Bo when he sensed there was a break in the harangue.

Then Bael hit the desk so hard that a picture in a frame fell over onto the floor and cracked. But the manager didn't even blink. "What the holy fuck do you think you're up to, boy? This ain't no South American bush league we're running up here. Do you understand me?"

Another pause. "Yes sir."

Bael almost jumped over his desk. In a moment he stood toe to toe with the curly haired hurler. "I'm not going to take insolence like that. Do you understand me? I don't care what people think of you. We own the media in this town and we can make people think anything we goddamn well please." As Bael talked he gestured dramatically with his index finger; jabbing it pointedly at the pitcher's sternum without touching it—but coming very close.

Bo kept his eyes on Bael's face and didn't budge.

"Up to now I've gone to bat for you, kid. They've wanted to give you your walking papers, but I told them *no*. I said you'd listen to reason and that you were just a big hick from Milwaukee with your head stuck up your asshole. But now I'm beginning to wonder at my judgment. I'm beginning to wonder if I shouldn't just let you go."

"You're the boss."

"You bet I am. And don't forget it." Bael pulled up his pants over his potbelly. "I'm damned good, too. Don't forget that— EVER!" Bael walked back to a team picture on the wall of the San Francisco Giants. The fat man seemed to stare at something in the picture almost as if it were nurturing him. Then he turned to face Bo again. "I can understand how someone can make a mistake. I waited to talk with you about your behavior last week because I wanted time to give it the consideration I thought it deserved."

The fat man approached Bo again with index finger extended.

"In fact, I'm going to give you a second chance. There's a fundraiser for crippled kids that Advanced Builders is sponsoring when we get back in July. I want you to be there shaking Balestrieri's hand. Do I make myself clear?" As these last words were delivered the finger was shot right into the star pitcher's sternum. Bo caught the hand and gripped it momentarily. His eyes rose from those fat fingers to the potent form they belonged to. Bo released the hand and smiled. He was late for a pitcher's meeting.

As Bo Mellan left the office of the general manager, he was startled to see sitting casually on a bench the columnist for *The Herald*, Joe Beezy.

"He doesn't like you very much, does he?"

The reporter's words were delivered in light, easy tones.

Bo paused a moment and started to say something, but shook his head and walked toward the other end of the locker room. "I've got a meeting to go to."

It was a typical outing for the Cubs. The wind was blowing out, and the northsiders jumped out to an early five run lead, but eventually lost 12-9 as the bullpen fell apart. The team was five games below .500 and had three games left on the home stand.

When it was over Bo dressed quickly. He wanted to get away from the park and go home. But this design was delayed when he saw someone he knew waiting outside the clubhouse. It was Bobbi Dowel.

"Hi, Bobbi. Sam told me you were visiting." The pitching coach's daughter was bright faced and full of vitality.

"I got a week before my summer job starts and, well, Daddy said he'd spring for the ticket."

"That's great. How's everything?"

"Well, about the same except that Daddy is calling a whole lot more often—he even talks to mom some of the time." The adolescent girl paused and then added, "You know she isn't always the way you found her the day you visited."

"Don't worry about it, Bobbi." smiled Bo.

"Sometimes I can get pretty hard on her. You know what I mean? Like when we talked."

"If I was held to everything I'd ever said, I'd be in a lot of trouble," winked the star hurler at the high school girl as he started to leave.

"Can't you eat with us or something? I'm sure Sam, I mean Daddy wouldn't mind. You're one of the best friends he's got as far as I can figure."

"I'd like to, Bobbi, but this weekend looks pretty full. Maybe another time."

The teenager's face made no attempt to hide her disappointment.

"I have to go now. See you around the ballpark. Enjoy Chicago!"

The hurler waved and smiled as he walked out of the ballpark and in the direction of the Addison Street 'el' stop. As he walked, Joe Beezy once more arrested his progress.

"What are you, a vulture?"

"That depends—" replied the youngish looking Beezy, who had smooth almond colored skin and thick wavy black hair that was attractively combed straight back, "—on who died."

Bo's mouth twitched nervously into a smile. The pitcher paid his fare and mounted the aging wooden structure. The reporter followed. When they had reached the southbound platform Bo turned to his somewhat shorter companion, "What are you going to do; follow me home?"

"I might. Any objections?"

"Must be pretty hard-up for a story."

"I don't think so. There's something about you, Mellan, that's red-hot material. I don't have the angle on it yet, but when I do, everyone in the city will be reading my by-line."

"Maybe they'll even make you sports editor." The pitcher's thin lips stretched out into a line.

The reported licked his lips and clucked his tongue. Then he took a step closer to Bo and asked in a softer voice, "Why did you walk out of that gala event for ABC last week? The club said you were ill, but no one believes that. What's really the trouble? What do you have against Balestrieri?"

"I've never met the man."

"But you know who he is, of course. It was his party you walked out of. Were you trying to make some sort of statement?"

"I'm a ball player, not a politician."

"But a ball player who's started an organization of your own. Some sort of venture capital operation for minority businesses, am I correct? So you're right in the middle of things whether you like it or not."

"Our People's Project is just a small group to help people who the other agencies ignore: the struggling businesses, people out of a job and teenagers trying to fit into the work place. I don't see how our little group has anything to do with Advanced Builders or Mr. Balestrieri."

"Are you saying you've got nothing against Advanced or Balestrieri?"

"I'm neutral. I endorse no one."

"Not even Krakatowa?"

"No."

"That's not what the big wigs around City Hall are saying. They're calling you a 'fig newton': light on the outside and dark on the inside."

Bo smiled. "A fig newton, eh? I'm sure that's probably the most polite thing they're calling me."

"What are you trying to do, Mellan? What's your purpose in this whole thing?"

"What does City Hall think my purpose is?"

"To divide the white political base in the city so that Advanced won't get the Loop Redevelopment money." The tracks began to rumble.

Bo shook his head.

"Do you deny it?"

The green and white subway train was approaching.

"I'm not in the construction business. The People's Project isn't making a bid on anything—except, I guess, at helping some of the disadvantaged of the city."

The train stopped. The folding doors creaked open.

"You mean the blacks, don't you?"

Bo got aboard and turned around to face the reporter who was still standing on the platform. "Look at the city. You tell me who most of the poor people are."

* * *

The train ride from Addison to Garfield Avenue takes about thirty-five minutes. Bo trudged home by way of the 57th Street Market to buy some food for dinner. There's a fishmonger there that always has the latest catch from the Great Lakes lying out in long tubs atop crushed ice. The fish lay motionless, their scales glistening and their translucent eyes eerily glowing.

Bo selected a buffalo fish and tucked the package, wrapped in yesterday's Sun, under his arm and made his way home past the Woodlawn Tap and Stagg Field. It was a pleasant night and Bo looked forward to sampling his fish. The former pitcher of the Elite Giants remembered the fare that Pedro used to cook-up when they played along the Mexican Coast. It was no restaurant, but nothing had ever tasted finer.

Cora was working late so Bo could count on a relaxing meal, alone.

It wasn't to be. About eight, just when the curly haired pitcher had finished with the dishes, there was a knocking at his door. Bo assumed it was Cora. He was surprised to find Razi.

The proud man of Ethiopian descent strolled, uninvited, into Bo's apartment. The co-owner of Krakatowa Enterprises looked about Bo's living room examining the sofa and the condition of the two chairs. He decided to stand.

Razi was dressed in a powder blue cotton suit with a flowing handkerchief decorating his breast pocket. His silk, navy tie sported white polka dots and was set jauntily with a pearl stickpin.

"I just came out of a meeting with our board of directors. We are prepared to lend you our complete support: money, office space, volunteers and some grease in high places." Razi carried his head high and seemed to look above the curly haired pitcher who was standing at the edge of the hallway.

"That's very considerate of you, Mr. Razi, but—"

"—Don't get me wrong, Bo. There's still a lot of people in Krakatowa who don't trust you. But then what kind of treatment have they ever gotten from whitey? Do you blame them?"

"I'm not in a position to blame anyone. That's my point; you see—"

"—That's what I told the brothers. Your People's Project is exactly as it looks. It isn't a front for Advanced or Dailey; even though you work for the plantation master, himself."

"I'm sorry Mr. Razi, but—"

Razi took out his handkerchief and waved the air at the mosquitoes who were drawn by his musk-scented cologne. The proud entrepreneur had two objects of his thought: his message and these insects that were attracted to him.

"You know our prophet, Elijah Mohammed, says white men are the devils that Satan sent to tempt and persecute his chosen people. We were created first. Eden was in Ethiopia and the true descendants of Adam were all black men. The only way whites could come about is by unnatural mutation. Contrary to nature. Contrary to the purpose of Allah."

"I'm sorry Mr. Razi, but I don't see how—"

"So it is not without some effort for me to persuade my brothers that you could be trusted. Even the Devil can be useful to achieve holy ends."

Bo leaned against the wall and watched the mosquitoes. One maneuvered itself through the Ethiopian's defenses and alighted on his hand. The smooth-faced businessman smiled and lifted his arm to better watch the mosquito's attack.

"They draw blood through the capillary action of their hollow stingers. The blood rises mechanically of its own accord. They have no control over it. When they're filled they exit." Razi then stretched the skin on his hand where the mosquito was doing just that. "But if their exit is impaired, then they are slaves to the very mechanical force that keeps them alive."

In a few moments the mosquito started to struggle as it attempted to escape, but it couldn't draw out its stinger because the tightly stretched skin held the instrument in place. The encounter was short lived as the supply of blood that kept rushing into the insect's abdomen finally caused it to explode and leave the blood spattered, mutilated body lying on the stage provided by the noble Razi.

"You see? It does not understand the forces of nature, the forces of Allah. So that when it becomes too proud and thinks it can go its own way, then splat! It dies with a bloody show: a victim of those very forces which allowed it to live."

Razi extended his hand so that Bo might see for himself the fate of the unfortunate insect.

CHAPTER TWENTY-FIVE

IT WAS LATE OCTOBER when Rainbow Billy Beauchamp was seized with a fit of malaria. The team was in Santo Domingo playing a round robin series against all-star teams from Haiti, Puerto Rico and a local squad. The engagement promised to be a profitable one with a guaranteed draw and separate winner's purse. Already the Pan-Am Elite Giants were 4-0 with only two games left to play (three if they made the November 2nd championship game).

Bo and Rainbow were together in a bar they liked to frequent that overlooked the slow moving Ozama River. It was a dark and musty establishment that was partially built into the hill so that it always smelled moldy.

The attack came when the two were drinking together and Rainbow was spinning yarns about some of the fine acts developed by the Indianapolis Clowns, one of the touring clubs that survived the demise of the Negro Leagues. Rainbow was describing how once they had just come from a stunt game in the morning to a straight game with the House of David (a team from Michigan that wore long beards like Orthodox Jews). The Clowns got confused which game they were in. They started going through one of their comedy routines in the second inning. This incensed the House of David, who proceeded to clobber the Clowns because they thought the Indianapolis team was trying to show them up.

"You always got to know who you're dealing with," said Rainbow when his left hand began to shake causing him to spill his drink over his hand and cigarette.

"What's the matter? Want me to get your pills?"

"Just get me back to our room." Rainbow's voice was impatient, but without force. The former Negro League star blinked hard several times and then shut his eyes.

Rainbow had to be carried back to the hotel, which was four blocks away. Bo slung the former star pitcher over his back and rested five or six times during the journey. Time was short before he must give him the amodiaquin.

Rainbow had had bouts with his malaria for as long as Bo had known the man. The pitching star had contracted the disease in Dominican Republic after he had gone down with Satchel Paige to pitch for the dictator Trujillo who had put up big money to buy a team that would win a challenge series. Everything had not gone according to plan and several of them ended up in a jail where malaria was rampant.

Ever since that time the cagey veteran of many seasons steadily refused to play, and later, to bring his team into a country with a strong man dictator, and Billy Beauchamp never set foot in the Dominican Republic again (despite some attractive offers).

Bo got the team leader back to the small grimy Santo Domingo hotel room and set him on the bed. The chills were already beginning. The pale blues searched for the pills and administered two straightaway.

Malaria affects everyone differently. The parasites live in the liver cyclically attacking the red blood cells. Some people can go months between attacks while others, like Rainbow, often had years of respite.

Though the attacks were far apart they could be severe. They would begin with chills and then move into heavy sweating and fever. Once, Bo remembered, this stage had also brought on convulsions.

"Isn't there any cure?" Bo had asked as a fourteen year old boy when he first witnessed one of Rainbow's attacks.

"Nope. Just gotta live with it, boy. Like it is with everything: accept what you got and do what you can with it. That way you're not wasting your fight on yourself, but saving it for more important things."

Later, Rainbow would tell Bo that it was the whole lousy deal that did it to him. "If I hadn't been in jail I wouldn't have gotten sick. If I hadn't gone to that god-awful Dominican Republic, I'd never been throw'd in jail. If I hadn't had such a nose for money, I'd never have traveled with Satchel in the first place. So there it is, boy. My own fault I'm sick."

All of these scenes played through Bo's mind as he sat up with his friend and mentor. After an hour and a half of chills the fever took over. Usually this lasted three or four hours until the medicine eased the symptoms. This time the fever was getting worse. By midnight the fever was as strong as ever.

The old man's sheets were wet with perspiration, as he lay quietly staring at the cracked ceiling. "C'mon Rainbow," the young man said softly. "You gotta pull out of this."

The prescription box said, "Two tablets twice a day until symptoms abate." There was nothing Bo could do but sit and wait. Around two the old man shut his eyes and seemed to rest. The disease was finally running its course, thought Bo as the young pitcher let himself drift off to sleep in the hard chair, which he had pulled up next to the bed.

At five o'clock the former All-Star hurler for the Grays awoke with a start. His eyes were bulging. Sweat was pouring down his gaunt face. His hands clenched the bedclothes tightly.

"What's the matter, Rainbow?"

"Turn on the lights. Turn on the lights. We've got to frighten them away."

"Who Rainbow? Who we got to frighten?"

"Turn on the lights. The bed bugs. The lights."

"There ain't no bed bugs in here, Rainbow."

"Old Gus says they hate the light. You keep the light on and you won't have no trouble."

"Settle down. I'll turn on the lights." Bo laid the sick man back down. His skin was fire.

"I got to get someone to see you. This isn't going right."

"No don't leave. It's so cold in here. I need another blanket." The thin man's teeth began to chatter. Bo got up and drenched a towel in water and sponged the sick man's forehead. Then he handed the cloth to Rainbow.

"Bite on this. It will calm you down." As Rainbow took the rolled up cloth, Bo hurried next door and banged with his fist until a sleepily Mellow Muenoz came to answer.

"Get dressed. Hurry. We've got to get a doctor."

Mellow didn't respond very well when awoken from a sound sleep, but Juice Johnson, who had been standing naked in the hallway, did. He rushed back and was ready to go by the time Bo had explained things to Mellow sufficiently.

Bo returned only to find Rainbow wrapped up in his sheet as if it were a shroud. In a moment the young man was over to the bed carefully unraveling the mummy.

"We've got a doctor coming, Rainbow. You're gonna get better. Hold on."

It wasn't long before the entire squad was in the room looking at what had happened to their indestructible leader. In all the years on the road he had never let anyone besides Bo and Pedro see him have an attack. The team knew he suffered from malaria, but aside from slowing him down a bit, they never knew what he went through.

Rainbow had always been so steady that no one had paid much attention to him. Of course he was the team owner and ran things his own way, but it had always seemed that the team was in the forefront. The team and the schedule they faced: over and over again they had to play up to a standard. It was a discipline they all had adopted. It was synonymous with the name of their team: The Pan-Am Elite Giants.

Now, everything was suddenly precarious. When they went to bed life was secure and certain. In a moment, it seemed, all that was gone. How could six years of dedication to an ideal be undermined so quickly?

Mellow and Juice had gone for a doctor. Roy, Harold and Candy stood in a semi-circle waiting. While before them the withered body of the man who had always stayed in the background writhed prominently in paroxysms.

The Hospital del San Francisco was closest to the hotel. There, in a room with six other patients lay the manager of the Pan-Am Elite Giants' Rainbow Billy Beauchamp. It was a hot room on the top floor of a three-story building. The only cooling influence were two large ceiling fans, whose broad wooden blades moved slowly around in a continuity that suggested perpetual motion.

The Elite Giants played that day, October 31st, without Bo and lost their first game of the round robin. The curly haired pitched stayed at the hospital.

Tests revealed anemia, and enlarged liver and spleen. Also, there was some developing puffiness about the old man's face. The physician said there was little he could do except treat the symptoms and that they had better hope for recovery soon, since after thirty-six hours into an attack the possibility for stroke and brain damage or death increased dramatically.

Bo stayed with Rainbow. The younger man sustained himself only with coffee (a drink he had never cared for very much). In Santo Domingo the coffee was potent from brown, full roasted beans. It was all the young man wanted.

For his part, Rainbow would go through seizures and remissions. Each time an attack would pass a glimmer of hope arose. But the hope was so delicate that neither patient nor nurse said anything for fear that the speaking might extinguish it.

After the game the entire squad came to the hospital to look after their leader. They talked about their plans for the last game of the round robin, which they had to win to get into the championship game that was to be played on Sunday. The weather had been very good and so had the crowds. Juice and Harold joked about how senoras Carmelita and Maria would spend their fat paychecks.

"Real fine," said Juice.

"For the girls, you mean. We won't see a centavo of it," responded Harold with a smile on his face. "Still, it'll be nice to relax a little when we get back in December."

"Relax," said Mellow. "Harold, you don't do nuthin but relax. Ain't that right, Roy?" But the tall Texan was silent. He stood with his hands made into fists pushing against each other inside the pockets of the team's chenille jacket.

"Roy thinks that's right," said Mellow, turning back to the others. One half of his mouth was turned up into a smile that vanished as quickly as it came.

"Yes, sir," said Juice after a long awkward pause. "I be looking forward to getting back home for a spell after our schedule."

Another pause. Some of the players looked at the figure in the bed—others at the chipped, gray linoleum floor.

"Nice to get back again, though," put Harold.

"Oh yeah. A month of home life is enough to drive a feller right out again." Juice started to smile, but didn't carry through.

Then the man on the bed sat up and cleared his throat. Bo leaned over from his chair and supported his friend's back.

"I want to thank you guys for coming by here." The old man was breathing heavily. Then he looked around the room. "What do they call this place, anyway?"

"San Francisco. It was the nearest one. The doctor we got works here."

Rainbow nodded and pointed to a small statue of Saint Francis on the wall. "When I get outta here we gotta get some—" The team owner was getting dizzy. The effort was weakening him. "—more players. We gotta have ten players."

No one said a word.

"Thank you for coming. I probably won't be well enough for Sunday's game. You better not run out of players. I want to rest now. Come back tomorrow after the game."

The team shuffled out. Roy asked Bo if he wanted to be relieved in order to get some rest. Bo declined. He wasn't leaving Rainbow.

At ten o'clock another seizure came on with chills and fever. Rainbow's eyes were getting wild. The soft browns had lost their hold. The young man sat in horror as he watched those irises turn as black as the coffee he was sipping.

The fit subsided around one. Almost immediately Rainbow fell asleep. Bo slumped in his chair and dozed a little.

At four-fifteen Rainbow touched Bo's arm. The young man's eyes opened at once. They were tired but clear. The former All-Star was sitting, propped up by pillows.

"Listen little Rainbow. My little Bo. I got to tell you how to negotiate money."

Bo gazed at his friend. His face and neck were bloated. This altered his entire appearance. "Really. It's not the time—"

"Let me be the judge of that," snapped the team owner. "I gotta tell you, and you gotta listen. Get some paper." Bo complied. "Now first, on cities we know. If they're steady take a draw; you'll get more. Up and down, a flat guarantee. You get less, but it's in the bank. Up front. Third inning at the latest. Local stuff's all extra. Remember that. We've always got the bus. We don't pay for what we don't need.

"Second, cities we don't know. Feel the promoter out. If he is keen on giving us a guarantee, take a percentage. If he wants us to take a percentage, take a guarantee. Gus Greenlee taught me that. Never forget it. Businessmen aren't like that saint over there on the wall."

Rainbow's voice was clear and light for the first time in over a day. Bo wrote furiously, and was just able to keep up.

"Third, if the team breaks up—"

"—Rainbow?"

"Shut up. Listen. I can't talk very long. No breath. If you go play league ball in Mexico or Puerto Rico or in the States, don't let them put you on a standard contract. Get one based on performance. Do it like this: take the top pitcher's salary and compare it to the top pitching statistics. Take the five top categories and divide the categories into the salary. So if the top salary is 100 grand, then 1/5 equals 20 grand. And if strikeouts is one of those categories and the best last year was 200, then you should get $100 per strikeout. That's the best deal you can cut.

"Money don't mean shit. But you can't give it away. Better not to play."

Then Rainbow slid down in his bed and went into a paroxysm of sweating. Bo took the ceramic bowl and proceeded to wash his leader's face, armpits and chest. Over and over: dip, wash, wring, dip… It was as if he were doing it in his sleep.

*   *   *

"My, it was quite a game. We was playing the Cubans and Smokey Joe Williams. Our bossman bet the store on that game and we knowd it. Talk about high stakes… ."

Bo opened his eyes again and Rainbow was talking in a whisper. But there was feeling in what he said. It was just like the old days on Medford Avenue when they used to sit on that cement slab in front of the garage while the older man spun tales about his traveling life.

"At that time the Cubans and the Grays were both just about ready to bust out and be the best club in baseball. We were both that close. This was going to be a real test. We played in Newark and the place was jammed with nearly 20,000. You hadda go outside to change your mind!" The old man's eyes rolled. Suddenly, they were not focusing.

"Edsell Walker started the game and pitched four innings before he got a bad blister. So I come in during the fifth. It was a scoreless tie till the eighth. You gotta understand how important a run was in a game like that. Smokey Joe fanned the first ten batters he faced. By the end of it he'd gotten more than twenty. The guy was amazing: a fastball better than Paige and a slow curve that broke down like Sam Streeter.

"Well, in the eighth they got a runner on with a hit and then he steals second and goes to third on a ground out. Then Russell gets up and powders a medium deep fly that Jerry Benjamin gets one-handed with his bare hand on the run and throws the guy out at the plate for a double play.

"You shoulda seen the way he piled into Josh. I tell you that Gibson could really take the punishment. He was more talented than any ballplayer ever lived. He's the only player to hit it out of Yankee Stadium over Centerfield. He cleared the scoreboard. A seven hundred foot shot. Can you believe it? I saw it. The greatest hitter ever born. I suppose that was the curse that did him in. How would you like to be the best ballplayer in the world and have people 'speculating' on whether you could make it in the white man's league?"

The voice trailed off. Rainbow closed his eyes and began to shiver. Then he began again. This time with a stronger voice.

"We was in the twelfth when we got our first hit. I had held the Cubans to five hits and they had gotten three or so off Walker. But the Grays had been hitless. Smokey Joe had his fire. Well, he strikes out Cool Papa, but the last pitch was wild and so Cool Papa races to first. He was so fast that he was halfway to second by the time the catcher had the ball. Then they struck out Vic Harris and Buck Leonard. That brought up Josh. On the first pitch Cool Papa stole third. The third baseman—he was just a kid—came in on the grass expecting maybe a bunt. From Josh Gibson!

"Josh stops the game and walks up the line to this green kid and tells him he better play back or he's liable to get killed. And sure enough, Josh hits a line shot that went no more than six feet off the ground, but was hit so hard that it made the wall 340 feet away on one bounce. That put us ahead. Our manager and owner, Cum Posey, brings me over and says, 'Rainbow. Stay with what you can do. Don't go outside yourself. We've got everything riding on this.'"

Rainbow's eyes came into focus. His breathing was short and rapid due to the chills. But there was a determined look on his distended face.

"I gottem out and we won. *We* were then the big team. 'Twas because I knowd myself and what I could do and what I couldn't. Bo, that's what pitching means. And when it gets tough—" The old man started to cough and slumped back into bed.

"Where does it hurt, Rainbow?"

The old man tried to smile.

"Your chest. Is that what's tight?" Bo was off for a physician. A very young man came and examined Bo's friend.

"It says on his chart that he has Malaria," said the doctor in Spanish.

"What about his chest?" Bo gestured to the ribs.

"Maybe I can prescribe an anti-coagulant, but I'd have to confer with an attending. One will be in at eight or so. Only a few hours."

Bo didn't understand. The intern began to walk away.

"Can us you help?" Bo asked in halting Spanish.

"Wait till eight," replied the doctor in slow, exaggerated tones.

"But he needs help," implored Bo in English.

The intern smiled and shook his head and walked determinedly away.

By now Rainbow was sweating again. His skin seemed discolored. He tried to talk, but his voice was too weak. Bo leaned near his friend.

"If I don't make it, Bo... if I don't, I want to be cremated and put in a metal box like a cigar box—got it? Have a crescent moon painted on it. A crescent moon with a cross in between. It's my sign. Take it to Le Bout and give it to Duvaier."

"You're not going to die," said Bo, trying to put conviction into his voice.

Rainbow closed his eyes and a faint smile reappeared. In a few minutes the convulsions began again. This time they were the most violent yet. Bo searched for the doctor, but he wasn't there. Back to Rainbow, who was now crying out with all his strength, though the volume was no more than ordinary talking. "The beginning... the beginning. . . is the End. . . The End is the Beginning." With one hand Bo grabbed Rainbow to stop his thrashing about. With the other he tried applying the compresses, but it wasn't working.

"Do you understand me, Bo?"

"We'll get you better; try to stay on top of it."

"Do you UNDERSTAND?!" It was screamed without volume.

"About the box, your sign, Duvaier?"

"The End!'" His body thrashed violently and bounced up and down high off the bed. "Is the Beginning... the Beginning is—"

And then he stopped. His body was quiet. Rainbow Billy Beauchamp was dead.

Chapter Twenty-six

TWO PHRASES WHICH DESCRIBE the height of pitching achievement are "no-hitter" and "perfect game." A no-hitter indicates that a pitcher held the opposition hitless for the entire contest. A perfect game is a no hitter in which no one even reaches base. The odds against someone pitching a no hitter are around 5,000 to 1. A perfect game is rarer still at 50,000 to 1.

There is a certain mystique surrounding these events that even has its own code of etiquette. For example, no one on the field or in the stands is supposed to talk about the possibility of a no hitter for fear of jinxing the pitcher. Part of that is common sense. Many pitchers throw three or four innings of hitless baseball so that it would be jejune to make such references at that time.

After the fifth inning people start to wonder, and by the seventh the tension and excitement begin to build with every out. Another unwritten rule is that the first hit of a ballgame must be a clean one. Any dispute between hit and error is to be decided in favor of the pitcher. This is because a pitcher in such a situation is likely never again to have this opportunity. These are rare and to be treasured. Every accommodation is made for the pitcher to complete his task and immortalize himself. Until the magic spell is broken, everyone in the stands and at home listening on the radio or television becomes tied to that hurler trying to buck the odds—just this once—and attain some goal which is just beyond our grasp.

Such is the aura of the no hitter.

* * *

It was the top of the eighth at Wrigley Field. Bo Mellan was dueling Manuel Hernandez of the San Francisco Giants. The wind was blowing in and the score was 1-0 in favor of the Cubs. The northsiders were striving to stop a losing streak and gain a chance at evening the series at one game apiece.

When Tom Spier, the Giants shortstop, came to the plate, everyone was paying very close attention. Bo Mellan had retired all twenty-one he had faced. There had been no base runners.

On the third pitch Spier hit a deep drive that sent the centerfielder almost 400 feet away to make a running catch before crashing into the ivy. The outfielder was shaken up but not seriously injured. There was one out.

The next batter struck out. Two gone. Then the catcher was due up, Rollie Katz. He hit a grounder up the middle that somehow the shortstop was able to knock down, pick-up and fire to first in time to get the slow-footed catcher by the slimmest of margins. The Giants half of the inning was over. Twenty-four retired. Bael sent Billy Sample out to get some work in the bullpen.

The score was the same in the top of the ninth. The leadoff man was a pinch hitter. He struck out. It was Bo's thirteenth of the game. The next batter walked on a disputed 3-2 pitch. In such situations, it is customary to give the pitcher the benefit of the doubt. But plate umpire, Joe Jerkin, thought otherwise, and sent the batter down to first breaking up Bo's perfect game.

There was one on and one out when Juillo Guillen came up. On the first pitch Juillo hit a sharp ground ball to second. It was a routine double play that should have ended the game and given Bo his no hitter.

Instead, the fielder fumbled the ball and couldn't make the play. It was an obvious error. Jeers followed from the disappointed crowd. The fumble-fingered second baseman picked up the ball and walked it back to Bo. That put the go-ahead run on base and brought up the league's leading hitter, Skeeter Barry.

Everyone was restless. Sometimes pitchers lose their concentration when things don't go their way, and then they make mistakes. But Bo Mellan was known to be a pitcher who didn't give up. Time after time during the season he had made the crucial pitch after his fielders had let him down or after his teammates hadn't scored any runs for him. The fans knew this, and began, collectively, to bear down with Bo.

Buddy Bael rubbed his tummy and spat tobacco juice out of the dugout. "Sam, go out there. He's had it."

In a moment the pitching coach was out of the dugout and onto the steps. The home plate ump called time. Then Sam Dowel paused, screwed up his eyes and turned back to Bael, "You want me to settle him down?"

"Hell no. I want you to get him outta there. Bring in Sample."

"But he's still got his stuff. The kid hasn't given up a hit."

"Yank him."

Sam half turned toward the field and then pivoted to face his boss. Sam's green eyes were wide open. "You don't take out a kid who's got a no hitter going."

"You've got five seconds to get your ass out there, Sam," threatened the pot-bellied man. The bulge in the manager's cheek bounced up and down. The plate umpire was approaching the dugout.

"This is just your personal feud. There ain't no reason to take Mellan outta there."

"You know what you're doing, Dowel?" taunted the bald headed manager and charity fundraiser. The umpire came over with his hands on his hips and facemask drawn up on his scalp. "What's going on here?"

"It's your team, Bael. But I'm not going to fight your personal battles long distance any more. Get yourself another flunky."

With that Sudden Sam Dowel, former Big League pitcher, walked back through the dugout door and away from Major League Baseball.

"We've got a ball game, Buddy," said the ump. "You going to do something?"

Bael looked up at Jerkin and then to his bench of players whose eyes were riveted on their manager. Bael spat tobacco Juice at a beetle, but missed. Then he sighed, hiked up his pants and trotted up the dugout steps. "We're making a pitching change."

"A pitching change?" repeated the incredulous Jerkin. "You're taking out the kid now?"

"Mark it down: 'Sample' for 'Mellan.'"

By now the audience was alive to something being amiss. Almost everyone could see Sam Dowel about to walk on the field and then heatedly discussing something with the manager in the dugout. What was happening? A low rumble could be heard as theories were spontaneously generated. This was the question uppermost in everyone's mind as Buddy Bael made his pitching change and denied Bo Mellan his no-hitter.

As Bo walked off the mound there was total silence. Why was the pitcher coming out? Was he hurt?

"LEAVE HIM IN THE GAME!" The solitary voice ignited a flurry of commotion. The fans didn't like what was happening. In the uncovered outfield stands the "bleacher bums" started screaming over and over, in unison,

"Hey, hey, let him stay!"

On the roofs of the apartment buildings just over centerfield, where residents regularly congregate for a distant (gratis) view of the game, there arose loud clanging as garbage can lids, large pans and any other metal object in sight became symbols of their discontent.

The noise grew until Billy Sample yielded a bloop single that loaded the bases and then walked home the tying run and allowed a sacrifice fly for another. As the team left the field there was a deafening roar of disapproval.

Bo had elected to stay on the bench and not to go into the clubhouse. He was surrounded by teammates who wanted to know if he were injured or why he left the game.

"Ask him," replied the curly haired hurler pointing to Bael.

All eyes were on the manager.

Bael was pouring over his line-up sheet.

"Get Jones up and throwing," ordered Bael to the absent Sam Dowel. "Did you hear—" he began turning his head to look for Sam. Instead, he saw the eyes of his entire team. "What do you want? Who's up? Porter, grab a bat on the double."

But nobody moved.

"What's the matter with you?" Bo sat on the bench surrounded by the entire team. "I can have the lot of you replaced in 24 hours, you know." Bael spat in the direction of his players. The tobacco wad was no longer moving up and down.

Once more the umpire walked over to the bench.

"What's the matter with you bastards? Don't you know who I am?" Bael started to walk menacingly toward his squad, but the ball team didn't budge.

"Listen, I don't know what's going on here," began Jerkin. "But I'm that close to calling this a forfeit. Either you get a team out there, right now, or the game's over."

The umpire stood on the grass overlooking the dugout. Bael stood alone in the middle; his team was bunched to the outfield end.

Then a voice was heard amidst the solid phalanx."Let's go out and score a couple runs." The tension was broken and all eyes turned to the figure on the bench who was exhorting his comrades. The figure was Bo Mellan.

In rare fashion, the Cubs came back to win in the bottom of the ninth. The win technically went to Billy Sample, but somehow that didn't seem important.

*   *   *

"I tell you, you got to back me on this."

"Bael, you're a child, a stupid blubbering infant."

"I had to show him. He needed to understand—" stammered the general manager of the Chicago Cubs in the office suite of Ruppert Cakos. A huge shining desk without anything on it separated the two men. Ruppert Cakos sat in a high backed swivel chair that was facing the floor length windows that formed the back wall of his brightly lit office.

"You put us in an awkward position. You were completely unjustified."

"But how else could I get his respect? That kid is no good. I say make a four or five-man deal and put Mellan in the middle of it. We'd get him out of town and—"

"—and lose the Loop Redevelopment Project. That's what'd happen."

"But we've got to do something. You've got to help me."

Cakos swiveled around so that he was facing Bael. "I think you've got things confused. You are my agent. Whatever I will, you put into effect. The order goes from me to you. From me to you. Got that?"

Bael was silent.

"Children must repeat in order to learn. Now you recite: from me to you."

"From you to me," mumbled Buddy, who was looking down at his folded hands.

"Fine. Splendid. There's hope for you yet. Now go along. I have ways to take care of this Mellan."

Bael turned to leave.

"Oh, one more thing," said Cakos. "Don't pull any more cute stunts. The ball team can go to the devil. We've got to keep things in perspective."

* * *

Sam came to answer the knock on his door. It was Bo Mellan.

"It's you," said Sam weakly after he opened the door.

"May I come in?"

"Be my guest. Bobbi's out getting some supper."

"Alone?"

"I wanted to be alone."

The two men stood in the hotel room that Sam rented by the week.

"I heard what you did for me today. I tried to find you after the game, but I guess you left right away."

"I had no reason to stick around."

"No. I suppose not." Bo looked around the room that had gold colored chairs in front of tan, grass papered walls. "Can I sit down?"

Sam made a vague gesture.

"I'm sorry if—I mean, your job and all. I know how much that meant—"

"Forget it."

"But it's your whole life. You've sacrificed so much..."

"Maybe too much."

Bo nodded. Sam got up and filled half of a twelve-ounce glass with whiskey and then dropped in a couple of ice cubes.

"I let that Bael shorten my career. I had one or two years left in my arm, but I let him pressure me out of them. Put me into Big League coaching." The former pitching coach laughed. "Made me a big league ass is what he did."

"You're being too hard on yourself."

"No way. Too easy would be more accurate. That man made me do whatever he said. He surrounds himself with flunkies. With 'yes men.' And I was the prize." Sam paused and took a long drink. "Sometimes this stuff doesn't do any good, you know it?"

Bo's lips tightened and Sam put down his drink.

"Shit, I don't want that. I've been doing too much forgettin' in my life. Too much accommodating. And it's made me into a fuckin ass. A goddamn spineless, fuckin ass."

"But today you stood up to him."

"Yeah." Sam grinned. "And I feel so—I don't know—so free. Like I can breathe again. Do you know how long it's been since I could breathe?" Sam picked up his drink and poured it down the sink. "It's like I'm meeting myself: a guy I used to know but hadn't seen for a long time. It's such a hard feeling to describe."

"What are you going to do for work?"

"Fuck the work. Something will turn up. Or maybe it won't. Tonight it doesn't matter. Tonight I'm a free man." Sam got up and stretched his arms wide. "You know being a free man makes me hungry. Want to join Bobbi and me in some chow?"

"Sounds good to me."

* * *

It was ten o'clock when Bo got over to Angela's. He hadn't seen her in several days and had got a message that she wanted to see him.

"Get in here," barked Angela. "We're in trouble."

"What do you mean?"

"I tried calling you at the ballpark, but they said they never deliver messages while the game's in progress. I don't know why. You don't pitch but once a week or something, do you?" Angela was pacing. She lit a cigarette and then immediately set it in an ashtray on her desk.

"Today was my one day a week."

"Maybe that explains it."

"They still won't deliver messages short of life or death." Bo moved into the apartment and straddled a chair with his arms resting on the back.

"Well this could qualify."

"What do you mean?"

"The death of our People's Project. I told you to get over here right away."

"Sorry. I'd have made it here sooner, but my bodyguards slow me down."

"Don't be funny. This is serious."

"All right. Who died?" The pitcher was still smiling.

"Our three largest grants, that's who."

"There are other grants."

"Not like these. All of a sudden I got this call telling me we're out of the running." Angela talked to the window. "It's so terrible. Why only yesterday I—" Then she pivoted to face the curly haired young man. "Oh Bo, we were so close, and they told me. . ." Angela lit another cigarette and placed it in an ashtray on the window ledge.

"Why don't you slow down and tell me about it?" Bo held out his arms for Angela to come, but instead she walked over to the copy machine and lit a third cigarette.

"Well, just a few hours ago—I was eating lunch when I got the first phone call. It was from the State Superfund for Community Development. Last week we were given preliminary approval for half a million. Today: nothing.

"Then there was the United Community Chest. They had as good as pledged us two hundred forty thousand, and like that they change their mind.

"Finally, around three, I got this call from H.U.D. They had verbally approved our request for three million dollars over two years. All we needed was an outside audit, which we'll have to have anyway for our tax exemption. Then they call me today and they tell me our proposal needs more work. Just a big song and dance to tell us we're finished."

"Maybe they have a point. Did you jot down their suggestions?"

"Oh you big moron. You don't know the first thing about any of this."

"Then why did you call me? You must have had a clever reason."

Angela uttered a loud sigh and pounded the copy machine. The four-foot metal cube turned on and took a picture of Angela's hand holding the cigarette. "Oh shit. Now the thing works. It's been on the fritz since yesterday." A black sheet of paper with an indistinguishable blob in the middle shot out of the slot and fell unnoticed onto the floor. Angela was now tracing a circuitous trajectory to her desk.

"We're just about ready to start-up. This could cost the credibility of the whole operation! Don't you realize? We've already pledged this money!"

"You pledged money you don't have yet?"

"That's the only way you grow, because each new grant is predicated upon your total liability. And that means pledged disbursements."

Bo began to scratch his cheek. At this time of night the stubble made a sound like sandpaper. Angela put down her third cigarette and picked up her first again. Then she opened a file folder.

"The more you give out, the more you get. It's that simple."

"It doesn't sound right to me," replied the hurler. The light in the apartment concealed his hair's golden-red highlights.

"That's because you're not an accountant. Believe me. This is the way things are done."

Bo stopped stroking his chin. "What do you want me to do?"

"Get us more money. After all, it was your idea in the first place."

"I guess it was at that."

"You've got to save us. Otherwise, I think we're finished. We're at the end."

"Well, for one thing, I've hired someone to do community relations. He'll start immediately and begin drawing pay in July."

"What! Another employee? Didn't you hear what I was saying?"

"You said you wanted someone, and the man I have in mind will do a good job."

"But what about our funding?"

"We'll go to the people. It's really their agency, anyway. If they want it to survive, it will. Otherwise, it was a nice—experiment."

"Experiment! Is that what you call it? All that money will be lost. And people too. We've already promised a bundle." Angela reached for cigarette number three again but didn't smoke it. She now held two at once. "And what about me! Not to mention that bubble-headed girl you hired. What's going to happen to us?"

"Sometimes you just have to act like the future's going to be there. I remember when we were in Mexico playing ball—"

" —I don't want to hear about your fuckin' baseball team. This is serious stuff. A lot of people's lives are at stake. This isn't some lousy game, Phil—or Bo—or whatever you call yourself."

Bo got up. "Is there anything else?" And without pausing for an answer, "Sam Dowel's our new community relations man. I'll start him drumming up business in the morning. He's a very capable guy." Then the curly haired man blew a kiss to Angela. "It'll work or it won't. Let's give it a fight."

Angela didn't look up. The two cigarettes she was holding steadily fumed as they burned down to nothing.

Chapter Twenty-seven

BO RETURNED TO DERONDA very conscious of the shadows about him. It was a warm night. Being somewhat near the lake, there was always a cooling breeze. But Bo did not feel the breeze. The heat numbed him.

When he unlocked his door he sensed something was wrong. Inside, he found his apartment in a shambles. The rooms had been thoroughly ransacked, and the furniture broken and thrown about. A view from the end of the hallway told the tale. The young man fell to his knees and buried his head in his hands. At the base of his skull a tightness began to throb.

"Oh my god," said Cora at seeing Bo kneeling on the hallway floor. She flipped on the light switch and a large roach, which had been right next to Bo's leg, scurried under the floorboards. The light also revealed the disorder and vandalism. "What happened?"

Bo lifted his head. "Someone left me a message."

"A message? Who?" She shut the door and helped Bo to his feet. "Bo, I'm scared for you."

"Such a fuss. Such a commotion...." The hurler was feeling dizzy. Cora walked Bo into the living room where a light had been left on by the intruders. On the wall was spray-painted a bunch of dots and squiggly lines. Cora smoothed the upholstery of the couch, which had been ripped with a knife.

Bo had only been home for a short while, but the hurler was visibly affected.

"Who are these people, Bo? What do they want?"

"They want me to sign up on their ball club. They're sending a man to make me an offer."

"What ball club? San Francisco?"

"There is no room for San Francisco in this town."

''Bo, I don't understand you. Can I get you something? Some coffee or something?"

"I want them to leave me alone."

Cora stroked Bo's face. It was damp and lifeless. She took a handkerchief and cleaned off his brow. Her hands stroked his cheeks with soft, easy motions beginning at his nose and moving downwards. Soon his eyes began to focus, and his facial muscles began to respond.

Cora took Bo's head with both hands and pulled him to her.

CHAPTER TWENTY-EIGHT

BO DIDN'T LEAVE RAINBOW'S BEDSIDE until after the doctors had confirmed what he already knew. The pale blues had lost two nights of sleep, but somehow they did not want to rest. The Pan-Am Elite Giants had a game against Haiti at noon. Bo wanted to pitch.

It was a tight ball game with the lead going back and forth. Mellan didn't have his good pitches, but somehow he kept in the game so that they were ahead 5-4 in the ninth. Bo hit the first batter and walked the second on four pitches. His control seemed to fail him. The fastball was flattening out. The last one was hit 400 feet foul. It was then that he used a three-fingered grip on the fat of the ball just under the seams. He had a 1-1 count on the hitter. It was a pitch Rainbow had taught him. A slow, big bending curve that looks too good to be true. The hitter's timing is off for such an easy pitch, but he figures to slam it anyway; until the bottom drops out and he's swinging at thin air.

It was a pitch Billy Beauchamp invented in the Negro Leagues and earned him his nick name—after the patented pitch: The Rainbow Curve.

"You gotta save it or they'll set up on it. But when you need it, give it to 'em. They'll think it's Christmas until they strike out."

Bo threw the pitch; the hitter got a piece of it and dribbled it in front of the plate. The catcher pounced on it and started a third-to-second double play. Two outs. Next batter; a fastball, slider and another Rainbow Curve and the Pan-Am Elite Giants were in the Championship Game.

*   *   *

The death certificate was routinely issued and the body was scheduled to be transported to the crematorium on Monday, November third. Bo took a walk to sort things out and to find a plain metal box.

*   *   *

It was not a restful sleep. Many things were still in doubt. For example, who ran the team? Was there even a team? Rainbow Billy Beauchamp wrote no will, but everyone knew he was closest to Bo. There were assets that had to be distributed if the team were to fold, but on Sunday morning November second, no one talked about that.

Would they beat the Dominican Republic to take the mini tournament? There was some discussion about whether to start Candy Laro or Luis Sanchez (a recent acquisition). Bo leaned toward Candy even though he had just pitched two days ago and lost.

Juice and Harold favored Luis. The team took a vote. Luis Sanchez won.

Bo would coach from the field. It probably didn't matter what they did: the Pan-Am Elite Giants were flat. The day before, the death of their owner had inspired them despite their anxiety and fatigue. The day after... there was nothing.

Three hits were all they could manage in a 6-1 drubbing.

After the game there was a team meeting.

"Tomorrow they gonna cremate Rainbow. Any of you who want to stay, the team'll pick it up. Otherwise, I'll get each of you your pay and boat ticket home and we'll take our December break early. It's a cinch we need time to pull this thing back together."

"Why not go down to Venezuela like we planned? Good money. Get a little Colombian action while we're at it. They're rich down there from all the drugs." The speaker was the rookie, Luis Sanchez.

Several of the others on the team mumbled their assent.

"Rainbow never liked going into areas like that. You know we've turned down Colombia before." Bo spoke with choppy, irregular tones.

"Rainbow's dead," chimed in another new player. "We gotta go where the money is. We only young once, right?"

"Dictators and criminals are a bad combination. It's only trouble," returned Bo.

"I heard they offer two or three times the money we're pulling in the Caribbean. Sure beats the chicken shit we play for in those Mexican bush villages."

"We eat all right," said the left-hander.

"Bull shit. How often do we go out to a first class restaurant? I think we outta be able to go first class. After all, we is first class."

Bo wanted to reply, but didn't know what to say.

The team split into three groups. The largest group, consisting of the new players and Mellow, wanted to go into the Colombian back woods where the cocaine barons lived in luxury from their illicit profits. They were willing to pay a premium for some sporting entertainment.

Then there was the group of Juice, Harold and Candy who were undecided. Finally, there was Bo and Roy who were opposed to Colombia. Ten players. Five wanted to go; two didn't; three abstained.

They finally decided to head back to Mexico and wait till January to decide. Bo agreed and went his own way, making a detour through New Orleans.

CHAPTER TWENTY-NINE

FROM THE OUTSIDE, Le Bout was just as Bo had remembered it. It was almost sunset. The curly haired young man rang twice. There was no answer. Bo stood his ground and waited. Finally, after a long interval, the sound of footsteps could be heard.

"Yes?" The door opened a crack and Bo could just see the eye of Duvaier. The face was mostly hidden, but the voice was unmistakable.

"I don't know if you remember me, but—"

"Mon dieu! Entrez, mon jeune ami."

A hand shot out and pulled Bo inside. There were no lights on. The only illumination came from the sun as it pierced through the windows and diffused throughout, growing faint in the farthest corners of the anteroom. The hand guided Bo into the hall foyer where the two men stood in shadows.

"You returnez, yes?"

Bo didn't answer, but set down his duffle and knelt while he started to unzip it.

"Ce n'est pas necessaire; attendez. You come." The two figures went through the leaded glass doors into the magic room. It was still. There was a quality about the space that Bo had completely forgotten. But now, in a moment, it all came back. It was the same, but even more. It was as if he were apprehending secrets that before were hidden, but now were looming like penumbral shapes that intruded upon the inhabitants.

The two men sat down at a table.

"He is dead now, no?"

"Yes."

"He joins Cadillac Joe and Dixie Lee."

Bo never thought to ask Duvaier how he knew. Amongst the shadows, this knowledge seemed completely appropriate. Bo took out the box and handed it do Duvaier.

The old Haitian nodded. "It was his sign. Now it is yours."

Bo tried to see into the darkness, but his eyes were not strong enough. "He died of malaria. It was not an easy death."

"I knew him the premier fois when he was bitten by the fly. It was I who helped him escape from jail and later from Haiti to Cuba. He will rest now with many others." Duvaier led Bo through the back door and into the kitchen; then down some stairs into a basement. In the cellar there was a false wall that revealed a shelved room that contained other metal boxes. "They retournent, toute le monde, to the earth. Le Bout is both their ending and their beginning."

"That's what Rainbow said—"

"Shh—" intoned Duvaier. "Speech inside this room is only permitted to me."

Bo returned with his host to the main floor where Louis Reed, now over ninety, had turned on all the lights.

"It is time to celebrate. We must all have a drink. Little Rainbow has come back to us."

Duvaier stretched his lips into an unusual expression while the natty Mr. Reed went to pour himself a gin and tonic.

Bo had only intended to stay the night, but he found himself drawn to Le Bout. There was a peculiar charm that proved to be a powerful lure. Johnny Rae had connections with an old scout that could secure a spot on the Braves roster in an instructional league that played in December.

"If you're good, you'll get invited to their spring training camp. A real opportunity." The petite Johnny Rae stood proudly erect as one night he made his offer over drinks.

"I've always thought it would be interesting playing in the Major Leagues," replied Bo. "But what about the Pan-Am Elite Giants?"

"Rainbow was dat team. When he died, so did the team. Besides, you already told us how the rest of them want to go off to Colombia. Let them go. It's their hides. You ain't getting no younger, boy."

"I know. But we've been through so much... and Rainbow... his dream...."

"You was his dream, boy. You and pitching in those white major leagues. If you want to do what he wanted, you'll go to Puerto Rico for that instructional league."

"I don't know."

"What'll it hurt? If you bomb you can go back to the traveling team. If you're good, then you've got one more option. In another year you'll be too old. Then, they won't give you the time of day. It's your last chance for sure."

Bo said he'd think it over. Many of Johnny Rae's arguments were persuasive. He could go into the December league and then make up his mind. The curly haired young man bought a freighter ticket to Puerto Rico and planned his last days while playing cards and enjoying midnight suppers in the hotel's anteroom.

Then the telegram came that changed everything.

Chapter Thirty

Trouble. Over our heads. Suarez has us in Grandcourt.
Roy Carnes.

THE TEAM HAD GONE TO COLOMBIA. Over the years they had been offered very lucrative sums to play an exhibition series. Before they had been rejected. Now, with Bo gone, they had accepted.

"What about baseball in Puerto Rico?" asked Johnny Rae as he fingered his diamond cuff link.

"I have to go to Colombia."

"The team is history. They have no tie on you."

"I have to go."

"You'll probably miss your chance at playing in the Big Leagues."

"Yes," said Bo with a heavy voice.

"You've probably sealed the end of your baseball career. It can take a long time to get someone out of jail down there."

"It may be the end of my baseball. But I'm going."

The frail old man smiled as Bo left the room. Louis Reed leaned against his silver tipped cane. "Jist like old Billy Beauchamp. A real headstrong boy."

From the corner the old Haitian whispered, "Au revoir my young man. Until I see you again. Commencez."

* * *

It was not an easy task to extricate the Pan-Am Elite Giants from the power of Pacifico Suarez. This man was one of the largest dealers in illegal cocaine within a country where coke is the principal cash crop. He had an isolated mountain kingdom named Grandcourt between Tolima and Cauca. His land holdings were massive and were supported by a private army of over five thousand. In all, Suarez employed over 20,000 people counting those involved in cultivation, processing and exportation of the drug. It cost him $200 a pound to bring pure coke into Chicago, New York or Los Angeles. The street value of that after the final cut was around 2.5 million dollars. It was virtually all profit.

This fantastic mark-up enabled Suarez to maintain a lifestyle that only a very few enjoy. He controlled people and money, and had powerful political clout in his native land. The man's passionate hobby was baseball. He had made offers to the Elite Giants before to play in a challenge series in his mountain citadel. Rainbow had always refused.

Bo knew little to nothing about Suarez. The golden haired pitcher went first to Bogotá and found out as many details as he could. From bits of information gleaned from official sources he understood a little about the power of Suarez. His scheme would not be easy to effect. Bo returned to Mexico City to question Carmelita and Maria, the wives of Harold and Juice.

From them he learned that Suarez had lured the team to Colombia with a promise of one million American dollars, as a team, for one month of baseball. The group had left in mid-November and then wired a week later that things were not going well. That had been all.

The golden haired young man liquidated all the team's assets and gathered in his remaining savings. He was able to raise nine thousand dollars. From this amount he gave three thousand to the wives and promised to return soon with their husbands.

It was a promise that took longer than that to keep. Bo tried communicating directly with Suarez, but was unsuccessful. The drug king did not wish to talk to Bo. Grandcourt was too secure to take by force so Bo had to wait for an opportunity. It was a long wait. Two and a half years passed. During this time Bo worked at odd jobs and pitched regularly in neighboring Venezuela. Through careful living Bo was able to increase his stake to twelve thousand dollars.

Finally, the moment came in which Suarez showed vulnerability. A drug war began when Suarez tried to gain greater control of the country's cocaine exports. Five smaller bosses ganged up on Suarez. There were some bloody confrontations. Parts of the mighty empire were captured. Bo was able to purchase the release of his comrades from a faction that successfully raided Grandcourt.

Three years. That's the time it took for Bo to bring Harold, Juice, and Roy home again. Mellow, Candy and the three newer players had died in captivity. One newer player had escaped early on, but no one had ever heard from him.

Pacifico Suarez was an intensely paranoiac and vindictive man according to the survivors' account. Suarez had become suspicious that the team was working for another drug boss. This suspicion drew out a deep sadistic tendency in the man. When they missed their first paycheck, Roy went to Neiva to send Bo a telegram. This, also, was misinterpreted and the entire team was pressed into the bossman's forced labor corps. It was a terrible life in which they lived at subsistence level and consequently were always getting sick. They did not know that Bo was in Colombia or whether they'd ever escape. Grandcourt was so remote and they knew nothing about the terrain....

"And we never saw a cent of that million," said Juice bitterly. The captivity had soured the former shortstop's once joyful and playful attitude on life.

"I thought we had seen the end," commented Harold blankly.

"It was the end. The end of our baseball team. The end of a way of life," said Roy.

"And we thought we were making a killing."

"I wish they had butchered that son-of-a-bitch, Suarez."

"Nobody ever get him. That guy got more tricks than the devil himself."

"We got to get back to Mexico City."

"What about our wives?"

"I've been in touch. They're waiting for you."

"Well at least I remember how to fix cars," drawled Roy. "It's been a long time since I was back in Texas."

Even as Bo was taking his friends home, a man was being tortured in the mountains of Colombia. The interrogator was Pacifico Suarez. His victim was the man who had freed the ballplayers and who had blown-up a cache of drugs that eventually might have brought 100 million dollars.

As the man was suffering the last stages of life, he uttered over and over one name. It belonged to the foreigner who had paid him money to release a certain group of men while he carried out his demolition mission. Over and over he repeated one name; a name, against which Suarez silently vowed revenge. Over and over was one name: Bo Mellan.

Chapter Thirty-one

SAM DOWEL SPREAD THE WORD far better than anyone had expected. In only three weeks time he had recouped three hundred thousand in contributions. This was quite an achievement since most were in small dominations. It was almost paradoxical that just when the People's Project was being shunned by the establishment, it acquired a general popular support.

Sam successfully enlisted the aid of Joe Beezy, who wrote a series of articles on the "no hitter," and why Sam quit, and what the People's Project was all about. These editorial columns in "The Day After" shot up *The Herald's* circulation at the expense of Cakos' rag *The Sun*. There were strong insinuations that Big Stick Dailey put pressure on the agencies to cancel the People's Project's grants because Bo was aiding the Sweet Sixteen—a charge that Joe also proved false with Sam's help.

Bo was a martyr hounded by a manager who didn't like him and by a mayor who was trying to sabotage a project of charity because it might upset a delicate power balance in the City Council.

Sympathy was running high for the golden haired pitcher: both on and off the field. On the field his teammates rallied behind him. The Cubs were playing for themselves and no longer for the bald headed, pot bellied manager.

When Bo was selected for the All Star team as the northsiders' only representative, all the Cubs took pride in him. They were a team with a mission. This mission was larger than Bo, but there was no denying that he was the man who had sparked it.

Off the field, Bo was the focus of national attention with his People's Project. The idea of tackling the problems of unemployment and minority business capital at the same time was novel and caught the nation's attention. In a year when inflation was raging and interest rates were soaring, this innovative initiative was one of the few positive foci for those Americans trying to live its nation's dream in a time of declining economic prospects.

It was the second week in July. The Cubs were just finishing a home stand with a Sunday doubleheader against the first place Mets.

The Cubs had taken the first two games of the series to draw to five games over .500 and seven out of first. Bo, along with first baseman Big Train Lincoln, was escorted to a benefit at the Parklawn home for crippled children. Also scheduled to be present was Tony Balestreri.

The event started at six on the grassy playfield that stood behind the red brick colonial structure. All sorts of people seemed to be milling about in suits that smelled of perspiration. It wasn't that it was really that hot, but the high humidity made everything seem very close.

The evening's guest list would have been familiar to a political insider. Various Party leaders and ward bosses sent out the word to higher-level patronage workers that a charitable contribution was in order. It was the way many fundraisers work in Chicago. Ward bosses and precinct captains hold well- paying municipal jobs. However, these positions carry a price. Part of this price includes handing out a century note whenever the Party wants you to. It isn't too bad a deal, really: you are overpaid by ten grand for the work you do, but you are expected to give up half of that in various forms for political and social fundraisers (all of which may be deducted on your taxes). All in all, most people thought it was a nice set-up.

When Bo walked through the crowd with Perry Reston, the publicity man on the ball club, he was astonished at how many municipal employees he was meeting. Every department seemed to have its representatives—from 'Streets and Sanitation' to 'Parks and Recreation.'

The golden haired pitcher moved through the crowd with alacrity. The air was thick as a certain heaviness prevailed that tended to elonegate all activity into a slow motion. This made the ease and swiftness of Bo's progress even more astonishing. Soon, the main guests had passed through the group and had made their way to the podium. The audience sat in metal lawn chairs and awaited the series of speeches for which they had each paid one hundred dollars to hear.

When everyone was seated, two crippled children were paraded forward for everyone to see. In the audience were two hundred well-healed Party regulars sweating beneath their tan and blue polyester suits. They were waiting. Tears formed in a bathetic display of compassion for the unfortunate children who had been put on show. The audience clapped and wiped their eyes and waited.

Sean Patrick O'Neil gave a rousing twenty-minute introduction to a ten-minute speech by Parklawn's director. Yes. Yes. Quite good. Well done. Clap clap. The main event was coming up.

Then came a few authentic Polish jokes (jokes, that is, in Polish) by Adam Wojciuk and the announcement of the presentation of some plaque or other to the Parklawn home for doing whatever they do. It was Mayor Dailey's "Chicago Medal of Honor."

"...And to present dis award is two very fine members of dis community: de pitcher sensation, Bo Mellan and de President of Advanced Builders, Tony Balestreri."

This was it. No one any longer felt the thickness of the air or the predatory mosquitoes that were venturing out into the early evening as they made their surprise attacks. Shadows were dissolving into the dusk as Bo moved quickly to take the wooden plaque into his own hands. The golden haired pitcher stood squarely behind the microphone and spoke in clear, well-measured tones. "I'm happy to be here tonight—a feeling I am sure Mr. Balestreri also shares." Balestreri had meant to meet Bo en route to the microphone and walk up together. Bo's quickness and premature movement to the podium, even before Adam Wojciuk's introduction was complete, had taken the president of Advanced Builders by surprise. The lieutenant of the Mob and City Council alike stood awkwardly behind the pitcher. It almost seemed as if he might move forward on several occasions, but each time the impulse teetered just beneath that unseen level needed to complete the action.

As Bo made reference to Tony Balestreri the short, broad chested man with his thick, dark hair managed a faint grin that made the fifty-five year old man appear to be a child. His smile fit exactly with his indecisive manner upon the speaker's rostrum.

"It is especially fine to be able to recognize this fine charity. When a city can give. That's real fine. Real fine, right?" Bo nodded at Balestreri as the pitcher looked around at his audience. "You know I've been in a lot of different cities, but I've been amazed these past few weeks at the solidarity of this city.

"Here we have an orphanage doing a good job and you all come out to support it. On the South Side we have our People's Project. A lot of men and women have put what they had into that. What they could afford. Maybe not a hundred dollars a head—more like ten dollars or so from folks who have to do without when they give it to you."

There was an uncomfortable restlessness in the audience.

"But they supported us. They believed we would help them. And that's what it's all about, isn't it? I'm sure Mr. Balestreri would agree." Bo turned his head, for the perfunctory assent. But it was not forthcoming. Tony Balestreri had left the speakers rostrum and was not to be seen.

* * *

The next day saw the Cubs sweep a double header and climb to within five games of the first place Mets. Bo Mellan threw a seven hit shutout in the opener and Willie Williams won 5-3 in the nightcap.

Then it was out to the West Coast for a twelve game road trip. This trip had added interest to Bo because Sam was also flying to L.A. to talk to a Hispanic Civic Organization about starting their own People's Project in Southern California.

Monday was traveling day and Bo had been invited to a dinner that Bobbi Dowel was throwing for her parents. Sam was non-stop about the new developments that were occurring within the organization as they drove out to Downey. Bo never knew the former San Francisco pitching ace had so many ideas and was so passionate about them. It made Bo dizzy.

The little house was different from the way Bo remembered it. The furniture seemed to have been shifted around and a great deal of cleaning performed.

Linda was also transformed. Her hair was short and neat and there was a marked alteration in her demeanor. The men entered and were shown into the living room. Sam sat in a chair next to his ex-wife while Bo rested on the sofa with Bobbi.

"Do you really think the Cubs can overtake the Mets?" asked an eager Bobbi.

Bo mumbled the usual platitudes.

"We don't get cable out here or I'd watch every game you pitch. I think you have an exciting style. You never seem to give-up. That's what I can't get over. Even when you get way behind you're out there scrapping just as if it were a 1-0 game."

The golden haired hurler modestly thanked Bobbi and suggested she might be exaggerating somewhat in her description. But Bobbi continued her panegyric with the bouncing enthusiasm of an adolescent.

Out of the corner of his eye Bo saw Sam and Linda talking earnestly and then quietly excusing themselves from the room.

There was no doubt to Bo that Sam was a new man since leaving the ball club. The resurgence of the People's Project was, in large, due to Sam Dowel. From the kitchen sounds of suppressed laughter could be heard and then footsteps leading to yet another room.

*   *   *

"Why do you have such a problem with my name?"

"Is it really that important?"

"Is anything really that important?"

"C'mon, Bo. See, I said it without hesitation."

The ballplayer smiled. He was sitting next to her and drawing closer.

"I can't tell you how important that P. Sue Kay grant is to us."

"You've told me over and over." Bo held her face in between his hands.

"But it will make all the difference. Now we can really take on something big. One million dollars. It makes that hustling of your buddy, Sam, look like small time."

"Without Sam's hawking, Angela, we'd never have gotten the P. Sue Kay grant."

"Maybe..."

"What's important is that we've stuck it out. They tried to shut us down and we wouldn't let them."

Angela looked into Bo's eyes even as he kissed her. The executive director of the People's Project allowed the tenant, who used to rent from her parents, to kiss her. There was some force within this person she couldn't comprehend. For a moment she was filled with wonder. This was the man who traipsed off into the bush with her crusty grandfather—the feisty old man who had driven a wedge between her parents. Who was he?

Little Phil. Before her now. His affection and devotion to her almost reminded her of a pet—and yet he was not in the least domesticated.

Hands touching skin. Firm young breasts that have never been suckled by a child. Frustrated passion *thwarted yet once more*—not by physical distance, but by the cool millions of P. Sue Kay.

Chapter Thirty-two

"WHY DO YOU LOVE THAT WOMAN?"

"Who says I do?"

"Isn't it obvious?" Cora got up and began clearing the dishes. She was not gentle in the way she set them on the chipped, white porcelain counter. Then she returned to the living room. "She doesn't love you, you know. That woman ridicules you behind your back. It's sickening." Another group of dishes fell to their place.

Cora came back for yet another trip when Bo stopped her. "Why are you saying this?"

Cora looked right through him, and then ran out of the apartment.

* * *

It was mid-August and the Cubs were in first place by two games over the Mets and four ahead of Pittsburgh. Bo was 19-6 and near the top of every pitching category in the league.

The team was in the middle of a home stand and had just won a 2-1 decision over Atlanta. Bo was eating dinner in a small Mexican restaurant on the north side with Sam Dowel.

"This place was always one of my favorites. Especially out here on the porch." Sam gestured with his hand to the crowded eating area that was bordered by a wooden fence and covered overhead with a matching trellis that sported dying vines. Beyond, was the vague smell of the alley.

"It seems very nice," replied the hurler.

They ordered, and Sam launched in on the latest news at the People's Project.

Bo began nibbling on his food. The pitcher watched a spider in the corner, by the fence, working on its web. "I wonder why spiders don't get caught in their own webs," wondered the hurler aloud.

"What?"

"Spiders. You know they weave their web..."

"What's the matter, Bo. You ain't yourself. All this talk about insects."

"I was just wonderin', that's all."

Sam screwed up his eyes and took a long look at his friend. "This pressure's been rough, hasn't it?"

Bo waved his hand in the air.

"I don't talk about that too much because I'm outta that now. You don't know how much better I feel. It wasn't so much baseball, I guess, but Bael. I tell you that man is evil."

Bo continued to listen, but his eyes wandered back to the spider.

"Since I've gotten involved in this People's Project, I tell you, it's a whole different world for me."

The main courses came, but Sam continued to talk. "I can't explain it, but for the first time in my life I feel whole. Things are great with my kid, and me and Linda might be getting back together. She's real proud of my new life and how I stood up to Bael."

The web was finished and awaiting its victim. Sam ate awhile, but then became full. There was food still on the platter.

"You know they are really interested in starting a People's Project in L.A. They'll know in another month if they have enough start-up money or not. I've been helping them with the preliminaries. Shit. Who'd ever think I'd be a guy who went around like this. You know, doing something real. A year ago I'd never have believed it. Hell, eight months ago I'd have said I was Bael's forever."

Sam smiled at Bo. The golden haired pitcher had taken his eyes off the web.

*　*　*

In the next couple of weeks Bo became a target of two newspaper crusades. The Cakos-owned *The Sun* and the Black Muslim *Awake* both took on the hurler from different angles.

The Sun found out about Bo's unorthodox relationship with Cora and Angela, and inferred that this sanctimonious pitcher for the Chicago Cubs was nothing other than a cheap two-timer, alternating between black and white when it suited him. Such a man is not only divided in his sexual proclivities but in his loyalties as well.

> The Sun claimed that Bo didn't know whether he wanted to be black or white. Some sort of deep psychological imbalance was suggested. This would be fine and good if Mr. Mellan were a private citizen but the fact is that he is not. Mr. Mellan has thrust himself into the public arena, an avenue that demands trust and honesty at the very least. What have we learned to expect from Mr. Mellan? Why he doesn't even use his legal name: Phillip 0. Mellan. He builds himself up upon tissues of lies. And this is the man who expects the Public Trust!
>
> It is time the People of Chicago really told this imposter what they think of his two-timing prevarications and sham morality. It is time we turned this city over to the men elected to run it:
>
> Eddy "Big Stick" Dailey and his hand-picked team, which has served the city well for over two decades.

Awake, which supported Krakatowa, came with equally serious charges.

> This man, who calls himself Bo Mellan, is a fraud. This man who pretends to be the friend of the black man, is a fake. Who is he but Satan in disguise? Satan comes to Earth to tempt Allah's chosen people. And this is Mellan's avowed goal. How can we say this? Look at the proof. We all know that Elijah Mohammed is the prophet of Allah. Elijah Mohammed supports Krakatowa as the instrument that can bring prosperity back to the black folk of this city. It is the

instrument of the people; their one hope for material
betterment just as Elijah Mohammed offers the hope
for true spiritual salvation.

This Mellan is a sham man. He doesn't support
Krakatowa. This means the man works for Dailey and
Cakos. He's a pawn for their evil designs. We know
many of you have supported this sham man. That's
an innocent mistake. But we must warn you that soon
you'll be forsaken innocents. Sham man is taking us
downtown and we must stop him before he stops us!

And so proclaimed both newspapers day-after-day changing the
phrases to create new charges; changing the charges to attack Bo in
new ways.

Soon, large groups formed and picketed the ballpark whenever
Bo pitched. Others flocked to the stadium to boo and curse the
golden haired hurler whenever he was slated to be on the mound.
Many of these people were the same ones who were wildly cheering
him only a month before. Now, with copies of *The Sun* or *Awake*
rolled up in their hands, they hurled abuse upon the newly elected
captain of the Chicago Cubs.

Once again, Buddy Bael became the favorite of the city. This was
the way things stood when the general manager asked Bo to step
into his office after a game.

"Well, boy, sit down," said the potbellied man as he made his way
to his own chair. "I guess you been getting back a little of your own
out there lately."

"I have a few critics."

Bael let out a loud laugh. "I guess you do, boy; I guess you do,
at that." Then Bael wheeled forward in his chair and leaned on his
metal desk. "Got a proposition for you. Now you have an attendance clause in your contract that has been paying you pretty good.
But you and I know that those people ain't coming to see you play,
but to cuss you out. They want your ass, boy."

"They buy tickets, don't they?"

"That's not the point. The point is you're not the all-fired star you're
cracked up to be. You know it and so do I. When you run out of your

good luck out there, that city will eat you alive." Bael smiled and took a pinch of tobacco. "Damn, I've never seen a man with so many enemies."

Bo shifted his weight as he crossed his legs.

"So maybe you'd like a little guarantee that you'll be making cash when the hitters in this league start walloping the junk you're dishing up."

"What's your deal?"

"Give up your attendance clause retroactive to June 1st and we'll write you a guaranteed contract of three hundred grand per year for four years. Plus a 200,000-dollar signing bonus. That's a 1.8 million dollar package. Pretty sweet for a rookie."

Bo started to speak, but Bael cut him off. "Oh I know you're going to say that you'll be making close to a million dollars this year alone and that our package is a pay cut. But let me remind you that a lot of things can go wrong to a pitcher. He can have a little accident, and puff, his career is gone."

"Do you have one lined up for me?"

"Are you willing to negotiate your future?"

"I'm satisfied with my contract."

"You know we own you for five years. You can't go to another club."

"I may not be able to go to another club. But you sure as hell don't own me."

"You're days in the Big Leagues are numbered, boy. You just don't go around acting the way you do and get away with it. You may have pulled a few fast ones on us, but sure as hell, you won't get away with it for long. I can end you like *that*." Bael snapped his stubby fingers loudly.

"There's only one way to do that, and I don't think *even you* would stoop to do it."

Bael leaned back in his chair and laughed.

*   *   *

"What's the matter?" Cora asked as she cleaned the dinner dishes.

"Why?"

"You've said next to nothing since you came home."

"I guess I really don't feel much like talking."

"All right. But you can't go around all the time with everything bottled up inside."

"Why not?"

"I don't know. They say that it will hurt you eventually."

Bo sat and sipped his coffee.

"It's so hot for drinking coffee," said Cora as she returned with a cold beer in hand. "Why don't you have something cold?"

"I don't like cold."

"Well, room temperature, then. Just a little drink to loosen you up a bit."

Bo smiled and touched Cora's hand lightly. "I can't hold it, Corey."

"You're a drunk?"

"I used to drink to ease up, but I hit bottom a couple times. Once in Guadalajara and once in Colombia. It just brings back bad memories."

"But you never said—"

"—Don't worry about it. I'm just full of thoughts tonight. I guess I want to be alone."

Cora pulled back in her chair and then got up and took one step forward and stopped. "Don't you want me to do the dishes?"

"I'll do them. I don't mind."

Cora walked into the hallway and checked her progress once more. "Are you going to see *her* tonight? Is it *her* turn tonight?"

"It's nobody's turn. I just want to be alone." Bo sighed and looked up at Cora. "I'm sorry."

Cora watched him intently and then shouted, without volume, "Would you be sending me away if I were black?"

"Don't be a fool, Corey."

"That's my problem, I guess. I'm always somebody's fool."

* * *

Bo never did his dishes. Instead, he sat up late with all the lights in his apartment turned off. It was a rather quiet night with few sirens or much street noise that might have drawn his attention. Bo just sat at the dining room table and looked out onto the alley through the ancient, rippling window glass.

Outside, from the street side, the men of Al-Sulami quietly thwarted a man intending to throw a bomb into the bedroom window of Bo's apartment.

Chapter Thirty-Three

NO MONTH IN A BASEBALL SEASON can have the thrill of September during a tight pennant race. This year had seen the favorite Pirates fall to the Mets, who then were overtaken by the surprising Cubs led by their new phenom.

However, September for the Cubs is always a month of trepidation. The '69 team blew a substantial lead to the miracle Mets that year and a couple Cubs teams since had folded down the home stretch. The so-called 'September swoon' was always in everyone's mind whenever the northsiders were in contention late in the season.

This year appeared to be no different. A five-game lead at Labor Day had evaporated to one game by September 10th, and by the 15th, the Cubbies were two games out. The team was not performing as they had during their sizzling streaks of July and August. People began speculating once again whether day baseball sapped the strength of this team at the end of the season and whether lights should be installed at Wrigley Field.

In the midst of all this, Bo Mellan threw three shutouts in a row on successive outings including a no hitter. It was just what his teammates needed. When Bo took the mound they felt they would win. In fact, during September Bo got five wins and extended his unbeaten streak to twelve games.

It all came down to the last game of the season when Bo and the Cubs beat the Pirates while the Mets fell to the Expos. The Cubs were in the playoffs: next stop the league championship series.

With the September jinx off their backs, the northsiders breezed through the league championship series and into the World Series to face the Detroit Tigers (their arch rivals from years past).

Bo's fabulous pitching during September seemed further to polarize the fans who came to see him pitch. He was depicted as anything from a devil to a saint with very few people holding neutral opinions.

The World Series was due to open in Chicago on October 5th. People everywhere were flocking to the north side of Chicago to see the first World Series game there since 1945. O'Hare was jammed with domestic and even some international flights from places as disparate as England, Germany, Egypt—and even Colombia.

Every hotel room was booked and the thirty-five thousand-seat ballpark was expected to hold forty—with even more across the street atop the apartment buildings that overlook the centerfield bleachers. The most sought after commodity, at any price, was a Series ticket to watch the Cubs.

The morning before the opening game, Bo Mellan was quietly eating a cantaloupe with Cora.

"Have you ever pitched in such an important game in your life?" asked an animated Cora.

"At least two come to mind. One was in Guadalajara and the other was in Santo Domingo. Every game is important, I suppose. But some change your life more than others."

"I wish I could come watch, but you gave your tickets to Angela and she auctioned them off for the Project."

"The money's important."

"That's not the point and you know it. She doesn't give a damn about anything but that old Project of hers. She acts like she started it."

"She did."

"But it was your idea and your money. Sam told me so himself."

"Well, I guess Angela's enthusiastic."

"But I love you, and she doesn't."

"Angela's different than most people. You have to understand her."

Cora bit her lip and then moved closer to Bo. "I'll be listening on the radio—I don't care what Angela says."

Bo smiled and covered both her folded hands with his left hand. His skin was prematurely aged; it was rough and coarse. Cora

gazed upon the golden haired man. She wanted to tell him many
things, but held her peace. In some ways, she thought, I can speak
more truly through silence.

*   *   *

It had been over a week since Bo had been to Angela's. He found
her very busy and interviewing perspective clients. The hurler
convinced her to meet him for lunch at a small ribs place down
the block.

"Over five million—can you believe it? I'd have never believed
it possible. L.A., New York, and Seattle want to start Projects of
their own..."

Bo nodded. Was this the woman who only a month ago had
stopped fighting him off? Now her attitude was different: indifferent.

—*They've got more than just an eye on you. They're after you.*

"We've got to hire more staff just to get the job done."

—*One contract has already been made on your life. You just don't embar-*
rass a Tony Balestreri the way you did and not be forced to pay for it.

—*He's going to kill me for that?*

—*To him being made a fool is no joke.*

—*But that's what they were trying to do to me. I just out maneuvered them.*
al Sulami was silent, but Bo understood his response.

"What about us, Angela?"

"Us?"

"Don't pretend you don't know what I'm talking about."

—*Sure I understand. I'm a marked man.*

—*Your end is near. I have people watching you, watching the hired kill-*
ers that Acardo and Razi have dispatched against you. But I'm afraid
it may not be enough.

—*There's nothing to do but submit to my fate.*

—*Al-Islam, but you could leave. I would smuggle you away.*

—*But then what would happen to all that I've worked on?*

—*Keeping you alive might mark their end—surely faith, prayer, charity,*
and fasting do not require such a pilgrimage as you suggest.

"Don't you know there are certain questions you don't ask of
a lady?"

"A lady?"

"One of them is the condition of her heart."

"But just last month—"

"Last month was last month."

"Then there's nothing?"

"I never said that."

—*La ilaha illa-allah: there is no God but Allah. Salaam Aleikum.*

"I see," said Bo. He paid the bill and left. Alone.

*   *   *

The next day saw the opening of the World Series in Wrigley Field. National and International television and press were on hand to record the athletic exploits of these two baseball teams contending for the title of best American/Canadian baseball team.

Bo Mellan was slated to start for the Cubs against Bucky Brewster for the Tigers. It was a beautiful October day. The sun was shining and a little wind was blowing from left to right field. The grass and ivy were full of vitality.

The stadium was packed beyond capacity. People were standing in the designated aisles, and beneath the cover of the stands it was a little cool.

But on the field it was a mild sixty-five degrees; a perfect day for baseball. The groundskeeper finished the infield. Introductions were made. The national anthem was played, and finally the Chicago Cubs took the field. The din was deafening. A few warm-up tosses, and they were ready to play baseball.

"Batter up!" yelled the ump.

And to the plate strode Mirah, the Tigers shortstop. Bo threw a fastball right down the middle.

"Strike one."

Then another. "Strike two." Two bad pitches followed and then, "Strike three." A second strikeout followed the first. Then with a 2-1 count on the third batter, who had led the American League in batting average and RBIs, Bo threw a change-up that was belted sharply foul. Two and two. Bo set. He needed this batter to establish the pace of the game. The crowd was screaming. For many, the Cubs pitcher was a hero, and for others he was a bum. Just now

they were verbally expressing themselves at a collective volume
that made O'Hare Airport sound like the Newberry Library.

Then Bo let go the pitch. It was a long, slow breaking curve ball
that seemed to hang forever. The hitter salivated even as he tried to
time the lazy bender. Then there was a mighty swing, even as the
ball sunk dramatically into the dirt. The batter twisted himself up so
that he fell over from the power of his swing. The catcher took the
ball (which he failed to catch cleanly) and tagged the unfortunate
batter for the strikeout.

The batter was aghast. It had seemed like such a tempting
offering. But he had failed to connect, and that fact had the hitter
bewildered. The pitch had been a slow curve; a rainbow curve. Bo
Mellan had struck out the sides with it.

It was the last pitch the hurler would ever throw. As he was coming
off the mound, the golden haired ball player fell to the ground. What
amazed everyone was that he didn't get up again. Suddenly, there
was a hush as the trainer rushed out from the dugout. Immediately
it became evident that something was seriously wrong. The security
forces were alerted. Everyone waited in anticipation. What had happened? Did he trip and fall? A heart attack? The theories came fast and
furious, but then somehow the word got out and spread even more
quickly: Bo Mellan had been shot.

And then some commotion occurred during which time three
men carrying weapons tried to make their escape.

Balestreri's man, Tommy	Razi's man, Jemahl,	Suarez himself
knew he might be	was afraid he would be	knew he must escape
arrested and	accused	because he had pulled the trigger
detained even though	he had not acted	But now
the deed was another's	Escape	the first priority

Get out of the Park	was all he could think about	He had to dispose of the weapon
So he went	At the first level ramp	there was a rest room
A large arched opening	then down to the main gate	he threw it into a refuse can
allowed him	his opportunity for escape	He went back
to drop down	except that police were there	Then he sat calmly
While handcuffs awaited	to take him away	as he innocently munched Crackerjack

"Bo's hurt!" cried Cora as she listened to the radio at work.

Angela continued writing at her desk.

"He's been shot!" Cora ran up to her employer. "Did you hear me? Bo's been shot!"

"What are you talking about?"

"Bo. You know. The one you're always calling Phil; the one who started this project in the first place; the one who... but you wouldn't care. You're so tied up in your fuckin'—business. That's all you're really after anyway."

"You're not making any sense."

"No. You're the one who doesn't make sense. You're an ungrateful—" Cora searched for the right word, but she couldn't find it. Instead, she got her purse and headed for the door, "One of these days, maybe, you'll realize what you missed."

"You can't leave; it's the middle of the day." The door slammed shut. "That girl's no good. Never has been. I only hired her because of Phil. He picked her up somewhere and just assumed she'd fit in here. That man is no judge of people. He has no discrimination at all." Angela walked to the window and yelled outside. "Don't come

back. You're through! DO YOU HEAR ME? Friend or no friend of—"
But Cora didn't hear a word of it. She was already gone.

Angela walked over to her desk and tried to work. The radio was still detailing the latest developments in the Bo Mellan shooting. Angela stopped. She didn't turn off the radio until the announcement came that the golden haired pitcher for the Chicago Cubs was dead.

Chapter Thirty-Four

IT WAS THE END OF BO MELLAN.

But it was a beginning for the Chicago Cubs who were so fired up over the loss of their captain and team leader, that they walloped the Detroit Tigers 13-4 for their first World Series victory in 34 years. Unfortunately for the northsiders it would also be their last win of the series as Detroit would come back to win four straight and take the Series four games to one.

For reporter Joe Beezy it was the start of a new phase of his career. After an anonymous tip, the sports reporter for *The Herald* did some fine investigative reporting on the man who was behind the scheme to shut down Bo Mellan. This turned out to be none other than Rupert Cakos. The link to A.B.C. was documented and it was shown that this billionaire abused his princely powers in order to win the fat federal and state monies slated for the Loop Redevelopment Project. Beezy inferred that a paranoid Cakos viewed Mellan's charity project as a threat and that the rich power broker put the forces into action that probably killed the pitcher (or at least created a climate of hate wherein such an event might occur). Krakatowa was also implicated.

These pieces came out in December and proved to be a Christmas present for the people of Chicago and a fatal blow to mogul Cakos. As a result of Beezy's stories Cakos had to split up his A.B.C.

Company under a court ordered reorganization scheme. Special safeguards were installed against future infiltration by Organized Crime. (These failed.) The Loop Redevelopment Project was shelved because of the controversy and one year later a new U.S. Congress would cut those funds entirely.

Further, because of the links with Organized Crime, Cakos had to sell the Chicago Cubs. (Buddy Bael also lost his job with the ball club, but was kept on by Cakos.) The FCC suddenly didn't approve of Cakos' ownership of T.V., Radio and Newspapers in the same city and threatened his license unless he sold his television station.

Rupert Cakos never again attained the power and influence he had once enjoyed. He died eighteen months later.

For his work, Joe Beezy won a Pulitzer Prize and became associate editor of *The Herald* and later moved to *The New York Times*.

* * *

An investigation into the murder was also instigated. The weapon was found with no fingerprints. The police had two suspects: a Mafia hit man and a killer hired by Krakatowa (a member of the so-called 'Fruit of Elijah Mohammed,' a squad of anti-white thugs and murderers). Neither man had actually killed Bo Mellan, though each had received money to do so.

The Mafia man was mysteriously cleared in a non-jury trial while the Kraketowa suspect was convicted of conspiracy to commit murder and 2nd degree murder (reduced by plea bargaining). The sentence was 40 years.

It was also the end for the real killer, Pacifico Suarez. After making his escape from the ballpark, the Colombian drug king took an overland route back to Grandcourt. When he got as far as Mexico City, he got a case of food poisoning and was admitted to a local hospital. Somehow, in the process of his treatment, he was injected with a dirty needle and died from complications arising from the ensuing hepatitis infection.

For Sam Dowel it was the inauguration of new success. The Hispanic Community of Los Angeles had launched their own People's Project and asked Sam to be the executive director. Sam departed Chicago and rejoined the city he had left years before. The former pitching star successfully guided the L.A. project in fruitful directions and eventually branched out as far north as Ventura and as far south as San Diego. In ten years it became the largest branch of the People's Project in the country.

Sam remarried Linda and enrolled Bobbi in UCLA. The Dowels were back together for good.

At the same time, it was the beginning of the end of Angela's tenure as Project Director. She found it difficult to delegate authority so that as the Project continued to grow, it became increasingly unmanageable. In less than a year's time she was supplanted from the head position by a smooth faced tan-skinned graduate of the Wharton School of Business who came in and increased the staff tenfold. Angela ended up in middle management, a bitter woman. Eventually, she married her boss and left the organization.

Cora headed south and became a radio disc jockey in Arkadelphia, Arkansas.

* * *

The aftermath also marked the demise of Krakatowa. The once burgeoning company had too precarious a financial structure to withstand the bad publicity following the Beezy investigative series and the murder trials. But this collapse marked the resurgence of all of Chicago's black population into the mainstream of Chicago's politics. Wilson Ice rallied these forces and created a workable political machine that was able to knock Dailey out of office two years later and install Chicago's first black mayor.

Along with Krakatowa's demise came the denouement of the Black Muslims. Most of this separatist group merged with mainstream Islam under al Sulami. Elijah Mohammed died and his own son and successor embraced orthodox Islam under the leadership of the mystical Arab.

One assassin's bullet put a stop to Bo Mellan and his phenomenal year in the Big Leagues. Many people still speculate what kind of statistics he would have had if his career had run its full course or if he had broken in at a younger age.

After the autopsy and investigation were over, an old Haitian appeared with a document that claimed proprietorship over the dead body. No one much liked letting a local star go like that, but the document was in order and had been legally executed by the pitcher himself.

The corpse was cremated in Chicago and then placed in a metal box. Thousands of people came by to pay their last respects.

In his life the golden haired man with the pale blue eyes had occasioned bitter division, but in death, it seemed, most of the rancor had abated.

Then the Haitian mysteriously vanished. The disappearance of the old man with the hurler's ashes added another enigma to a life that was already very puzzling. It is true that a bullet stopped the man in the faded chenille jacket. It stopped the career and activity of a man nobody really knew. But the reverberations of that death were not soon to be silenced. It was the end of Bo Mellan, but it was the beginning of a legend.

Other Novels by Michael Boylan

The Extinction of Desire (2007) What would you do if you suddenly became rich? *De Anima* #2

To the Promised Land (2015) Are there limits to forgiveness: personal, corporate, political? *De Anima* #3

Maya (Forthcoming) Follow the fate of an Irish-American family through three generations. It's the story of immigrants. *De Anima* #4.

Naked Reverse (2016) There is a backdoor to the ivory tower. Find out what happens to one professor who escapes. *Arche* #1

Georgia (Forthcoming) A novel told in three parts. Explore racial identity through a murder mystery set in the early 20th century. *Arche* #2-4